Wedding Bandits

Oswald Black

Published by Oswald Black, 2024.

This is a work of fiction. Similarities to real people, places, or events are entirely coincidental.

WEDDING BANDITS

First edition. June 4, 2024.

ISBN: 978-1738061709

Written by Oswald Black.

Chapter One

Angie Robertson peered across the breadth of the Cedar Falls Reception Hall from her loveseat throne at the elaborately adorned head table. Inundated with joy, she watched the scores of friends and family attending her wedding as they encircled an archipelago of smaller numbered tables next to their respective peers and loved ones and dined on pan-seared duck, dished out by the wait staff promptly and with Broadway-worthy synchronicity. The men of the assemblage flung their suit jackets over their backrests and feasted heartily. The women, who did not have the luxury of degowning at will, tended to restless children and ate sparingly between sips of Domaine Joseph.

Daddy had instructed that each table receive a bottle.

"Daddy, that's over two hundred dollars a bottle!" Angie gasped the day her father suggested the idea. Her family no doubt had the means for such a thing, but the thought of so much money going toward something as trivial as wine was jarring.

Her father responded with a familiar warm and husky laugh that, compounded with his crown of dense silver hair, resembled a white wolf yawning. "Your baby only gets married once."

Angie shook her head and smiled impishly. "Wait until I tell Pierre...,"

The decorator—a short, balding Portuguese fashionista named Pierre—was an absolute gentleman and a formidable creative consultant. In spades and style, he wrought to fruition Angie's vision of a reception party ensconced in the color purple. He and his enthusiastic assistants, infixed with a work ethic comparable to that of Snow White's seven dwarfs, had diligently draped the tables with rich purple cloth and rolled the polished silverware in matching purple lap napkins. They dripped purple icicle lights from the rafters among purple balloons and purple streamers, evoking the air of a million fireflies flitting across a meadow of lilacs and bubblegum. They upholstered the dais under her feet in a lustrous and regal coat of shimmering purple velvet and meted out cute little purple bow ties for the necks of the wait staff.

It was perfect.

Next to Angie at the head table, dapper in his purple groom's tuxedo, sat Clyde Morrison. Clyde's sapphire eyes glinted under icicle lights as his adoring gaze drew her in. His smile revealed a dimple on the right side of his face and a flawless rail of pearly whites that evoked in Angie's belly a pleasantly warm sensation, suchlike a batch of gooey chocolate chip cookies baking within its walls.

The words 'I love you, Mrs. Morrison' floated off Clyde's full lips in a rapturous cadence and kissed Angie's ears with the sweetness of honey drizzle on a curled tongue.

Mrs. Morrison.

The proclamation of her inherited moniker made Angie want to break out into fits of zany laughter, to throw her hands up in the air and shout at the rafters as loud as she could, as hard as she could, until not a whisper of breath remained. But more than anything, she wanted to feel her husband's children swimming in her stomach, which they would be tonight after they consummated their union.

Yes. Sex. Finally.

It had been hard to deny their prurience during their year of courtship. Clyde was a devout Orthodox Protestant and bound to abstinence outside marriage. But tonight, all that was going to change. Tonight, after they returned to the chalet, Angie was going to show her lover that their bout of patience and good faith had been well, *well*, worth the wait. If Clyde thought that just because Angie was a big girl, she didn't have any bedroom tricks up her sleeve, he was in for a *very* rude awakening.

As it had many times before, visions of their future together fondled her imagination and plucked at her heartstrings. Babies. Birthdays. Vacations. Graduations. Grandkids. Sunsets. Growing old together on their front porch, hand in hand, in sickness and health, 'till death they did part.

Angie squeezed Clyde's hand and whispered helplessly: "I love you like crazy, baby."

Rhonda Mallory, Angie's longtime best friend and the evening's maid of honor, nestled in close with the newlyweds and shrieked. "You two are so good together! I love it!"

The purple bridesmaid dress hugged Rhonda's taut figure while voluminous platinum-blonde hair rolled past her narrow, naked shoulders and rested above perfect little b-cup handfuls. Her lips were plump, pink, and wet with shimmer. Her skin was slick, tanned, and freckled just enough to make the attribute attractive, like a coffee creme granite countertop with a high gloss finish. And despite the subtle signs of aging that had begun to announce themselves on her visage in the form of rigid brow lines and tenacious crow's feet, Rhonda could still turn heads and put the asses in seats. Effortlessly, it seemed.

Growing up together, Angie was lucky enough to have been granted a front-row seat to Rhonda's inherent hold over the opposite sex, whether she wanted it or not. First, in grade school, when Valentine's Day brought her more cheesy Hallmark cards and cinnamon hearts than she could cram inside her backpack, then onto high school, where every boy with a license and a morsel of self-esteem was fighting over who would take her to the drive-in Friday night, and then, as her roommate in college, Angie witnessed more hot action from her bed across the room pretending to be sleeping than a porn theatre projectionist.

Angie found it difficult to precisely recall how many times in the tenure of their friendship Rhonda had abandoned her at a party to partake in a dalliance in the bathroom or bedroom with Scott or Matt or Greg or whoever her crush happened to be that week, while Angie stayed on the couch, nervously pulling her dress over her pale and varicose knees, and tried to force awkward small talk with Scott's, or Matt's, or Greg's creepy best friend, who, more often than not, was concentrating less on the conversation at hand and more on sneaking less-than-sneaky peeks at her cleavage. The twins were the only thing on Angie's body that solicited the boys' undivided attention. Like the rest of her, Angie's chest was loud and full. Alas, it always seemed the boys peered upon her endowments with more novelty than desire, as if they were flipping through a National Geographic rather than a Playboy.

And yet, here was Angie, sitting at the head table in the flowing white dress while Rhonda was still scrounging through the local bar scene in search of Mr. Right. Sure, Rhonda had a great career in marketing, but she had no one to call her own, no one to kiss goodnight, and no one to wake up to in the morning. And what good was all that success if there was no one with whom to share it? Angie concluded that it was not much good at all.

The bride pursed her lips and blew her maid of honor a kiss. "Thanks, bae," she sang. "You're the *best*."

Rhonda raised her flute, brimming with bubbling champagne. "Cheers to the both of you," she proclaimed. "I love you both so much. I love it, I love it, I love it! Ugh! I love it!"

Angie and Clyde barely raised their flutes before Rhonda drained her glass to suds.

Husband and wife shared a covert grin.

Angie pouted at Clyde's flute, bearing water. "Are you sure you don't feel weird? With everyone drinking?"

Before Clyde could respond, a succession of four high-pitched pings, like the reverberant jingle of a servant's bell, oscillated throughout the reception hall.

The attendance of over a hundred guests turned their attention to the front of the room where Angie's father stood behind the speaker's podium: imposing and broad-shouldered in a three-piece, pinstriped, Italian stitched suit. It was the one with the thin lapel, one of Angie's favorites. It made him seem slimmer at the waist and more pronounced at the chest. Daddy was also wearing the gold Rolex that Angie's mother, God rest her soul, had gifted him on their tenth wedding anniversary.

Daddy placed his flute on the podium and cleared his throat. His smile was slothful and inebriated. His eyelids drooped listlessly. It was getting a bit late in the night for the construction tycoon consistently roused before the sun or even the birds. But a man built as heavily as her father did not succumb to the tranquilizing effects of wine and whiskey so easily. There was life in the old man yet.

"Attention! Attention!" her father bellowed into the microphone.

A brief shriek of feedback replied. Daddy recoiled.

"You da man, Uncle Sly!" yelled Cousin Ralph from table eighteen near the bathrooms.

Daddy reveled in the fanfare. He lurched over the podium like Richard Nixon and delivered his best Elvis Presley: "Thank you! Thank you very much!"

Good humor pervaded throughout the assemblage.

Daddy's expression twisted as though he might weep. He bit down on his lip, squared his shoulders, and continued: "As the father of the bride, I would like to say a few words. I hope you'll bear with me."

He wrestled the cordless microphone free from the mount, stepped out from behind the podium, and regarded the newlyweds.

"Angie, my love," he addressed with eyes almost as misty as his daughter's. "I am so very proud of you. I only wish that your dear mother could be here to see it for herself, her baby girl starting a family of her own. I am beside myself with joy. And I know your mother is looking down on you tonight, smiling, with all the other angels in heaven."

Many family, friends, and associates in the room had known Angie's mother well. Each of them had been equally devastated by the news of her accident. Understandably, nods of esteem from tearful and tender faces spanned table to table. Even Angie's brother, Sebastian, a younger, flashier dressed version of their father and the most enigmatic and equivocal man Angie had ever known, softened like wax under candlelight as their father paid his respects to their late mother.

Beside Sebastian at the Robertson table perched Clyde's sister, Magda, who had flown in from New York to witness her little brother tie the knot. The young woman was a painfully beautiful blonde and filled out a strapless pink dress with a body that made most Hollywood starlets look like trailer trash by comparison. She had her hair pulled back in a tight cinnamon bun, and her skin was raw sienna and radiant. Her makeup was simple yet elegant, and her eyes were like brilliant blue flames.

"And as for the groom," her father continued, dropping his tone and arching a suspicious eyebrow at Clyde.

Beguiled expressions humored Daddy's playful galling of his new son-in-law. Clyde, however, looked pale and squirmy, clearly discomfited. Daddy broke from his glowering facade and let out a raspy, disarming laugh. At this, Clyde's shoulders relaxed. The color slowly returned to his cheeks, though he remained slightly guarded.

Daddy flashed Clyde a playful wink. "Today, my boy, I am proud to call you son. You're family now." He pivoted to address the room like Steve Jobs was unveiling the new iPhone. "When Clyde showed up just over a year ago, a new face in the Falls, I had my suspicions about his intentions with my Angela. So, naturally, I did a little digging into Clyde's past, as a man of my lifestyle should, and I have to say, I was not very happy with what I found. But before I had a chance to confront the young man, Clyde came to *me* and told me all about the dark moments from his past with complete, unfiltered honesty. He said, 'Mr. Robertson, I may have had some dark days behind me, but I'm a changed man, and I'm looking ahead. I'm ready to work hard and take on my responsibilities as a man. And all I need is the love of a good woman and, well, sir, I believe that your daughter is that good woman'.

"When I heard that, my heart went soft. I saw a man in need of a fresh start. In need of someone to believe in him. So I gave him a chance to prove himself, and I wasn't let down. Clyde showed me time and time again that he is a man of discipline, of strength, and, most importantly, a man of his word."

Steadfast in his gaze, Daddy found the head table and said to Clyde: "Today, Clyde, I give you the most precious gift I could ever give. My only daughter. My sweet baby. And I know you will treat her like the queen she is."

"I will," said Clyde as he used a knuckle to wipe the tear from his eye.

Out of microphone range, Clyde's assurance to her father failed to register with the guests. Nevertheless, the message was delivered clearly to the person who needed to hear it.

Daddy tidied his posture, flexed his chest, and, like a circus ringmaster, proclaimed: "And tonight, I am giving you both *another* gift!"

Expressions of wonder fell like dominoes on myriad candlelit faces. Clyde and Angie were equally as surprised as the guests. The entire reception hall waited intently for Daddy to show his hand. A valet boy in a white dress shirt and red vest jogged obsequiously across the dance floor and carefully approached her father. He whispered in Daddy's ear. Daddy nodded equivocally and relieved the nervous-looking messenger. Resuming his theatricality, he announced: "I've just been notified that your gift is waiting for you outside. Clyde, your Civic is nice, but I think a 911 Porsche convertible—a *four-seater*, for when the first of many grandsons is born—would do you better." He raised his glass accordingly. "The keys are in the glove box. I wish you both a lifetime of happiness."

Angie was speechless. Clyde, evenly stunned. A 911 Porsche was the near pinnacle of luxury, with a price tag of over two hundred thousand dollars. Between Daddy's more-than-generous gift and the sundry cash and checks made out to the newlyweds stuffed in a purple sack near the dance floor, Clyde and Angie Morrison could count on a healthy financial start to their new life together.

When the guests finished applauding Daddy's magnanimity, Clyde's best man and longtime friend, Roger, was called up to say a few words. Roger had traveled along Clyde from New York to Cedar Falls, and the two best friends were similar in many ways. Roger, like Clyde, was a recovered alcoholic making the best of his second go amid the comforts of small-town living. Like Clyde, Roger had a lean exterior, chiseled jawline, healthy dentition, and an enviable shock of chestnut hair. However, unlike Clyde, who frequently adopted a frustratingly reserved and mousy disposition, Roger possessed a razor-sharp wit and a relentless silver tongue that had gotten him in hot water with contractors on the job site more times than Angie could count.

Roger rose from their table. He and Rhonda shared an aslant glance and a smile. Angie caught the exchange. The two had been playing eye tag all night long. Angie had a feeling that she and Clyde wouldn't be the only ones among the wedding party acting out their pent-up sexual urges later on in the night.

Daddy returned the microphone to its stand and tipped an imaginary hat to relatives sitting nearby as he strode back to the Robertson table. Roger ambled to the podium and surveyed his audience with a grin. "Mr. Robertson, everybody," said Roger, respectfully extending a hand to Angie's father. "Owner of a multi-million dollar, nationwide construction empire and still pays his clean-up guys fifteen an hour. What a guy."

And the mouth makes an appearance, thought Angie.

The room united in surprisingly boisterous laughter. Daddy's Rolex clattered off his wrist as he shook a lumpy fist at Roger goodheartedly. Sebastian sat stiffly in his seat and glared at Roger from under his salient familial brow.

Roger, glowing off the success of his first joke, gripped the sides of the podium and rolled on sanguinely with his speech: "Being the one who introduced the newlyweds is quite a special honor. Honors have been a rarity in my life, so it made me really happy to know that my best friend had finally met the girl he wanted to spend the rest of his life with...I thought things couldn't possibly get any better...then Clyde asked me to be his best man. And I can think of no higher honor *in the world* than standing up for your best friend when he needs you the most." Roger broke from the concourse and spoke to Clyde directly: "I will always be there for you, Clyde. Together, we have seen hard times, and together, we will share brighter days. And I know, if the day ever comes that *I* find the girl I want to spend the rest of my life with, you will be right up here standing up for me, probably making a much better speech than the one I'm making now."

The two best friends shared a meaningful look. Roger put on a devilish facade and returned his attention to the room. "But, I must be honest," he said lightly, "when I first introduced Angie to Clyde, I didn't think it would end up with the two of them getting married. I was just trying to get my buddy laid."

Angie ejaculated a burst of laughter. Some of the teenage cousins and beer-guzzling knuckleheads from the StrongBolt family joined her in jest. Others, like Sebastian and Daddy's investors, were less than entertained.

"I'm just kidding," Roger chuckled. "We all know how the Protestant Church has changed Clyde's life for the better." Roger raised his glass of water to the bride and groom. "I wish you both a lifetime of happiness. And I will wait until you get back from your honeymoon to collect my finder's fee."

This time, Roger's wittiness was received correctly. He was seen back to the table with ancillary applause from all but Sebastian.

Roger stopped short at the newlyweds' throne and shook the groom's hand.

"That was perfect," said Clyde.

"That was beautiful," said Angie as Roger folded into his seat.

"Not as beautiful as you," noted Clyde. He pressed his lips softly on Angie's cheek. His eyes remained on her as he patiently receded. The feeling of warm cookies baking in Angie's stomach returned if indeed it had ever left. Clyde guided her hand to his lips and kissed the flesh. His warm breath glided across her knuckles, melting Angie's heart like butter in a hot pan.

With the speeches concluded, the big band began orchestrating the classic Frank Sinatra song *I Did It My Way;* Angie recognized the musical arrangement well. After her mother's accident, her father listened to the record often. Angie imagined the song reminded him of the days when he and her mother were young and fervidly in love, the way she and Clyde were today.

As the concourse broke from their tables to stretch their legs and converse, Angie separated from Clyde momentarily, elevating her flowing gown and carefully descending the dais. On the floor, she shuffled intently through a dizzying tumult of congratulations and goodwill. Angie nodded and smiled graciously at familiar and unfamiliar faces as she went but sustained a determined gait toward her target. Magda was away from her seat at the family table, and Angie wanted to speak with her father before her sister-in-law returned, as Angie was more than intimated by the woman's staggering beauty.

When Angie arrived at Daddy's table, he and Sebastian were busy in a private discussion. "Your speech was beautiful, Daddy," Angie interjected. She lurched over and swallowed her father in her arms. He disappeared under her pendulous rolls and folds. Daddy was used to it by now; Angie had been bigger than him since the age of seventeen.

"You may be bigger than me," he would say when Angie would mope about her growth. "But you're still my little girl."

Sebastian leaned away, clearly discomfited with his sister's schmaltzy display of affection toward their father. "You sure about this guy, Angie? He's not even Catholic."

"Oh, can it!" Daddy snapped from under Angie's prodigious limbs. Angie released her hold, and Daddy emerged from the veil of flesh. He arrowed his finger at Sebastian and rebuked his boy trenchantly: "This is a big day for your sister. A big day for all of us. Show Clyde some respect. It takes a lot of courage to admit you're an alcoholic, to go through all those steps and start over."

Sebastian scoffed. "Yeah, he fucked up his life like every other fiend. He's a real hero..."

Daddy raised the back of his hand as if to slap Sebastian across the face with his rings on. "You show some respect, you understand?"

Sebastian flinched for the slightest measure. He picked up the toothpick next to his plate and set it between his lips before glancing transitionally around the room. "Got it, Pop."

"*Yes*, I'm sure," Angie answered her brother pointedly. "When are *you* going to settle down, Sebastian? A handsome man like you would have no problem finding a wife, and you'd make a great father."

Sebastian glanced at Daddy, hardly at all, then tilted his head at Angie. "Someone's got to take over the family business."

Angie swatted a hand to reject her brother's tenuous exculpation. Daddy had raised a family and made himself a millionaire from the ground up without help from anybody. All Sebastian had to do was keep the business afloat. But she wasn't about to start *that* argument on her wedding day.

Angie waved merrily at the elderly bald man in all-black attire growing nearer as he cautiously navigated the meandering canals between tables. "Pastor!" she cried out.

Pastor DeMarcus regarded Angie and shined to the best of his ability. He, like Sebastian, was a very joyless man with a personality about as colorful as the vocational black garb draped over his cadaverous stature. "Angela, so good to see you," he greeted, slow as molasses. "I was just on my way to the buffet for a few more slices of that delicious cantaloupe."

Angie attended him affably. "Oh, wonderful. The caterers have done a fantastic job. I won't hold you up, then. I just wanted to thank you for making the trip from New York. Clyde was insistent that it was you who married us. You two must be very close."

"Yes. I was the minister at the orphanage where he and his sister were reared all those ages ago."

Angie put a soft hand to her heart and pouted sweetly. "That's beautiful," she said.

Daddy leaned in and usurped the conversation rather abruptly. The smell of whiskey trailed off his crooked lips as he praised Pastor DeMarcus for his service. Angie was embarrassed by her father's boisterousness, but Pastor DeMarcus responded with regal propriety.

"Bless your heart," the pastor imparted on her maudlin padre. He exhausted himself in his attempt to curl out another smile, which at best appeared as if invisible fishhooks were tugging upward at the corners of his mouth. He regarded Angie politely and puttered onward to the buffet.

Angie glanced back at Clyde. Presently, he was up from his seat and folded over the breadth of the head table, having a private word with his Greek goddess of a sister. Angie decided it was time to face her new sister-in-law, intimidated or not. She started back for the dais, but not before turning to Sebastian and pointing accusingly at her father. "No more drinks for him!"

Magda smiled opposite Angie as she approached. "Angie!" she cried with arms outstretched. "You look stunning! The most beautiful bride in the world."

Angie was almost insulted that a girl as aesthetically flawless as Magda would have the brass ovaries to comment on her at-best homely appearance. "Thank you so much," she returned thinly.

"I saw the Porsche parked outside when I was out for a smoke," Magda went on. "You two are going to love it."

"I was hoping to have a look myself," Roger chimed in beside Clyde. He had shot alive at the talk of cars.

"Totally," said Rhonda beside Angie. She fired Roger an electric glance.

"I can't deny that I'm a little curious myself," added Clyde. "What do you think, babe? Want to go take a peek?"

Angie replied for the second time that night: "I do."

The group of five ventured eagerly for the exit. Angie invited her father and Sebastian to join the parade as she passed their table. The group of five grew into a group of seven. There was an acute sense of two families becoming one during the short jaunt to the door. Angie even saw Sebastian patting Clyde's back on their way.

To protect her wedding dress from the elements, Angie stood inside the reception hall and leaned out the doorway while the rest of the group dispersed into the warm night. Daddy and Sebastian stepped off to the side and lit cigars. Magda joined them, igniting one of her thin menthol cigarettes that further accented her daunting femininity. Like hyenas around a discarded carcass, Clyde, Roger, and Rhonda circled the four-seater convertible. The retracted top exposed cream leather seating. The glossy cherry paint job and chrome rims gleamed under the streetlamp like a game show prize. Clyde ran a finger along the low, subtle curvature of the hood as he glanced over to Daddy, sheer bafflement across his face. "Mr. Robertson, this is...this is amazing. Thank you so much. I don't know what to say."

White smoke billowed from the thick stub of Daddy's cigar as his cheeks inflated in short bursts. He took a moment to admire the bedazzled evening sky. The constellations were dense and aglitter as though each celestial cluster had made an effort to show out for Angie's big night. "You said 'I do', son," grinned Daddy. His gaze remained fixed on the studded panorama. From the corners of his mouth, tendrils of thick smoke ascended to the heavens. "You've said all you needed to say."

His eyes found Clyde's as he reached to remove the stogie from his mouth.

Angie grew panic-stricken. "Oh, no! Daddy! Look at your hand! Is that *blood*?"

Her father scanned his flesh and noticed the blotch of rust dusting his palm and wrist. He reacted disarmingly and slipped his bloodstained hand back into his pocket, using instead the right hand to pull his cigar. "Nothing to worry about, dear," he assured. "I must have opened up a cut. I'm always dinging myself when I'm at the sites. I'll go to the bathroom and wash it off when we get in."

Angie sighed. It was worrisome to have her father around all that dangerous equipment, especially as he matured in age. But what could she do? Daddy had his own addictions. He was a workaholic.

Presently, Aunt Lisa's acrylic nails scratched against the acne on Angie's bare back, letting her know that husband and wife had been summoned inside for the first dance. Angie braced a surge of innervation and hurriedly instructed everybody inside.

Time stood motionless in the reception hall as Clyde and Angie took the floor. The big band commenced a rendition of Ed Sheeran's hit love ballad *'Perfect,'* which had been chosen by the bride. The rosy-cheeked ginger had been Angie's first love before Clyde, and his posters still unabashedly plastered her bedroom walls.

Clyde smiled at her, closed the gap between their bodies, and touched her corpulent waist. For an instant, Angie felt overcome by a paralyzing surge of negative emotions. She felt insecurity over the doughiness of her love handles, shame that her husband could not get his arms around her midsection, and guilt for being so tall and sizable. She stifled her anxieties and breathed deeply, reminding herself she no longer needed to worry over such menial, superficial insecurities. Clyde had chosen *her,* love handles and all.

She gazed down at her husband's affectionate stare and took a moment to admire his cheekbones, dimples, and soft, kissable lips.

Magda didn't inherit all *the looks.*

The guests watched on with enraptured smiles over licks of candlelight as the newlyweds swayed in slow circles over the dance floor. The tables dimmed and blurred kaleidoscopically in Angie's peripheries until all life in the universe had reduced to a population of two.

"I can't wait to get you back to the chalet," Clyde said softly, safe and sound in his wife's encompassing embrace. "Tonight is going to be a magical night."

He rested his head against Angie's chest, and together, they glided along in each other's arms as if floating on a cloud while sweet horns and strings guided their melded hearts.

ANGIE AWOKE IN THE chalet, tangled in cool bed sheets, her head pounding and groggy, her mouth chalky and bone dry. She felt confounded, ill, and confused about how she arrived at her present position. The last thing she remembered was standing in the parking lot outside the reception hall, saying goodbye to the last of the straggling aunts and uncles. After that, she and Clyde loaded the purple sack of gift money into the Porsche trunk and started for the chalet.

Okay, she thought. *That's how I got here. Then what happened?*

Slowly, fragments of her recall started to assimilate. She remembered that she and Clyde had come up to the suite. Clyde poured them each a glass of champagne and...

Angie felt her body. She was out of her wedding dress and wearing an extra-large cotton nightshirt. She shot up ninety degrees and threw the mess of curls out of her face, twisting to wake Clyde and finding a vacancy on his side of the bed.

She flattened her palm against the mattress. The sheet was cold. She gasped at the sight of her hand. Her engagement ring and wedding band were gone, and a creased valley of discolored skin remained in their wake.

Her heart thumped faster. *Just what the hell is going on?*

"Clyde?" she called out.

No response. The only movement in the room was the webbed silhouettes of swaying tree branches dancing on the hardwood floor atop squared sheets of light beaming in through the French doors leading out to the balcony.

Angie clambered out of bed and set her feet on the hardwood. It was cold on the flat of her bare heel. She made a move for the vanity and checked the alarm clock. It was one in the afternoon. She had been sleeping all night and nearly half the day.

Out of the corner of her eye, Angie noticed the purple sack, which she remembered she had placed beside the bathroom door upon her and Clyde's return, was unaccounted for.

A dull lump weighed heavy in her throat. *No*, she thought. She banished the inconceivable from her mounting suspicions and began a string of grappled reasoning: *He couldn't have. There's just no way. Not Clyde. We must have been victims of a robbery.*

She rubbed the back of her head. No lump. No tenderness. The room showed no signs of a struggle. The dresser and night table drawers remained undisturbed. There were no chairs tipped over, no glass broken.

She called out again for Clyde to no avail.

Observing the bathroom door slightly ajar, Angie tip-toed across the room, pushed the door open circumspectly, and switched on the bathroom light with a blind hand before guardedly stepping inside.

No intruder waiting to spring. No Clyde. No anything.

Well, there *was* something.

Two empty long-stem champagne flutes were abreast on the granite sink counter; one exhibited a lumpy white residue at its bottom.

Suddenly, Angie felt nauseous and dizzy and struggled for air. She ran out of the bathroom and raced to the French double doors. She swung them open and dashed out onto the balcony. Without the sentry iron railing to arrest her, her speed and momentum would have cast her off the platform's edge toward the parking lot twenty feet below. She was careless, vertiginous with suspicion and worry.

The afternoon sun enveloped her in its warmth. A slight breeze caressed her face. She breathed deeply and filled her starving lungs.

The roar of truck engines in the distance alluded to a day well underway. She peered down at the succession of inert cars. Sun rays glinted off curves and chrome lining. The space that should have contained a 911 Porsche convertible was suspiciously empty.

Angie's heart hammered violently against her chest as if it were seconds away from breaking through her breastbone and tearing through her flesh like one of those aliens in that sci-fi movie from the '80s. The parking lot blurred behind a backlog of tears. Angie's jaw clenched. Her cheeks trembled. At the climax of her despair, in one great release of pain and anger that sent the crows perched on the crooked branches of nearby trees squawking for safety, Angie lifted her head to the clouds and screamed until not a whisper of breath remained: "Dadddddddddddy!"

Chapter Two

Clyde sat behind the wheel of a cherry red Porsche 911 convertible, top down, pushing one hundred miles per hour down a long, deserted southwestern highway. Eyes lost behind dark sunglasses, a satisfied grin edged his face while the arid wind rustled his cotton undershirt and flailed his inky bangs wildly across his brow like the sporadic tentacles of an octopus.

Laura, whom the evening previous had played the role of Clyde's estranged orphan sister, 'Magda', was stretched out in the passenger seat, soaking up the intrusive sunrays beaming down on her from a cloudless blue sky. The wind pummeled her unfettered hair, throwing aimless strands of gold indiscriminately over her face, and pinned her tank top to her lithe, sinuous exterior, defining every bend and contour of her carnal femininity. Her long, shimmering legs propped up on the dash, exposing bare feet and the fresh pastel-blue nail polish applied to her toes that morning.

In the backseat, Joey 'The best man' and John 'The Pastor' flanked a purple sack filled with almost two hundred thousand dollars in cashed wedding gift checks. One might speculate that it would be a tricky thing cashing all those wedding checks addressed to Mr. & Mrs. Clyde Morrison in the middle of the night. However, the kids behind the glass at the 24-Hour Checks Cashed places always smiled when a guy showed up in a tuxedo, a purple one especially, looking to cash in his wedding money to take the Mrs. on a shotgun honeymoon to Vegas. Of course, all the necessary identification would be readily available. This time, 'Clyde Morrison' and his government IDs were out of there in less than half an hour.

"What are you thinking about, Mitch?" Laura asked, head canted listlessly against the creme leather headrest. The blue contact lenses she had donned for the part of Magda now removed, her natural jade irises glimmered boldly.

Hearing his real name fall off Laura's gloss-wet lips after assuming the identity of Clyde Morrison for so long was like the strumming of a poignant chord. The proverbial 'music to his ears'. It meant they had completed their job successfully, and could once again behave as themselves after more than a year to the contrary.

Mitch focused steadily on the seemingly infinite straightway before him. Lane separators zipped under the Porsche at bullet speed. "Thinking about getting to the buffer town," he answered over the engine's roar. "You?"

Laura smiled dreamily beneath lacerating whips of blonde. "A cold beer."

"I'll second that," said Joey from the backseat. He had broken from his fixation on the glassy body of water on the horizon beyond the guardrail, below the rocky escarpment, where daylight sparkles dappled the water's blue-green surface like a swarm of diamonds washing upon the shore.

Mitch glanced briefly at his protege in the rearview and returned his eyes to the road. The summer heat radiated waves over the pavement's surface like a screen of translucent jelly. "The township of Sandy Acres is a half hour out. We'll set up, get this car out of sight, and then we can grab some beer."

"Beer first," Joey countered.

"We have to switch cars, Jo," Mitch remonstrated, asserting an authoritative tone and throwing a longer and more pertinent glance at Joey through the rearview.

Mitch's eyes shifted behind his sunglasses and met John's. Now out of his religious garb and resting easy in a pair of slim jeans and a vintage *Lynyrd Skynyrd* t-shirt, John appeared much more like his old-fashioned cowboy self, besides the ashy goatee he had shaved off reluctantly before the wedding ceremony. The two founding members of the team shared a glance as if to roll their eyes and say: *Kids...*

Joey's dimples cracked as he grinned at his superiors. "Nope. Beer."

"ANOTHER ROUND OF SHOTS, sweetheart!" Joey howled at the waitress working the Sandy Acres Bed N' Bar. He slapped a crisp fifty-dollar bill on the wooden table littered with myriad suds-lined ale pints and four shot glasses brimming with Jameson Irish Whiskey.

The waitress, presumably in her fifties by the coriaceous wear of her skin, was clad in a black t-shirt and washed denim skirt. Her hair was styled into a beehive, excessively hair-sprayed, dehydrated, and brittle. A piece of chewing gum smacked and popped in her mouth as it bounced between her yellowed teeth. New lines appeared on her face as she squinted down at the four shot glasses on the table. "You haven't drank your first ones yet," she observed casually.

"You just worry about the drinks, honey," Joey said outright. "Let us worry about the drinking."

Without a response, though vividly indignant, the waitress picked up her tray and jaunted slowly back to the bar to make sure Joey understood she was in no rush.

Despite being a Wedding Bandit for nearly eight years now, Joey always got his back up when arriving in a new town, *especially* the buffer town, due to its inherent lack of consequences. He wanted to establish right off the bat that he wasn't a pushover and leaped eagerly at the opportunity to prove as much to anyone who sought to contest his alpha-male status. Even if that 'anyone' was a middle-aged, worn-out waitress from a small southwestern township in the middle of butt-fuck nowhere.

Mitch watched the nervous glances from a few nearby patrons slide in and out of his direction. The foursome's decision to take the corner table in the back of the ramshackle tavern had been an attempt at keeping their presence low-key. Three rounds of beers and whiskey shots later, that attempt had been in vain.

"Ease up, Jo, eh?" Mitch murmured to his protege. "No need to put a sign on our backs right away."

"Give 'im a break," said John. He stamped his empty pint on the faded coaster graphic. "He's just celebrating a job well done."

The elder bandit perched tall in his seat and scanned the sparse and seasoned clientele. "Speaking of celebrating, I need to find a new connection."

Mitch tried not to sound too much like a mother when he said: "You gotta lay off that cocaine shit, John. It'll be the death of you."

John stroked his non-existent goatee out of habit and replied with a familiar shrug of apathy. "Better than a bullet in the head, Mitch. You goddamn babyfucker."

Shortly thereafter, the waitress served out the fourth tray of shots, only to have Joey send her back for a fifth. Each time she returned, she regarded Joey with a little more esteem. This pleased Joey, and he'd send her back to the bar for more.

Within an hour of this perpetual ego-driven rotation, Mitch was certifiably drunk and doing everything in his power to keep the room from spinning. John had found himself a lead at the opposite end of the tavern, and Joey was leaning against the bar wood, flirting with their waitress, who, at this point, had more than thawed from her chill. Laura had been incrementally nestling closer to the warmth of Mitch's body. Presently, her head rested against his chest.

"So...here we are," she purred. It was the tone Laura used when she wanted to play house. "Another town."

Mitch swallowed a slow sip of suds. "Yup. Another town. Another job well done."

Laura caught Mitch as he again conducted a visual sweep of their surroundings, a habit of all crooks and fugitives picked up from years on the run. Normal people called it 'paranoia'. She smirked at his predictability and adjusted her face so they were nose to nose. "You ever get tired of this? The grind? The lies? The starting over?"

"I've been running almost my whole life," Mitch replied without much consideration. "That's like asking if I'm tired of life."

Laura's emerald gaze fixed on him and, twitching left to right, searched for a tell of dishonesty.

"So, you're happy?"

"I am."

Satisfaction curled upwards on Laura's ripe mouth. She rested her head back on Mitch's chest, nestled a little tighter, and closed her eyes. "Good."

A beat of silence.

"Are you?" asked Mitch.

Laura raised her head so they were again nose to nose. This time her eyes weren't searching; they were telling. "Fuckin' right, I am."

She pressed her lips against his and sent a rushing wave of strawberry across Mitch's tongue.

THE DOOR TO MITCH'S motel room swung open wildly and thudded off the wall with such force that Mitch wondered if the knob had punched a hole in the drywall. He and Laura shuffled blindly into the room, bodies intertwined, heads canted, mouths at work. Mitch used the toe of his boot to shut the door behind them.

The latch sealed underneath the soundtrack of their smacking lips and soft, short moans.

Mitch squeezed Laura's shoulders and posted her against the wall roughly. The room shook, and next to them, a small frame encasing a picture of a sailboat hopped off its nail and jettisoned to the ash-stained carpet beneath their feet. Laura gasped and looked up at Mitch with galvanic eyes.

She could take the pain. If anything, she got off on it.

She lunged forward and returned her mouth to his, nibbling his lower lip and taking it with her as she pulled away. Serpentine coils of blonde hair fell wildly over her face. Mitch closed the gap between them, drawing Laura in by her hip so that her pelvis interlocked with his own. He felt her feminine heat permeate.

Tumbling through the motel room, bouncing off table edges and closet doors, Mitch explored the curves and slants of Laura's textbook body. He had conducted expeditions through those hills and valleys many times before. Nevertheless, an anatomy such as hers was a work of art, meant to be indefatigably admired, analyzed, and appreciated.

The spring creaked as Mitch dropped onto the mattress. Laura crawled over him on all fours like a prowling jungle panther. She whipped the entirety of her quilted mop to one side of her head with a single snap of her neck, grinning down upon her recumbent quarry with a hungry appraisal.

There were two things in life at which Laura was indisputably unparalleled: Lying and sex.

Suddenly, the door to the motel room swung open. Mitch and Laura at once became a pair of deer caught in headlights. Mitch anticipated SWAT or FBI, but it was only Joey, entangled with the middle-aged waitress from the bar. With exemplary precision, Joey performed the 'close the door with your foot' technique Mitch had executed only moments earlier. He, indeed, was Mitch's protege.

It took a moment for Joey and the waitress to realize they weren't alone in the room. First, Joey peeked open an eye, then his paramour, sensing Joey's distraction, peeled open herself, caught sight of Mitch and Laura on the second bed, and shrieked.

Joey's lipstick-smeared visage held the innocent despondency of a young boy who had stumbled in on his parents eating his Halloween candy. "Guys? What the frick?"

Mitch and Laura remained frozen in each other's arms as if trying to outwit a T-Rex.

Joey resigned to the circumstances. "Whatever..." he shrugged. He pulled the waitress close and shut off the lights with the flap of a palm.

A creak of a mattress spring and a lilting giggle trailed in the darkness.

THE NEXT DAY MITCH was up before the alarm. Thick linen curtains over the windows deflected the sun and the overnight air conditioning had chilled the room to a temperature slightly too cold for comfort. Mitch clambered out of bed, careful not to wake Laura, whose soft features presently resembled a child amid a pleasant dream.

He extended his arms to the stucco ceiling and stretched.

The Bed N' Bar waitress had discharged at some point in the night, and Joey remained sprawled across his double bed like a chalk outline. He had passed out before getting under the covers.

Poor kid, Mitch thought with a smirk. He was proud of his protege for all the work he had put in on the last con. Working construction for a year couldn't have been easy for him, the early rises and the demanding labor, but the boy had stayed the course with surprising consistency and minimal objections. It almost made up for his face-palming blunder during their job in Martydale.

Quietly, Mitch dropped to the floor and pumped out fifty push-ups and fifty crunches. He was heading into the bathroom for a shower when the alarm clock started to buzz, and the languid forms of Joey and Laura began to flip and turn like steaks on a grill.

By the time Mitch was dried and fitted into a blue button-down shirt and khaki slacks, the other two had come to life and were looking to get in their showers before the hot water ran out. When it came to seedy roadside motels, as the team had learned over the years, it was always a toss-up when it came to bathing. Water temperature, water pressure—you never knew what awaited you upon the showerhead's ejaculation. Mitch's wash that morning had been surprisingly pleasant, relaxing even. Joey and Laura picked up on this fact immediately.

Once Laura usurped the advantage as the next to bathe, no surprise to Mitch—probably no surprise to Joey, either—Mitch used the room phone to call the Lobby.

"*Yeah?*" shot the receptionist on the other end. She was an older female and, judging by her granular timber, a heavy smoker.

"Room 28, please."

"*Hold on a sec.*"

The phone rang seven times without an answer.

Mitch hung up the receiver and went for the door. "Get movin', huh?" he said to Joey on the way out.

Joey motioned helplessly to the steam vapor pouring out from the half-inch of space between the bathroom door and the carpet.

ENCROACHING SUNRAYS had Mitch squinting as he strolled along the motel's second-floor mezzanine in the morning bake. The railing overlooked the tavern and parking lot. The cherry red convertible parked amid rusted pickup trucks and early model station wagons with sun-bleached side paneling stuck out like a sore thumb, rekindling Mitch's urgency to get the car out of sight as soon as possible.

Upon approaching John's room, he heard noises indicative of a struggle inside the unit. He put his ear to the door and discerned multiple exasperated grunts and skin slapping against skin. He considered returning to his room to retrieve his pistol but knew there was no time to waste if John was in trouble on the other side of that door.

Carefully, Mitch twisted the doorknob. The door opened barely half an inch. Mitch released the handle, closed his eyes, and drew a breath. Instinctively, he pinched the golden medallion hanging from his neck and recited a short Celtic prayer in his head. Then, he turned the knob and shouldered through the door.

What Mitch saw next made him gasp and shudder in horror...

John was standing at the edge of the bed, back to the door, slim jeans crumpled around his ankles, his chicken legs and rosy rump naked as the day he was born. An unknown heavy-set blonde woman lay prostrate on the pitted mattress, a massive oily lump of pizza dough, too many folds and creases to tell one body part from the other. On the night table, beside the reading lamp, was a small mound of white powder. Cut from the pile were three thin white lines portioned out at the ready.

John had found his coke.

And a prostitute to go with it.

John's bald head, slick with perspiration, whirled furiously to Mitch at the entrance. "Close the damn door!" he screamed while his manhood, neither fully erect nor flaccid, drooped from his clutch like raw deli sausage.

Mitch pivoted out of the room forthwith and slammed the door shut behind him. Shortly thereafter, the grunting and slapping inside recommenced without lag.

After a drawn-out exhale, Mitch's heart rate gradually slowed. He let out a sharp laugh, embarrassed more at himself for thinking the worst than at John's salacious and repugnant indiscretion. With an impish grin and a shake of his head, Mitch started back in the direction from which he had arrived.

When Mitch returned to his room, Laura, in a black tank top and jean shorts, watched herself in the vanity mirror while pulling her hair into a ponytail. Her face was void of makeup to maintain an unremarkable countenance, the modus operandi until they figured out what kind of people they needed to become for the next job. She let her arms down, broke from the mirror, and met Mitch's gaze curiously.

The rushing of shower water came to an abrupt end.

"That shower was fucking freezing, Laura!" Joey yelled from inside the bathroom.

Laura's eyes remained on Mitch, analyzing. "Are you okay?"

Mitch rendered an assuring smile. "Yeah. Yeah, I'm good."

Chapter Three

Mitch and Joey perched in the front seats of the Porsche, top-up, A/C blowing, watching Laura under the low brim of their baseball caps as she bartered with the willowy old rube who ran the Sandy Acres junkyard. The sun's glare tinged the earth gold and galvanized Laura's unfettered limbs. The old man's ashen, rutted skin took to the heat less easily. His jutting chin dribbled with tiny droplets of sweat that dripped onto the oil-stained dungarees sagging off his gaunt frame. Every few seconds, the lot owner would glance away from Laura into his shaded workshop, wantingly, as if yearning to enjoy the coolness waiting for him under the shed's corrugated tin roof. For one reason or another, the old man did not act on the inclination. Mitch suspected Laura's full breasts sweating in a black tank top might have had something to do with his decision to remain stationary.

"Do we really have to stash this thing?" asked Joey over the hum of the dash vents.

Mitch's attention stuck with Laura and the yard owner. He replied flatly: "Yes."

Joey huffed like a child at the supermarket after his mother told him to put the toy back where he found it. "It's a crime, is what it is."

"Identity fraud is a crime, Jo. Enough time has passed that the Robertsons know what's going on. They'll be looking for this car."

"Yeah, yeah," Joey groaned. "It was a joke. Just a joke."

Mitch knew it was just a joke. But when it came to Joey, it didn't take much for a joke to turn serious. And then from serious to a problem.

Laura parted from the yard owner and approached the Porsche. She was patient with her stride, listlessly kicking up dust with the toe of her cowboy boot and letting the sun kiss her skin as she admired the sky behind aviator sunglasses.

Mitch rolled down his window at her request. She leaned in, speaking covertly: "He says he'll park it. Twelve hundred for the year."

"Did he ask about it?"

She retained a healthy smile for the rube's benefit. "Yup. I told him you're a collector, and you picked it up at a car show in Texas. He didn't ask much more."

"Great. Do it," said Mitch. "And since we're 'collectors' and everything, see if he's got any unique fixer-upper opportunities he wants to get rid of."

"Already did, babe," she crowed.

Laura regarded the old man with a raised forefinger in a plea for patience. The yard owner tugged on the straps of his overalls to convey his obligation. Laura then explained to Mitch through the open window that a '69 Dodge Charger needed some body work; the guts were fine, and he was willing to get rid of it for seventeen thousand.

"*Seventeen grand*?" sneered Mitch.

Laura reacted contemptuously to Mitch's parsimonious reflex. "You'll make triple that when you find a buyer for the Porsche. It's a beauty car."

Mitch's arm didn't need twisting. He loved the Dodge Charger. And even needing restoration, seventeen thousand was a steal. He and John could do the work on their downtime and flip it for a profit before heading to the next buffer town.

"Yeah, fine. Get it."

Joey, who had already been counting through a band of hundred-dollar bills for the parking fee Laura quoted, did a quick recalculation and removed another two small stacks of hundred-dollar bills from the purple sack at his feet. He loaded the bricks into Laura's awaiting palms. She sauntered toward the lot owner with full hands, adding a little flair into the popping of her hips as she went.

Maybe it was for the lot owner.

Maybe it was for Mitch.

GRAVEL SPRAYED FROM beneath squealing tires as the charcoal-painted '69 Charger peeled onto the main street. Once the tread had kissed the pavement, traction hugged the road, and the rusted body centered. Mitch engaged the gas pedal and braced the neck-snapping tug of the two-barrel engine as they lunged forward. He tittered surreptitiously in a fit of puerile nostalgia, yielding to his longstanding deference for Bo and Luke Duke from the old television show *Dukes of Hazzard*. Before Mitch's mom had walked out on him and his dad all those years ago, Mitch and his parents used to watch the program on the thirteen-inch technicolor in the sitting room every Friday after dinner. It was one of the few good memories he still carried from his childhood.

"John's going to love this thing," said Mitch. His grip tightened on the wheel.

Joey, presently sprawled out lethargically in the back seat, agreed.

"So we got the car," said Laura over the rumbling engine and ruffling wind flooding into the cab. She put her hand headlong out the window and let her fingers surf effortlessly against the current. "Let's go *shopping*."

BY THE TIME THEY RETURNED to Room 28, arms heavy with plastic shopping bags, John's mound of cocaine had diminished to a small hump, and the ashtray next to the powder was a hill of cold, gray ash and cigarette butts. John was at the nightstand on a phone call. A billowing yellow stub dangled from his chapped lips. The doughy prostitute from earlier had since shipped off, leaving only a thick torrent of sour sweat and stink in her wake.

Laura's face twisted as if all five senses had been offended simultaneously. "Maybe you should open a window in here," she suggested as she unloaded the new phone boxes from their plastic bags onto the unmade bed.

John hung up the phone. "Maybe you should shut the fuck up," he grumbled back at her.

Despite the elder bandit's uncanny ability to transform a few grams of cocaine into many hours of thorough, productive work, enduring the raging discontentment that accompanied his high's decline was invariably arduous for anyone who dared to step into its orbit. This account was no different.

Laura shook her head and bounded for the window. She thrust it ajar and sipped the fresh air like water from a public fountain.

"I got your IDs," John announced in a hoarse murmur indicative of a night laden with narcotics and cancer sticks.

He squashed a cigarette butt into the small mountain of dead smoke and lit another. Laura watched him, nauseated. Joey lay on the bed, beside the phone boxes, and interlocked his hands behind his head. Mitch shuddered. He imagined Joey might have reconsidered his place in the shade if he had witnessed what played out on its breadth a few hours earlier.

"And what unlucky souls will we be possessing this time?" asked Joey, blinking his toes.

Laura, briskly wafting the outside air into starving nostrils, said: "Another one of John's long line of down-and-out junkies."

Mitch often wondered if the junkies ever bothered to ask why John's constituents in New York were trading hundreds of dollars for their banking and social insurance information. Or what the junkies would do if they happened to check their accounts while the wedding money was filtering through. The thought of it had kept Mitch up at night during the con's infancy. But after twelve years of smooth sailing, apart from the Martydale incident, which undoubtedly had been a problem more human than technical, Mitch had learned to quit outwardly searching for black clouds and had begun, in the words of his sultry female teammate, to 'go with the flow'.

John neglected the other team members and conferred with Mitch directly. "You get the car?"

Mitch nodded.

"What is it?"

"A Prius," blurted Joey.

Mitch couldn't help but grin at the sheer contempt growing on John's sagging countenance.

"No, it's not," said Mitch, for Joey's sake. "But you're going to love it."

Mitch lobbed the key chain across the room. John snatched it from the air.

"I goddamn better," he groused. "Meanwhile, find us a mark, and let's get to the new town. I'm out of drugs, and we've overstayed our welcome."

Starting for the door, he stiffened at the team's continued idleness. "Get the fuck out of my room!" he barked.

Laura put her hands up defensively. "No one's fighting you on that."

Joey rolled lazily off the bed to his feet and followed Laura out the door. Mitch was right behind them, patting John on the back as he left.

"Don't touch me, boy," huffed John, breathing through his nose like a gorilla. Remnants of sweat still shone on his brow. "You don't know where I've been."

Mitch shook his head ruefully. "Unfortunately, I do. But believe me when I tell you that I wish I didn't."

HALF-EXCAVATED CHINESE takeout containers littered the vanity, mattress corners, and window ledges of Room 23. Inside the MSG-slicked Styrofoam octagon, Joey sat cross-legged on the bed, back against the headboard. His spacey gaze was transfixed on the pale blue glow of his laptop screen as his index finger sliced surgically across the touchpad. Laura leaned against the wardrobe and used a hand to fan her sweat-glistened neck, the signs of heat exhaustion prominent on her flushed visage. Mitch sat beside her, in a backward-positioned desk chair, and assumed the quarterback role while taking shallow pulls from a 40oz bottle of Wild Turkey.

"I got one," clapped Joey. "She's from Moss Lake, just over a hundred miles away. Thirty-four. Single. Profile pic looks like she's probably going to stay that way. Her father is an investment banker, happily married, doing very well for himself—according to his Instagram and personal website, at least. He's got a large property, a boat, a few collector cars. He's just the kind of rich we're looking for. You should look at this property, geeze...it's stunning."

"Stunning," huffed Laura as she accepted the bottle of Wild Turkey from Mitch's outstretched hand. "I'll stun *you*, bud."

She took a swig. Her face curdled. She stepped forward and offered the bottle to Joey. "Does she live with him?"

"She does *not*," answered Joey. He retrieved the bottle and used his shirttail to clean the nozzle before indulging. Laura's expression instantly soured at the insinuation. "She bought a condo. Saved up from her teacher salary. She's a teacher. But from looking at her *LinkedIn* account, I see she has been working steadily for the last two decades, doing an array of different shit. Bank teller, insurance salesperson, cashier at the grocery store, clerk at the video store...she's a worker. Been at it since high school."

Mitch shook his head with a stiff lip. "It's no good."

Joey arched a curious eyebrow at his mentor, slipped his lips around the neck of the whiskey bottle for an encore, and tilted bottom-up.

Mitch elaborated: "It sounds like her parents had her working at a young age to instill proper habits and for her to learn the value of a dollar. Parents like that are no good. You're looking at minimal contributions. The dowry would be no more than a congrats and a handshake. No, what we need is a leech. A train wreck, daddy's girl. She needs to still be living at home with no immediate plans on leaving. She needs to be lazy and not very cunning. She needs to be the type of girl whose parents will throw large sums of cash at any man who'd be willing to take her off their hands."

"Like sweet little Angie?" said Laura in a baby voice.

Joey laughed. "Little? I don't think so."

A rocket blasted up Mitch's esophagus. "Hey!"

Joey and Laura jolted out of gaiety.

"What's the golden rule?" Mitch demanded curtly of his wise-cracking pupils.

Bleary-eyed and visually labored, Joey and Laura recited in languid chorus: "After the con, they're gone."

Mitch remained firm. "That's right. What's done is done. We don't look back. The only way this works is if we keep moving forward."

His teammates' queasy glares pleaded no contest. Almost immediately, Mitch felt guilty for his overemotional outburst. But dragging the girl's weight was overkill, and he would not permit it. The team had already taken her and her family for hundreds of thousands of dollars. They more than likely had torn this girl's whole world, not to mention her heart, to shreds by what they had done. Adding insult to injury was arrogant and bad karma.

Mitch took a breath and recollected himself. "I'm sorry, okay? It's just...the rules are important. It's the reason we've gotten this far."

Joey wasn't the remorseful type, and Mitch knew that like he knew how to tie his shoes. His protege couldn't give a damn about a mark's emotional state after the getaway. Still, he adopted a frown and furrowed his brow apologetically to evince that he was at least attempting to show contrition. "You're right. I know," said Joey. "It's the last you'll hear about her, I swear."

Joey handed the bottle of Wild Turkey to Mitch. Mitch took a swig. He paused and let the burn settle in his chest before placing the bottle on the table next to the map of the region's municipalities and additional takeout containers. He wanted to erase the last few moments.

"Wait, wait," said Joey. His excitement sliced through the hovering tension. His head inched toward the luminance of his laptop screen. Small squares of white light reflected in his doe-eyed pupils. The more he scrolled, the more intrigued Mitch was by his protege's newfound curiosity. Joey nodded vigorously as if cognitively patting himself on the back for a job well done. "Oh, *baby*. We got a live one."

"Let me see," said Mitch. He lurched for the laptop.

Joey picked up the computer like a newborn baby and twisted away from Mitch until the laptop was out of reach. "Back off, Mitch!" he snapped. "Back off!"

Mitch desisted mid-pursuit, mildly entertained by Joey's newfound enthusiasm.

Joey shooed him and Laura away. "Go do something. Fuck off. Let me work my magic. This could be the one."

Mitch was pleased with Joey's confidence. Like John, when the kid was focused, he was a veritable tour de force. Mitch stepped back and disarmed. "That good, huh?"

Joey returned to his cross-legged position and set the laptop before his socks. "Oh yeah. This young lady is just what we're looking for. Give me a few hours and we'll know everything there is to know about her."

Satisfied, Mitch shrugged and stuffed his hands in his pockets. He turned to Laura. "Coffee? I'm buying."

Laura cackled at the gesture. "Wow, buying me a coffee, you're *so* generous. What would I ever do without you?"

"I don't know...bar tend, maybe?"

Laura gasped with the pleasant stupefaction of a slap in the face during sex. "I think you're wound-up enough. Let's get a *real* drink."

MITCH AND LAURA SAT at the wood inside the small tavern where they had tied one on the previous evening. Luckily, the waitress Joey had brought back to the room wasn't working. From the way the bed's headboard had been smashing against the drywall, Mitch assumed she was most likely on the couch at home with a pack of ice under her backside. The New York Yankees cap Mitch had worn all day was still low on his face, and Laura had Joey's Red Sox cap pulled deep on hers. She had untied her ponytail before they left the room, letting strands of gold rest causally on the shoulders of her new denim jacket. In front of them, the third round of foamy pints slowly depreciated between breaks in the conversation.

Mitch watched Laura as she threw her head back in wild laughter at his recollection of the moment he had walked in on John and the prostitute. There was a hint of madness in her cackle.

"Do you ever think," Mitch started as he ran his thumb across the layer of frost over his glass, "about how your life might have turned out if we never met in the pool hall that night?"

Laura paused to conceive the proposition. She appeared less than pleased with the results. "Married. A couple kids. Trying to turn my daughter into the figure skater I never was. Unhappy. Unfulfilled."

She turned the spotlight on Mitch. "You?"

Mitch fantasized and shrugged with a grin. "Probably take home a bigger cut."

She slapped him on the arm. "Shut up. You love me."

He willingly conceded. "It *is* nice to have a female on the team. I don't think I would have made it this far with just Joey and John."

Laura winked. "And John's prostitutes."

"Yes. And John's prostitutes."

Laura's face fell deadpan. "Have you been indulging with him?"

Mitch fought the urge to laugh. He settled with a firm "No" that distinctly translated his indigence.

His defensiveness satisfied the inquisitor. "That's right," she said slyly. "Joey told me you've been saving money from the last two jobs. What are you putting money away for? A 401K? Retirement? We're not normal people, you know. I don't know why you keep trying to be."

Mitch shrugged and broke from her gaze. "I don't know...Having a plan never hurt anyone. I mean, do you want to be doing this your whole life? Running?"

"I don't mind the running," said Laura, straightening out. "It keeps me in shape."

Their attention abruptly whirled when a voice coated with a thick Southern accent said from behind them: “Hey! Where’s that cherry convertible y’all were in the other day?”

It was one of the bar’s regulars, an older sort, sloven and haggard, comically stout and toting a keg-sized gut like a baby in the womb. He reminded Mitch of an elephant seal someone had dressed ironically in a flannel shirt. At a more prolonged glance, Mitch recognized the barfly as the coke dealer whose services John had rendered the previous night.

Mitch immediately switched into character. Laura, the same.

“Excuse me?” Laura asked pointedly.

The barfly effectuated a retreating bound, unprepared for Laura’s sharp reproach. He cowered like an amateur boxer on the defense. Mitch registered the depths of his intoxication from the reek of whiskey on his breath and the rocking of his shoulders and hips as he attempted to remain balanced. He tried again to be convivial: “You guys were in here last night, ain’t ya? With a couple other fellas. Your friend was over at my table yapping; what was his name?”

Laura flicked her hair behind her shoulder, smiling politely under the Sox cap and keeping her face out of full view. “Sorry, you must have us mistaken for somebody else.”

She touched Mitch’s arm softly. “This is my husband. We’re just passing through on the way to visit some family.”

The sloven barfly examined them good and hard. “No, I could have sworn it was youz.”

“Sorry to disappoint you,” said Mitch, shutting him out. “But if you don’t mind...”

Luckily, uncertainty and a sudden lack of interest befell the man, possibly due to the disapproving glare beaming down on him from the bartender, a soldier-looking type well over six feet tall. Mitch was grateful for the assistance. The barfly apologized and continued toward the bathrooms.

Mitch and Laura paid their bill and left.

MITCH ADMIRED THE DOOR bulb's incandescence on Laura's soft cheeks as the two stood at the entrance to Laura's room. She caught him staring and tilted her head sideways demurely.

"What?" she giggled.

"Nothing...You're just pretty, that's all."

"You know, you could stay the night."

Mitch denied his primitive nature. "No, I better get back and see where Joey's at with the new mark."

"Okay, well...Sweet dreams, Robin Hood."

Robin Hood.

Mitch appreciated the comparison. However, there was a key difference between himself and the legend of Sherwood Forest. Robin Hood stole from the rich and the *corrupt,* while Mitch stole from the rich, regardless of their moral credibility. Some of the people he cleaned out were commendable members of society who didn't deserve the destitution that Mitch and his merry band of thieves so heedlessly and indiscriminately delivered. For example, Mr. Robertson, Angie's father, had forged a lucrative construction company from nothing but a dream and some elbow grease. He was a self-made millionaire. He provided jobs and service to the community. He wasn't just some asshole who inherited his money without any sacrifice and treated the lower class like fecal matter.

Mitch severed the thought before it unfurled any further and recited the Wedding Bandits' bedrock mantra: *After the con, they're gone.*

EARLY THE NEXT DAY, the team reconvened in Room 28, which, to Laura's unabashed relief, had aired out overnight and was now a much more breathable atmosphere. Fresh off a good night's sleep, John handed out brown paper envelopes containing the character profile and identification of their soon-to-be assumed identities.

"Read 'em. Learn 'em. These people are you for the next year or so. Get into character. No fucking around."

Mitch tore a strip off the envelope and removed a letter-sized sheet. A new driver's license was paper-clipped to the top left corner of the page.

"Roy Hawkins," Mitch read off his manifesto. "Another ex-alcoholic looking for a fresh start in a new town."

"Think you got it down by now?" teased Laura across the room. Her provocative gaze narrowed.

"I'm Sean Forrest," smiled Joey, theatrically glib, round-eyed as a child opening their first gift on Christmas morning. "AA buddy, extraordinaire!"

Laura looked up from her paper with a frown. "I'm on recon again? Joey should be on recon; *he's* the screw up."

Joey's celebration halted. His brow furrowed over a wounded countenance. "...the heck, Laura?"

John sat down on the bed and, for the first time in two days, inhaled a breath unsquandered by anxieties or stimuli. "Okay. I did my part. Your turn. Who's this mark?"

Joey gathered the papers from the vanity desk and kissed his teeth impertinently at Laura before beginning: "The mark's name is Meryl Chestwick, daughter of Nick Chestwick. He's the Sheriff of Oak County, the town we'll be operating out of."

Laura slumped forward in her seat, elbows on her knees and hands clasped together. Her expression sagged. "A Sheriff? Doesn't sound very lucrative."

"On the contrary," said Joey in a pointed reproach. "The Chestwick family is worth over ten million."

John's eyes expanded as he thumbed out a cigarette from his pack of Player's and inserted it between his lips. "No shit! Ten million! How'd they manage that on a law enforcement salary?"

Joey explained as John alighted: "Some years back, an extremely wealthy oil tycoon was kidnapped by some bandits tied to Mexican drug cartels. It was big news. There was a huge manhunt trying to find this guy. The kidnappers were hiding out with him in Oak County, and it was the Sheriff who saved him single handily, turning the Sheriff into something of a local hero. Years later, the oil tycoon died, and, being that he had no wife or kids, he left his entire fortune to the Chestwicks. The Sheriff went from small-town hero to multimillionaire overnight."

"Great," said Laura as she stood to stretch. "Tell us about Mitch's new sweetheart."

"Meryl works at a call center in town. They sell commercial shop-vacs. Not very exciting stuff. Unfortunately, her sedentary lifestyle over the years has helped her put on some pounds. She stays inside the mansion mostly. Spends a lot of time on her phone and on Netflix. Her Instagram and Facebook are a ton of cat stuff. Very few pictures of herself. She's all about *Law & Order*, too...won't shut up about it.

"As for male callers, there are none to speak of. Maybe it's because she's the Sheriff's daughter, but I'm guessing it's something else. Either way, the last time she had a boyfriend was during the Bush administration."

"Bush Jr., I hope," chuckled John. He swatted an invasive stream of smoke from his eye and shot quick expectant glances at each team member.

"Yes. Bush Jr.," repeated Joey, pampering the senior bandit's want for validation.

"The big girl is going to love you, Mitch," teased Laura. "Don't you worry about *that*."

Mitch absorbed Laura's light-hearted slight. He knew it was coming. It always did. The razzing, the jokes. Now was the team's one chance to take uncontested shots at their leader.

"You think Mitch has it bad? I have to *work* at this call center!" groaned Joey. "I can only imagine what kind of train wreck monsters are lurking inside those walls."

Laura flashed him a wink. "You might even find yourself a nice bearded lady, Joe."

The four bandits remained inside the hotel room for the next hour and enjoyed each other's company. Mitch took the brunt of the gags and jabs casually tossed around at his expense. He didn't mind. It was better they got it out of their systems now while they could. It had been fun while it lasted, but vacation time was over. The next job was about to get underway.

It was time to refocus.

Chapter Four

Under a hot sun and a clear morning sky, Agent Quinn sat inside the unmarked Crown Victoria parked on the avenue leading up to the gated Robertson estate. The middle-aged FBI workhorse grunted and lurched forward to retrieve his coffee from the ash-cluttered center console. Lynyrd Skynyrd's *Free Bird* crackled modestly through the worn dashboard speakers. He turned the volume knob and filled the cab with the classic southern honky-tonk swagger.

Quinn drifted into a wistful reverie of childhood summer holidays at his parents' cottage. In his mind, the sunlight dappled and danced nostalgically off Lake Ahote's gently undulating surface. His legs dangled off the edge of the pinewood dock, toes skimming the frigid waves. A warm breeze caressed his face. His father stood by the charcoal grill with a bottle of Corona in one hand and a meat-speckled spatula in the other. The amber lager shone like liquid gold. The sweet fragrance of fresh-cut grass and his mother's department store perfume permeated the air. Wafts of sizzling beef enchanted his senses and roused his appetite. His mother's tender voice lilted from the screen door leading into the den, near the picnic table ladened with various condiments, paper plates, and cold cans of Pepsi and Ginger Ale, encouraging him to come inside and wash up for dinner.

Quinn opened his eyes and languidly stroked his slick crown. Reality settled, heavy and hot. The tension in his shoulders pinched at his portly neck as he took his first sip of coffee. The mud water had gone cold from neglect but was rewarding nonetheless.

As *Free Bird* came to a close, a commercial for StrongBolt, the construction company owned by the man Quinn was presently staking out, followed. The ad called for employment seekers to 'live a life they respect'.

Build Strong. StrongBolt.

It was a touching little campaign, especially for a man under investigation by the FBI for money laundering, extortion, drug trafficking, and murder. The air-time for the frequently run ad spot most likely would have set back Robertson a considerable sum, not unlike the wedding and reception he had thrown for his heifer of a daughter a couple of days previous. Quinn had staked out that event, too. And what an event it was. A panorama of inordinate extravagance and opulence, paid in full by the broken dreams of dope heads and junkies.

Live a life you respect...heh, right, thought Quinn with a derisive snort.

Quinn took another sip of coffee, smacked his lips, and exhaled with a resounding 'Aaaah.'

Unlike most of the agents on McAllester's task force, Agent Quinn did not resist the seclusion that accompanied reconnaissance in the field. In the confines of his federal vehicle, Quinn was free to partake in a multitude of taboo behaviors that his collectives might have found unpalatable had they been present. He could smack his lips after a sip of coffee as loudly as he pleased. He could scratch his undercarriage for as long as he felt necessary, if not longer. Heck, if he really wanted to, he could pull out his Johnson right there on the side of the road for a spunky good morning tug, and there wasn't anything anybody could say about it.

But of all the privileges that came with isolation, Quinn most enjoyed the fact that he could smoke a cigarette, tip to filter, without enduring the relentless lectures from his cohorts over the plurality of health defects he was imposing on his body by indulging in such a disgusting habit.

Quinn snorted. *What body?* Forty-four years old, high blood pressure, baggy-eyed, and double-chinned—he was a bald mass of lard and hair, and his idle manhood was ever-so-slowly disappearing behind a great barrier reef of belly fat.

He caught a glimpse of himself in the rearview mirror and shuddered. The pack of cigarettes on the dashboard called to him, and Quinn gladly surrendered to its siren song.

Pulling out a crisp Camel, Quinn parked the coffin nail between his chapped lips and scraped the lighter from the ashtray. A flick of his thumb produced the lick of a flame. He smoldered the cherry and inhaled deeply. Smoke coiled down his throat and muzzled his growling stomach, which was currently in the thralls of a violent protest against his decision to skip breakfast in exchange for an extra hour of sleep in his FBI-provided motel bed.

Quinn sucked back another long haul off the cigarette. The burning ember tumbled closer to the cotton filter like lava descending the slope of an ivory volcano. Amusing himself, Quinn drew his mouth oblong and deftly blew out a trio of swirling smoke circles. The geometric specters dwindled as they expanded outward, drifted into nothingness, and enveloped the cab in a haze. Quinn relaxed, pleased with his work. He took a slow sip of coffee and gazed through the windshield at the imposing estate on the crest of the hill.

The epicenter of the lavish property was the five-bedroom, four-car garage, Victorian country home, sidled by an Olympic-sized pool, lounge bar, and guest house. The crawling vines and primped emerald hedges wreathing the stately manor helped breathe life into an otherwise brooding fortress of ashen stone and mortar.

A team of gardeners in matching white uniforms were currently servicing the expansive rolling landscape within the prodigious borders of the wrought iron fence. At a squint, Agent Quinn thought he could discern amid the clutter of regimentals the civilian informant McAllester had recently recruited to keep tabs on the alleged underworld kingpin.

The informant was a skittish nineteen-year-old Spaniard by the name of Marvin Diaz. The local authorities arrested Marvin after catching him smoking a joint in a supermarket parking lot. Upon learning of the kid's access to the Robertson property, the Cedar Falls Sheriff's Office, aware of the pending investigation against Sylvester Robertson, notified the FBI. And wouldn't you know it? The kid was willing to cooperate with the feds in any way possible, just so long as his ironically anti-drug alcoholic father stayed in the dark about his less-than-commendable recreational activities.

Marvin, Agent Quinn chuckled to himself. *You dumb bitch.*

The sudden crackle of a walkie-talkie in the passenger seat jolted Quinn's ample backside out of its pitted cushion. The tinny voice mashing through the speaker belonged to Quinn's superior and task force leader Agent McAllester. He sought an update on Quinn's progress.

"I got nothing," Quinn said into the hand-held. "Ghost town over here. Bunch a hermits, these guys. Lifestyles of the rich and famous, my ass."

"Any sign of that Porsche from the wedding?" McAllester followed promptly.

"Negative," answered Quinn. "The daughter came back in a cab the next morning. No groom. No Porsche."

McAllester transmitted again, this time wielding a pointed tone that felt to Quinn as if his task force leader meant to undermine the thoroughness of his police work. "You don't think that's strange?"

Agent Quinn groaned privately and shook his head at the familiar micromanagement in motion. "We don't put eyes on the daughter. She's a civilian," he replied brusquely.

Silence on the line. A crackle of static shot out from the transceiver. "Stay on it. Out."

Quinn's belly rumbled. He wasn't going to make it until lunch. His weary bones demanded sustenance. He recalled the earlier commercial he had heard on the radio for the new breakfast sandwich from Ben's Burger House: Bacon, Ham, and Sausage.

Three different kinds of meat.

The corners of Agent Quinn's mouth began to moisten. His tongue grew wet. Processed meat and battered fried onion rings weren't the best things for his hypertension, but neither were coffee and cigarettes.

He decided to grab a quick pre-lunch lunch and return to his post before anyone knew he was gone. Other than the hard-at-work gardeners, the estate was a graveyard.

And besides, Marvin was on the case.

Satisfied with his reasoning and succumbing to visions of three different kinds of meat prancing through his head, Agent Quinn started the car and made a quick three-point-turn before heading back down the one-lane road to find the nearest Ben's Burger House drive-thru.

MR. ROBERTSON HAD JUST gotten off the phone with his Head of Security when the door to his office opened, and Sebastian stepped in from the hallway, dressed in a black turtle neck and jeans, hair ostentatiously fashioned. Following him into the office were his younger sister's inconsolable sobs emanating from her bedroom at the end of the hall. She had sequestered herself within its confines for the last two days, refusing to see or speak to anyone.

Behind an executive desk crafted of rich mahogany, Robertson grunted gravely. With a pained expression, he instructed his son to close the door. Sebastian did so and dropped in the leather armchair across from his father. Signs of fatigue were present on the younger Robertson's face, which was to be understood; the last couple days had been a long and grueling test of their family's strength. For a moment, father and son sat in silence as if to collectively gather their heads. Sebastian glanced disinterestedly over the three tiers of leather-bound titles occupying the bookshelf against the wall. Mr. Robertson sighed and watched the whirling ceiling fan.

Sebastian disrupted the dead air. "You know I don't like the guy," he said. "Never did from day one. But is it possible maybe he got kidnapped? By one of our enemies? Like what happened to Mom?"

Mr. Robertson's gaze drifted to the closed door. He watched the panels measurably.

"She can't hear me. She's crying," Sebastian assured.

Mr. Robertson exhaled and shook his head slightly. "I just got off the phone with my contact in New York. He put word out on the street for any information on the whereabouts of Clyde Morrison. He got a bite. Apparently, Clyde was at one of our establishments just last night."

Sebastian's angular jaw clenched. His stare iced over.

"I'm embarrassed I didn't see it coming," Robertson admitted with no subtle disgrace. "Once a junkie, always a junkie."

"So...cops? Or are we going to hire someone for the wet work?"

Mr. Robertson reclined in his velvet-upholstered armchair and pressed his fingertips into a pyramid. "No cops. No trigger men. I want to handle this myself. Clyde deserves that much."

Sebastian's gaze was narrow and focused, eager to begin the hunt. "I want to come with you," he said compactly.

The corners of Mr. Robertson's lips twitched upward. He gazed across the breadth of the desk at his seed with great reverence. He was a headstrong and courageous young man, just like his father had been in his youth. One day, he would take over the family business.

"Of course," said Robertson. "Go pack some things. We need to leave now. Tony just called, said the Fed watching the house headed out."

Sebastian rose and marched out of the office without another word.

Chapter Five

"You lost him? What do you mean you *lost* him?"

Agent McAllester closed the door to Assistant Deputy Director Martin's office to curtail the audibility of the inexorable berating he was about to receive. Desk agents on the floor who no longer gleaned their thrills off the capricious nature of FBI field work supplemented their need for emotional stimulation with overcaffeination and an astute ear for fresh office gossip. McAllester had no doubt that some of the aforementioned could have started their own supermarket tabloid and done very well for themselves. In addition to this motive for privacy, McAllester also moved to close the door to buy himself some time while he contrived an adequate response for his currently, and understandably, irate superior.

McAllester knew he would not be in this situation if he, rather than Agent Quinn, had gone to Cedar Falls to stake out the Robertson place. Unfortunately, his knack for getting things done had pulled him off the street four years ago and situated him behind a desk. Since then, he had been promoted three additional times, most recently to head the task force responsible for investigating Sylvester Robertson, a task that had special significance to McAllester considering his relation to the fabled Tyrant, whom Robertson's Number Two, Eric Baldacci, had fingered the StrongBolt CEO to be before a Latino gang-banger serving life for murder drove a homemade shiv into his jugular. But, as with the rest of the waking world, this connection between cop and criminal was unknown to ADD Martin. His superior only knew that one of Agent McAllester's field agents had lost track of the target. Understandably, he wasn't happy about it. Neither was McAllester. Nevertheless, it was a leader's job to stand before his team and answer for their shortcomings, even if he wondered how some of them, Agent Quinn being a prime example, ever got their badges.

"Our CI reported the Robertson's SUV leaving the property, but—"

On his feet between a paper-cluttered desk and a large, cumbersome file cabinet, Assistant Deputy Director Martin fanned the pile of informant reports in his hand. A vein bulged from his rippled forehead. Even his grizzly mustache looked angry. "I read the reports! Where was the tail?"

McAllester cleared his throat. "Agent Quinn reports he was in the bathroom at the time, sir."

At the drive-thru was more likely, thought McAllester. *Maybe a strip club*.

ADD Martin's aggressive pose disengaged. The red drained from his face. A massive coronary mishap seemed less likely with each passing second. He took a deep breath and said: "Hank, you're a good agent. You've been under me for ten years, and I've never seen you back down from a challenge. So when I told you that the Assistant Deputy Director position was yours to lose, I hope you didn't take that as a dare."

Even though his soon-to-be-retiring mentor had softened the blow of his dissatisfaction by wrapping his reprimand in a silk bow of dry humor, it stung McAllester all the same. He lowered his gaze. "No, sir."

The dress-down continued: "It took a long time to get the DA on board with going after Robertson. All we got is the testimony Eric Baldacci gave in exchange for a lesser sentence, and now that he's on ice, that testimony is all but useless. This investigation is hanging on by a thread. The DEA says it's a goose chase, a red herring, that

Baldacci was the Tyrant, and he fingered Robertson out of desperation for a plea bargain. If we come up empty on this..."

"We'll look like fools, I know," sighed McAllester with no subtle sensitivity.

"You," answered ADD Martin flatly with a pointed finger and an ominous stare. "*You* will look like a fool. Are you sure this guy is worth risking that promotion?"

Right then, McAllester's blood boiled with hatred for Agent Quinn, the one responsible for landing him in this precarious position. Regardless, the task force leader's militant expression held steadfast. "Yes, sir. This is our guy. I know it. He's smart and lets a lot of other people get their hands dirty before him, but he'll slip eventually. And I'll be there when he does."

A glint of contrition evinced itself in Martin's gaze. Maybe it was only exhaustion. His tone settled wearily. "Get back to it. I want this sorted out."

Back at his desk, accompanied by an out-of-date Macintosh computer, a foot-high stack of manila file folders relevant to the investigation, a coffee mug in need of filling, and framed photographs of his wife, Julia, and daughter, Jeanine, McAllester got on the two-way and instructed Agent Quinn to fall back until the Civilian Informant sent word of Robertson's return. "In the meantime," added McAllester, intentionally curt with his subordinate. "Find out where this missing groom is. Knock on doors if you have to. I don't care if you have to pull his dead body out of a dumpster. Find me Clyde Morrison."

Chapter Six

Clyde Morrison was losing his high. He needed more coke, and he needed it soon. He was concerned, however, that the gauntish slug with the greasy black hair and thrift store general's jacket, who for the last hour of the evening had been circling 8th Avenue and 35th Street and eyeing Clyde's spot over the steam vent next to the A-C-E subway entrance, would swoop in and usurp the prime real estate upon its vacancy.

A gaggle of five midtown pedestrians, a young couple up front, and a trio of retired women in the rear, passed over Clyde on the sidewalk. The woman up front, a husky redhead in her thirties, garbed expensively, shot him an impudent glare before commenting to her willowy date on how Manhattan had gone to hell over recent years. Clyde might have laughed had his mind not been preoccupied with the more important matters at stake.

What did she know about hell, in her diamond earrings and stilettos? he wondered to himself fleetingly before the need for cocaine overpowered all inferior thoughts.

He considered enduring the trek to Central Park. On the plus side, he was familiar enough with those dealers to avoid purchasing a half-gram of dish soap. On the negative, they pushed that Fentanyl-laced stuff, which was risky, and usually not much better than the dish soap.

Next, Clyde thought about Trevor. His spot was further away, but the product was top quality, immigrated from south of the border. Just the thought of the stuff had him more energized. Also,

Trevor might feel a bit generous, considering Clyde had aided him last year with that little identity fraud scheme he was cooking up. Sure, he had long since spent the money Trevor paid him for his social insurance numbers and bank accounts, but even still, he had helped Trevor in his time of need, which should at least be worth something.

Clyde watched the yellow cab traffic pour down 35th Street. More pedestrians traversed the sidewalk and ignored him. A worn brake pad squealed. The sound pierced his eardrums and rattled his skull. Instantly, Clyde's ambition, as if through a straw, was sucked from his essence. Fatigue crushed his spirit with the accumulated force of an anvil dropped from the top window of the skyscraper above him.

He needed sleep. He wanted cocaine, but he *needed* sleep.

His eyes closed, opened, and closed again under equal fight and forfeit. The steam rising from the street vent warmed his skin and placated his weary mind like the lullabies his mother had once sung to him as a child. His head collapsed into his chest, and he began to slip away from the hard and unforgiving metropolis into a soft, beautiful dream.

A voice spun in silk and velvet echoed through the void: "Wake up, Clyde. Come on. Wake up..."

Clyde peeled open his eyes and struggled to lift his head. The midtown streets were still spry with foot traffic and chattering crowds jostling in and out of the underground. The night air splashed his toasty cheeks like sink water. His neck hung stiff and heavy. He wondered how long he had been asleep. Two minutes or two hours?

Crouched at Clyde's feet was a man dressed in an expensive navy-blue suit and brown leather shoes. His features included slick hair, a prominent brow, and a pair of the most intense chestnut eyes Clyde had ever witnessed. These eyes examined Clyde with surgical precision, probing for some distinct peculiarity. Clyde noticed another stately-garbed gentry standing a few feet away, surveying him strangely. This one had hair white like the moon. The two moguls looked as if they could have been twins, save for the fact that the silver fox on his feet was much older than the blue suit squatting. The latter appeared closer to Clyde's age.

"Is it him?" asked the silver fox impatiently.

"Yeah, it's Clyde," replied the blue suit with grim finality.

Clyde wondered how the blue suit knew his name. Maybe he was an off-duty cop who recognized him from walking the beat. Or perhaps he volunteered at the homeless shelter and recognized him from the soup line. The truth was Clyde didn't care too much how the man knew his face. He was too exhausted to care too much about anything.

He shrugged off his spectators and closed his eyes.

The same guttural voice sailed calmly above the city's murmurs: "Wake up, Clyde...Talk to me..."

Clyde's eyes dragged open once more. The silver fox leveled his eye line this time. The blue suit stood watching the street. Clyde was stunned at the likeness of their faces, and for half of a second, in his bemused stupor, was convinced he had fallen asleep for thirty years, and in that time, the blue suit had switched outfits and withered exponentially. Clyde knew this to be a foolish thought, delirium invited by his want of repose.

"Go away, man," Clyde whined. His head heaved left to right. "I ain't done nuthin'..."

The silver fox repeated himself, this time with palatable malevolence. "I need you to talk to me, Clyde. Wake up."

Sleep was pulling Clyde under. Blankets of steam enveloped him, lulling him deeper and deeper into darkness. A sweet escape from a dismal, inequitable reality awaited him on the other side of consciousness. Cop or not, volunteer or not, this nuisance had to go. Clyde mustered the totality of what little energy remained in his sapless bones and, his eyes still shut tight, yelled: “Leave me alone, old man!”

Clyde heard titters from a group of young girls treading past. A horn honked in the distance. The roar of traffic rose and fell. He thought he heard the old man ask his partner if this piece of shit really just called him an old man, but disregarded as much without further deliberation. Sounds became echos and bedimmed as slumber’s warm clutch pulled him further and further into nothingness.

Suddenly, the sting of a hard slap across the face crashed into Clyde’s flesh like a lightning bolt. A dull, lingering throb consuming the entire right side of his face followed the blow’s initial white heat. His eyes flicked open, forcing him to witness the fuming aristocrat upon him as if for the first time. The three-quarter moon backlit the lurching menace’s broad shoulders and seamlessly commingled into his furry crown. Solid and immaculate teeth ground furiously between full parted lips. Dark eyes smoldered with rage.

Clyde spotted the threatening grip of a pistol protruding from the mogul’s waistband, and knew immediately that his man was no cop, no soup kitchen volunteer.

Lumpy fists yanked Clyde off the ground by his wrinkled collar. The geezer curled his one-hundred-and-thirty pounds without so much as a grunt. Clyde whiffed expensive cologne and wondered how someone so violent could smell so sweet. A callous hand around his neck forced him to an awaiting black Cadillac SUV with its hazard lights flashing at the side of the curb. The blue suit opened the back door, and a rough nudge knocked Clyde inside the vehicle. Bystanders watched the abuse as it unfolded but, as usual, refused to intervene.

The silver fox clambered into the backseat behind Clyde and slammed the door. The blue suit assumed the wheel, started the engine, and squealed onto 35th Street.

"Who the fuck are you, man?" Clyde wept as they drove.

"My name is Mr. Robertson," the silver fox dutifully replied while studying the details of Clyde's face. He gestured to the driver. "That's my son Sebastian. And we came a long way to find you, Clyde. Only thing is, you ain't look like the guy we're looking for. So I'm gonna ask you a question, Clyde, and I'm only going to ask it *once*. Why in the *sweet fuck* would somebody be carrying around your IDs and using your bank accounts?"

Clyde had never confessed to anything so quickly in his life. He told his captor everything he wanted to know and then some.

The silver fox listened intently and cracked a macabre smile once Clyde had finished. He reached into the hip pocket of his charcoal slacks and emerged with a clear plastic baggie filled with white powder and chunks of ivory rock as soft and pure as the first New York snowfall. Clyde's veins tingled at the bounty dangling in front of his eyes. The silver fox rested the baggie on Clyde's lap. Clyde shivered and glanced at his captor cautiously, waiting for a double cross.

"Take it," urged the silver fox, 'Mr. Robertson' he had called himself. "I'll help *you,* and you help *me*. Now why don't you take some medicine and instruct me where to go to find this *Trevor* of yours."

SYLVESTER ROBERTSON perched in the rear seat of the rented Escalade, hands interlocked between his thighs, peering through the tinted window to the small corner general store across the street. A closed sign hung in the window, and the storefront lights were off. Next to the general store was a second, nondescript door, painted the same black as the building brick, that led seemingly nowhere. If Clyde, shivering next to Mr. Robertson in the back of the SUV, had not singled out the camouflaged entrance with his dingy and tremulous finger, Mr. Robertson would have overlooked it entirely.

"That's the place?" asked Robertson as he glanced down with displeasure at the soiled hand reaching across his chest.

Clyde nodded, alert and self-assured. The cocaine Robertson generously provided had invigorated the boy's spirit and returned a feisty disposition to him. His knee bounced in a trice. His jaw cut left to right like a handsaw. "Not the convenience store. The door beside it. You ring the buzzer, and a guard lets you in. Takes you into a hallway. There's a room at the end of the hall where they sell the drugs. Trevor should be in there. He's always in there."

For a minute, Mr. Robertson sat quietly and watched the black door through the torrent of road and pedestrian traffic. The leather seating crunched under Clyde's bottom as he shifted his weight from one side to the other, eyes dead ahead on the back of the passenger seat headrest. He had an abstract elation about him, appearing suchlike he was enjoying a beautiful song muted to all but himself.

Before long, a young man wearing a bright t-shirt, beanie, and tattered blue jeans exited the black door. He glanced left to right guardedly before heading down the street with his head in his chest and his hands stuffed deeply into his pockets. Soon after, the black door received another visitor: an older man with a cataract of pearl-white hair that shimmered metallically under the streetlight. He approached the door from the street, rang the buzzer, and waited.

Robertson sighed with disappointment. It pained him to see men from his generation wasting their lives on drugs. They came from a better time. A more honorable time. A time when men were men. They knew better than to defile themselves with that garbage...or at least they damn well should've.

A few seconds later, a diminutive, stocky man with a buzz cut and tattoos running up his sleeveless and shapeless arms appeared at the door. He gestured the aging hippie inside, and the black door closed on the remainder of Washington Heights.

"Okay, Clyde. Let's go," Mr. Robertson hailed the junkie. He had waited long enough.

Clyde froze as if someone had pulled the plug on his imaginary record player. His brow knitted as he pleaded: "Ah, no, man. Come on. I brought you here. I gave you Trevor. It's his scam, not mine, man. Can't I just go? Please?"

His captor offered a reassuring smile. "No problem, Clyde. You just come inside with me real quick and point this Trevor out to me. Then you'll be on your way home."

The fiend looked deeper into Mr. Robertson's eyes in a desperate search for signs of knavery, then to the front seat where Sebastian watched him intently from the rearview. "Yeah. Okay," he swallowed in resignation. "I'll show ya."

After yielding to a string of passing cars, the three exited the SUV and ambled across 168th Street. Clyde led up front. Robertson and Sebastian brought up the rear on either side of him. At the entrance, Clyde pressed the buzzer and positioned himself in front of the peephole.

The door cracked open, and the same short, stocky man with tattoos skimmed over Clyde and his company. Mr. Robertson examined the artwork running up the thug's flabby arms. Naked girls with devil horns and skulls on fire. The words 'Loyalty' and 'Strength' printed in classic calligraphic font amid a crucifix and a rosary between praying hands. One glance into the doorman's shifty, raccoon eyes and Robertson knew that 'loyalty' and 'strength' were not the decorum by which the run-through strong-armer conducted himself.

"These are my friends," Clyde preemptively told the leery doorman. "They're looking to score."

The doorman appraised Mr. Robertson and his son for an instant before cowering under the weight of their unflinching gazes. He opened the door and motioned the trio inside.

"Down the hall," he grunted.

They stepped out of the night into a sparsely-lighted hallway subjugated under thick shadows. The narrow corridor was wet with humidity. Vulgar graffiti riddled the walls. A distinct reek of tobacco, marijuana, and mold permeated the air in waves. At the end of the hall was a second doorway where another goon with an infestation of tattoos on his arms and neck stood sentry next to a plastic palm tree that looked well out of place amid the squalid surroundings. He smoked a cigarette with one hand, held a 9mm pistol with the other, and stared down the trio as they approached. Mr. Robertson grinned at the guard's futile attempt at intimidation. Sebastian kept an eye on the first doorman, who nodded his approval to his partner.

The guard stepped aside wordlessly. Clyde led the way into the room.

About seven or eight people stood in line, including the white-haired hippie that had come in off the street. Clyde found his place in succession, and Mr. Robertson and Sebastian remained abreast. Robertson peered about the bedroom-sized space. The small operation was nothing fancy or even sanitary, but it fulfilled its purpose with impressive efficacy. At the far end of the room was a cash table. Behind it sat a Negro clerk receiving orders and money. He was a worn sort, and had shed most of the nappy, cotton-swab-like hair atop his crooked skull. Like the tattoo-riddled doorman, the Negro clerk had dark circles carved out under his eyes and a permanent frown that further sank his hollowed cheeks. He wore a sling holster over a red form-fitting long-sleeve which sheathed a 9mm pistol under his left arm. He was lean and sturdy and carried himself with an authority that Robertson felt lacked in the other employees he had crossed thus far. But that didn't surprise Mr. Robertson; the Negros were a race of pride and spirit.

After the Negro took the orders, he wrote denominations down on a ticket before putting the collected cash into a thin-slotted steel box. Then, a wide-shouldered, short-necked Irishman systematically appeared from a curtain-cloaked area next to the table, retrieved the steel box, and disappeared behind the curtain. Moments later, he returned with sealed envelopes for the Negro at the desk and took back with him the new set of orders. There was no loose cash switching hands, no product in sight. They ran a tight ship, which Mr. Robertson found agreeable.

What bothered him and disgusted him immensely was the establishment's slouched, jaundiced, and obsequious patronage. Repugnant, loathsome leeches, the lot of them. They were the diseased-ridden rodents of modern society. A chain gang of anemic posture and long faces, poor hygiene and ironic fashion sense. They were cowards who used mind-depleting substances to escape from simple problems they were too feeble or too stupid to sort out upfront, always cynical and quick to blame the prosperous for their deficiencies. They were a plague, a sickness, however necessary to his professional attainment they happened to be.

He addressed Clyde and, suddenly impatient, asked: "Which one is Trevor?"

Clyde's gaze held steadfast on his battered sneakers. "The white guy," he muttered.

Robertson nodded, and, breaking from the line, he grabbed Clyde firmly by the arm and escorted him up to the cash table like a teacher would accompany an unruly student to the principal's office. Those in dutiful formation shot nasty glares at the two line-cutters but did not dare say a word, for Sebastian followed close behind his father and glowered at each one of the lock-stepped cadavers until they understood the proper state of things.

The Negro recognized Clyde without any trouble. He wagged his head tiredly as if the mere sight of Clyde invoked a pulsating headache. "Back of the line, Clyde or I'll ban you," he ordered curtly.

"We're here to see Trevor," said Mr. Robertson plainly.

Presently, the Negro took a deeper notice of Robertson and his son. Following a spry glance of appreciation for their imperial haberdashery, the Negro's expression ebbed cold. "Like I said, back of the line. No exceptions."

"I think you might make an exception in this case," Mr. Robertson sagely remarked.

He motioned Sebastian forward. Sebastian stepped to the table, reached into the inner breast of his suit jacket, and emerged with a pistol. Before the Negro knew what was happening, Sebastian extended his arm, pressed the gun barrel against the Negro's forehead, and pulled the trigger. A deafening pop echoed throughout the room. The Negro's head flung back. A mist of blood streaked across the back wall, adding splashes of vermilion to the monochromatic graffiti.

Mr. Robertson calmly observed the ensuing chaos. Those in line shrieked and scattered like the rats they were. A swarm of suddenly animated bodies flooded the hallway in a mad dash for the exit, the street, and finally, the underside of a soggy blanket waiting for them at whatever derelict, vermin-infested lodgings they called home. He pulled out the .38 Special from inside his coat and aimed it at the doorway. The sentry from the hall pushed upstream through the panicked mob and fought his way into the room with his 9mm drawn. Robertson was waiting and fired off two well-aimed shots. He put a bullet through the guard's left cheek and another over his right eye. The haggard canvas of crude artwork crumpled dead to the ground.

Robertson remained still, acutely aware of his pounding heart and coursing bloodstream. It had been so long since he had killed someone; he had forgotten how exhilarating and fulfilling the act could be.

Nothing got your heart pumping like murder. Not gambling. Not sex. *Nothing.*

He stood over the contorted cadaver splayed on the floor, satisfied with his marksmanship and manifesting a thin, almost nostalgic smile. He replaced the .38 in its holster and checked the hallway. Surprisingly, the doorman with the words 'Loyalty' and 'Strength' inked proudly on his arm was nowhere to be found.

Mr. Robertson returned to Clyde and Sebastian. Clyde quivered where he stood, breath heavy and erratic. Sebastian gripped Clyde's arm with one hand and pointed his pistol at the curtained-off backroom with the other. Mr. Robertson adjusted his tie and lurched across the breadth of the table. To his left, the dead Negro remained sprawled in his chair, head over the backrest, watching the ceiling with unseeing eyes.

Robertson called out to the backroom with a paternal inflection: "Trevor! Get out here. Stop wasting time."

No response.

A few seconds elapsed before the jutted metal nose of a 9mm pistol peeked through the curtain. The wide-shouldered and short-necked Irishman, followed. He squeezed the butt of the gun in both hands in an attempt to mitigate his tremulous disposition. His savage bloodshot eyes shot from Sebastian to Mr. Robertson, Clyde, and finally to his dead partner. His lips sputtered and quaked.

"Drop the gun, Trevor," said Robertson sedately. "We're just here to talk."

Trevor passed a hostile glance at Clyde. Mr. Robertson witnessed the exchange and smirked. Mortified and stuttering, Clyde promised Trevor they would be okay as long as they did what Robertson asked.

Sebastian's gun-wielding arm pivoted ninety degrees and shot into Clyde's right temple. The bullet entered Clyde's skull like a nail in a stud. He tipped over and crashed off the table edge to the concrete floor. The resounding blast echoed off the walls. Clyde's blood stained the cash table as if evidence of the wound.

Trevor jumped instinctively. The 9mm fell from his hands, hitting the ground with a doubling clunk. "What do you guys want?" he choked out. Tears gathered across his eyelids.

Mr. Robertson smiled innocuously. He noticed and appreciated the intensity of Trevor's Celtic blue irises. "Just some information, that's all."

Still shaken, colorless, and perspiring, Trevor uttered: "I'll cooperate...But you s-s-should know that all this cocaine belongs to the Tyrant. If you don't know him...he's vicious. A rabid dog. A real killer. He'll find you."

Mr. Robertson contemplated Trevor's warning. "Tyrant, eh? I think I hurda him. Connected to Mexican cartels, right? Big importer? No one's seen his face or something?"

Trevor swallowed, stole a shuddered breath, and said: "Yeah, that's him."

Mr. Robertson nodded slightly in deliberation. His bottom lip protruded as he pretended to weigh his options. He blinked twice. "You know what, Trevor?" he said with a decided assertion. "I think I'll take my chances."

Chapter Seven

You're Sean. Think like a Sean. Be like a Sean. Don't fuck this up, Joey...I mean Sean.

Joey sat in one of the three uncomfortable plastic chairs lining the call center's closet-sized waiting room. He gazed up at the tiny holes in the mineral fiber ceiling tiles, the dull buzz of florescent lights in his ear like a fly. This was his moment. The ball was in his hands. It was imperative he land this job without a hitch. Since the Martydale incident, the team had been looking at Joey like the weak link in the chain, and he was more than tired of their waning faith. Yes, he messed up. But who hasn't? Mitch? His *darling* Laura? Fuck those guys.

So, big deal, Joey went for a few drinks after a wedding. Was it his fault some guy at the bar was in a bad mood and threw fists at him for talking to his big-nose girlfriend? *No.* Was it his fault the owner of the bar called the cops? *Hell no.* It just happened how it happened, and if it had happened to anyone else on the team, Joey would be the first to throw on a ski mask and bust them out of county holding—and he wouldn't keep bringing it up all the time, either.

Joey wasn't *really* angry at the team. He knew they were just looking out for the best interests of the con. But man, could they bust balls. And if Joey didn't land this job with the mark, that would mean Laura would have to step in, and Joey did *not* want to be sitting in a car in the heat of summer with a pair of binoculars following people around all day. Recon was the worst.

He let out a sigh. *Think happy thoughts. Think happy,* Sean *thoughts.*

"Sean Forrest?"

Joey's daydream was abruptly replaced by a trim maroon suit and skirt standing in the doorway. The woman occupying the outfit, presumably in her late thirties, had chestnut hair with auburn undertones; cut short; 80s short. Her milky skin appeared even more so contrasted with the clown-red lipstick applied to her thin, frowning lips to which her declining rouged cheekbones seemed to point. One thick eyebrow arched over the other, evaluating Joey with no lack of scrutiny.

What's the point in praying? he wondered.

"Yes, that's me." Joey smiled.

His cordial nature seemed to further repel the woman. Her bulging eyes remained fixed on him quizzically as she nodded at the doorway whence she appeared. Joey translated her gesticulation as a command to follow. He stood and covertly tucked the back of his dress shirt into his slacks before shadowing the icy woman into the next room: the phone room.

The space consisted of two rows, three desks long. Each desk contained a phone, an out-of-date computer, loose memos, a pad and pen, and other miscellaneous office supplies. A water cooler stood guard outside the supervisor's office, the name Joyce Winter blazoned on the foggy glass, and a small kitchenette housing paper towels, a microwave, and some cupboard space cut out the far corner.

On the way to the office, Joey passed his new co-workers, each of whom was already busy on calls. Despite the supervisor's swift pace, he managed to descry a younger Asian male with thin black hair styled in a bowl cut, a cocky teenage white kid who was eyeing him sideways on the phone, a robust orange-haired lady who spoke rapidly and with a punchy, falsetto phonation, and the most critical team member of them all, the mark, Meryl Chestwick. Joey knew *her* very well. Her office attire was unremarkable; hair and makeup equally so.

The aesthetic inside the supervisor's office wasn't any more lively than the phone room. The tight space possessed a single desk, a dented file cabinet, a slightly less ancient computer than the models on the floor, and a phone. The same buzz from the florescent lights that plagued the waiting room was equally prevalent in here, with the added ticking of a looming dollar-store wall clock.

No wonder this girl looks so cheesed, thought Joey as he sat across her desk. *She's working in a stress box.*

Folding into a cushioned armchair more luxurious than Joey's version, she drew his resume close. As she examined his credentials, she reclined and crossed her legs.

She *did* have some nice long legs, Joey decided. They were especially attractive presently lined in grainy pantyhose, a consolation for the woman's joyless face and brick-wall personality.

"So, what makes you want to work for Vacuserve?" she asked, glancing up from the resume.

He took a breath. *Okay, Sean. Showtime.*

"Well, I just moved out to Oak County from New York. I'm looking for work. I've had some experience in the field and I thought I could make a good addition to your team." He cracked a smile, revealing a level rack of pearly whites.

Her return was a deep freeze in August.

"I see you've worked at several different sales jobs. So, you're familiar with what we do here?"

He hadn't been, but a few hours scrolling Google while the whitening stripes worked their magic rectified the situation.

"I am. In fact, as you'll find on my resume, I spent two years telemarketing Anti-Virus software with Comp Tech."

"Yes, I see. I tried contacting your reference, but it seems the company is under new ownership, and they don't have access to your employment records. Actually, every single company that you have here on this resume is either under new management or has since dissolved."

Joey widened his eyes and tried not to oversell. "Wow. Imagine that."

"Maybe you're bad luck," she pitched at him.

"With a little hard work and focus, you'll find we make our own luck," he replied. He held back a commemorative wink for fear of looking cocky. She didn't seem the type to be flattered by chauvinism. His restraint proved fruitful. Her gaze brightened, seemingly affected by his words.

Boom, thought Joey. *Knocked it out the park.*

Joyce inhaled sharply and set his resume on the desk. "Okay, Mr. Forrest. I'm going to take you on. We could use the boost of an experienced salesperson on the floor. The job pays minimum wage plus a three percent commission on monthly sales. You get a forty-five-minute lunch break. If you want benefits, you'll have to pay into them off your check. I'll need your banking information for direct deposit as soon as possible. Okay, then?"

Joey contained the urge to jump from his chair and howl. *No re-con for this guy,* he grinned. *Suck it, Laura.*

"That sounds great—Joyce, is it?"

"Mhm."

He reached out to shake her hand, pearls on full display.

Bulging eyes glared back at him questionably. "Find yourself a station. Chad will get you started."

Joey withdrew, retaining an affable smile. "Sounds great. Thanks again, Joyce. You won't regret it."

Upon Joey's exit from the office, the chatter from the four other employees, now off their phones, hushed on a button. Blank stares gripped him and held him in place.

He raised a hand. "What's up, guys? My name's Joey."

Shit.

"I'm totally just kidding. My name is actually Sean. Sean Forrest. Sorry, it was a bad joke."

Joey waited tentatively for a response. Not a blink or a twitch roused from the audience.

He relaxed.

Nailed it.

"I was told to see Chad for training?"

The white kid that had smart-eyed him on his way to the office sluggishly announced himself.

Joey drew a plastic chair and perched next to his teenage trainer, evincing a keen interest.

Chad examined him strangely. "You're not from around here, are you?"

"How'd you guess?"

"I can just tell these things," he replied. The comment might have been misconstrued as arrogance had the kid not exuded such overt languor. "Where you from?"

"New York."

Joey focused on the monitor displaying the telemarketing software. There were two text boxes for the prospect's name and number, a larger box for notable information and order history, and a time code at the top-left of the screen.

Chad jutted his chin. "So, do you know Jay-Z?"

Joey almost laughed at the question. "No..."

The kid's brightness expired. "Oh..."

A brief silence elapsed.

"What about Nas?" he asked with a second wind of resilience. "Do you know him?"

Joey shifted restlessly in his seat, debating whether the kid was intentionally having fun at his expense or suffering from some form of mental retardation. "No. No, I don't know Nas or Jay-Z, I'm afraid. But there's nine million people walking around, so sometimes faces get lost in the shuffle."

Indifference surmounted the boy's curiosity. "Okay," he said. "So, the job is pretty standard telemarketing. We got the product, the script, and the call list. Right now, we're pitching the X-12 Dual Control Shop-Vac. It's got solar capabilities and dual uses. Most vacuums just suck. This one sucks and blows."

"Who needs a girlfriend, right?" Joey quipped lightly.

His attempt at lowbrow humor failed to entertain his trainer, and instead of validation, Joey was shown a clipboard on the desk with the marketer script leading and the call list running three columns per page on the second and third papers.

Chad reached for the phone and peeled up the first page, locating his place on the list.

"Watch me," he instructed. He wedged the phone between his neck and shoulder while he punched in the number.

As he waited, Joey casually surveyed the room. The other phone jockeys were again busy on calls and paid him no mind. His gaze flitted over Meryl's quintessentially average character as he stole a moment to marvel over her mastery of mediocrity. The bulk of the Bandits' previous marks retained a flare for the gaudy and ostentatious in an effort to display their wealth, and presumably to draw attention away from their less governable physical defects. Meryl's wardrobe, however, appeared an attempt at assimilation rather than distinction. Joey pondered if this variance of character would also impact her receptivity to manipulation.

As if Meryl had felt his eyes upon her, she glanced awkwardly over her shoulder and met Joey's stare. He smiled benevolently and continued a perfunctory sweep of his new habitat until the mark's gaze returned to her monitor.

With a stretch and a yawn, Joey felt optimistic regarding his new temporary vocation. Despite the spine-debilitating chairs leaving something to be desired, he imagined the grind at Vacuserve would be far less arduous than the construction job in Cedar Falls, which demanded of Joey more toiling than a cunning criminal should have to toil. Here at Vacuserve, the loud jackhammers converted to the rhythmic clicking of keys, the roar of the bulldozer converted to the hum of an A/C unit and hard-working computer processors, the blistering sun converted to fresh, predictable recycled air, and an angry boss converted to...

Joey looked over his shoulder at the supervisor's office; door shut, blinds closed. The name 'Joyce Winter' printed ominously on the glass. A shiver ran down the nape of his neck.

Well, maybe that part is still the same.

Chad straightened his posture and cleared his throat while waiting for the call to patch through. Upon connection, text stating the lead's information appeared in the vacant slots on the computer screen.

Dufton Custodials, Nevada.

3 previous calls. 0 sales.

"Good morning, sir," greeted Chad, who sounded to Joey like the stoner kid in high school presenting a project to the class that he had scrambled together the night before. "Am I speaking with the management of *Dufton Custodials*?...Okay, thank you."

Joey curiously observed as Chad replaced the phone on the hook.

"What happened?"

"Told me to fuck myself," answered Chad, seemingly unnerved.

Joey raised an eyebrow. "Wow. Really? Just like that?"

"Yup. Said, 'Not interested, go fuck yourself.'"

"Kind of mean, no?" said Joey. He straightened and leaned obliquely in his chair, elbow on the backrest. "Is everyone in Oak County that nasty?"

The kid's face twisted as if he had just taken a whiff of fresh wet dung. "We sell nationally. It's just the center out here. Geeze, you ever done this before?"

Joey's throat tightened. In an attempt to save face, he proffered a casual nod and raised his chin somewhat haughtily. "No, I had a few call center gigs back in New York. Just more local companies. Smaller clientele."

Chad appeared amused and didn't pry further. He went for the phone and started dialing. As he put the phone to his ear, Chad glanced at Joey nonchalantly and said: "But yeah, people tell me to fuck myself all day long."

After an hour or so of listening to Chad complete his calls, or at least *part* of a call before he suffered the same fate as he had with Dufton Custodials, they broke for lunch.

Joey offered to buy Chad a sub from Subway down the street as a consolation for the unfruitful morning. They walked the short distance, squinting under the sun, saying little. Inside, Joey ordered a couple of foot-long combos at the counter: chips for himself and chocolate chip cookies for Chad.

"You're a cookie guy, huh?" said Joey, tray out before him as they fit into a booth. "I would've pegged you for a chips guy. Maybe *Sun Chips*?"

"Nah. Cookies are the best," Chad replied. The talk of side dishes had the kid brimming with an enthusiasm incongruous with the personality to which Joey had been familiar hitherto.

The bandit went to work: "So, tell me about this supervisor. Joyce. What's her deal?"

Chad swallowed a prolonged sip of Pepsi as if quenching a parched throat in preparation for a detailed briefing before speaking earnestly: "She's your typical bitch boss. Wound up too tight. Needs a dicking."

'Needs a dicking', he says. Listen to this kid, thought Joey grinningly.

"She's a real man-hater, though," Chad continued. "Which gets in the way of getting that dicking, I'm guessing."

"I guess so."

"Hey! Why don't you take her out? Get her off all our backs."

"Not my type, kid."

"What is your type?"

"Young, beautiful, puppy-eyed women with nice butts and vanilla-scented moisturizer."

Chad laughed with a mouth full of cold cuts. "That's good for you. But this is Oak County. There's, like, three hot girls here. Everyone else is a hick."

"Well, call me Prince Podunk," Joey said with a wink. The kid seemed to appreciate the confidence. "What about the girls at the office? What are they like?"

"Nothing worthwhile. Not unless you're into big girls."

Joey's face brightened. "Actually, the guy I moved here with, he loves big girls."

"Yeah?"

"Loves 'em."

"Wow."

"Yeah."

Chad weighed his thoughts. "He might be into Meryl, then."

"Which one's Meryl?"

"Not the orange-haired one with the crazy eyeshadow; that's Tammy. She's hopeless. Meryl sits across from us, kind of chunky but has a cute face."

"Oh yeah? What's her deal? Does she have a boyfriend?"

"No. She's single. And she's rich. Very rich."

Joey snacked on a runaway pickle. "How's that?"

"Her dad. The Sheriff," Chad informed before clamping down for another loud slurp off his straw. "He saved some business guy a while back from some kidnappers. It was in the papers and everything. Well, that guy died, and he left her dad millions and millions."

"So, her *father's* rich."

Chad shrugged. "She still lives with them in that big mansion by Oak Bluff hiking trail. You've never driven by it?"

Joey shook his head.

"Word," said Chad. He raised an eyebrow. "Hey, you smoke weed?"

The kid reached into his hip pocket and pulled out a crinkled joint that looked like an eighteen-wheeler on the freeway had run over it.

Joey smiled, scolding Chad with his eyes. "Chadwick...of *course* I smoke weed."

MITCH RETURNED TO THE rental house just after one in the afternoon. He was in high spirits after successfully gaining employment at the hardware store on the town's main strip. It was the last task on the initial to-do list after getting John and Laura into the motel they'd be living out of for approximately the next year. Together, unfortunately. Neither was too happy about it when Mitch and Joey departed, but they also understood it was the only financially viable option. The team scored a lot of money out of weddings, but there were four of them, and it cost a lot to set up shop in a town for a whole year, even with the added paychecks from their cover jobs.

Next, Mitch and Joey needed to find another used car, having left the Charger with the team's other half. Something inconspicuous, which they found in a newspaper ad, cabbed to the seller's home and bought with cash. It was a silver 2002 Corolla sedan which, after some haggling, the seller let go for just under ten thousand.

Upon returning to their new abode, they moved in what little provisions they had to a main floor, two-bedroom suite Joey had previously arranged for them online through Craigslist. They paid the first and last month's rent by e-transfer to Miss Jenkins, a widow of sixty-four. Despite a genial correspondence online, the elderly woman grew as cold as Superman's fortress of solitude the minute Mitch and Joey pulled the Corolla into her driveway. Mitch surmised it was their youthful virility that imbued her stark change of favor, that two handsome men in their thirties living together was a sign of a lifestyle choice better left to the heathens in the big cities. Whatever the widow's clandestine motives, it seemed Mitch couldn't do as little as get in the front door through all her finger-wagging and crabby you-better-nots.

Presently, Mitch carefully removed a TV dinner from the microwave and made his way to the newly acquired thrift-store couch, which was satisfactorily maintained, excluding a blotch of slight discoloration on the seat cushion and a small tear on the right armrest. He set the steaming paper dish on his lap and rested his feet on the thrift-store coffee table, which was also commendable for second-hand furnishings. Mitch was glad. The pertinence of frugality in his line of work could not be understated. After spending almost thirty thousand dollars on vehicles, he was not fain to spend an arm and a leg on amenities that, like the new mark, would inevitably be abandoned after the con.

Enjoying the silence of an empty nest and the hearty aroma of his apportioned linguine alfredo warm on his crotch, Mitch permitted a few slow breaths and felt the knots in his neck and shoulders melt away.

His moment of zen-like oneness was at once subdued by garbled, albeit familiar, theme music and crowd applause pouring through the ceiling indiscreetly from the floor above. He was to learn that day that his crotchety landlady had an unwavering daily regiment of tuning into *The Price is Right* at three-thirty and enjoying the program at exceedingly high volume.

Considering that this lilting, retro soundtrack would not soon discontinue, Mitch decided to flip to the channel on the thirty-two-inch television, also a second-hand acquisition, and watch the program with her.

Near the conclusion of the Showcase Showdown, Joey came home cradling a pizza box and a bottle of tequila. His head-in-the-clouds demeanor, red eyes, and laden eyelids had Mitch instantly suspicious. And if Mitch was smelling what he *thought* he was smelling, his suspicions were very potently justified.

He waited until Joey sat down on the couch and set the pizza box and bottle of tequila on the coffee table before he commenced his inquisition.

"Tell me you're not high."

Joey's infantile grin grew broad. "I'm not high."

"You're *super* fucking high."

Joey chortled as he lifted the pizza box's cardboard lid and broke off a cheesy slice from the steaming pie. He guided it carefully to his mouth with both hands as if it might elude his grip at any moment. "Okay, I'm a little high," he said. As he chewed, he slovenly smacked his lips, further infuriating the bandits' leader.

Mitch let out a weighted exhale. "What the hell, Joey? We're supposed to be two guys who met in AA. And you come home stoned with a bottle of tequila."

"It wasn't my fault!" Joey exclaimed, unable to flatten his cockamamie smile. "A kid from work had a joint, and then we smoked another one after the shift. The little bugger's actually starting to grow on me. He kinda reminds me of me. Like the *old* me. Before you abducted me on this crazy journey."

"I didn't abduct you. You found *me* out, remember? You begged to come with me."

Joey scoffed. "Begged. Please. Who's the kid gonna tell, anyway? You think he's going to go around the office telling everyone he smoked a joint with the new guy? Kids are a little cooler than that. Or don't you remember?"

"And the bottle?"

"The *bottle* is for the BBQ we're throwing tomorrow. I invited the whole office. Except for the supervisor, she's a real C-U-N-Tea bags in hot water, if you know what I mean." He chuckled idly at his wit. "But it's perfect. I'll introduce you to Meryl, and your torrid love affair can begin."

Mitch crossed his arms, eyes on the television. His pout was only semi-put on. "It's about time."

"Will you relaximus?" said Joey. He lobbed his crust into the grease-puddled pizza box and retrieved another slice. "Everything is going to be just *fine*."

Chapter Eight

Two days elapsed without Robertson or his son's return. As per McAllester's instructions, Quinn had started knocking on doors in search of Clyde Morrison. He even stopped by the home of one of the Robertson aunts, who also lived in Cedar Falls. The visit was unfruitful. The sartorially dressed, unmarried fifty-something-year-old, Lisa Robertson, hadn't even known that Clyde had been missing. When she tried to bring up his Facebook page on her tablet, she promptly discovered the account had disappeared along with the groom. Agent Quinn got out of there when he realized the pearl-necklace-toting spinster had more questions about Clyde's whereabouts than he did. Clearly, the family was just as in the dark as the FBI.

Luckily for Quinn, later that same day, Marvin notified McAllester that Angie Robertson had taken leave from the estate. Following the orders of his task force leader, Quinn tailed her to *The Flamingo*, one of Cedar Falls' swankier drinking establishments. The cocktail lounge was not unknown to Quinn. During his stint in the small town, he had found himself soliciting its easy comforts many a night after his shift, surrounded by cheap plastic palm trees and gaudy prismatic streamers, sipping a short tumbler of double Jameson on the rocks, watching the bar screens impassively and trying to forget the last ten hours he had spent sweating his life away in a hot car.

Stepping into the dimly-lighted interior, Quinn sighted Angie's broad figure at the bamboo bar. She guarded an apple martini at her fingertips and donned a tragic expression on her bloated visage. A trim blonde, not too hard on the eyes, stood beside her with a comforting hand on Angie's expansive back.

Quinn nonchalantly approached the wood and settled on a stool a couple of seats apart from the girls. The bartender, a fit young Italian boy in his thirties, dressed smartly in all black, made his way over with Quinn's double whiskey. Quinn liked that the kid had picked up on his drink of choice and prepared it without request.

As far as the bartender was concerned, Quinn was a salesman named Harold Williams doing a stretch in Cedar Falls for business. The bartender had introduced himself to Quinn at some point; however, Quinn had instantly forgotten the name and did not want to go through the embarrassment of admitting his lapse, so he supplemented the handle with 'bud' or 'man' whenever he could not avoid a personal address.

The barkeep smiled as he placed Quinn's drink on the coaster. He had a pretty face that made Quinn hyper-aware of his own glaring imperfections.

"Hey, Harold. You're early today. No meetings?"

"Not today," said Quinn.

The bartender nodded affably and left Quinn to unwind. Quinn looked up at the bar screen and pretended to watch the football highlights while he nonchalantly eavesdropped on the conversation between Angie and the blonde.

"It just doesn't make any sense," sobbed Angie. "We were so in love. We were going to buy a house and even talked about starting a family...Now his Facebook account is deleted, number is out of service...It's like he's disappeared off the face of the earth!"

The blonde gave her tearful friend an encouraging pat on the shoulder. "Be brave, hon'. Things will work themselves out. Have you contacted the police?"

Angie wiped the tears from her eyes with the back of her hand. "Daddy said he was looking after it. He must have. Aunt Lisa said the FBI came to see her this morning. The whole family knows now. They won't stop calling the house. And Daddy is away on business. Sebastian, too...I just don't know what to do."

"Getting out of the house is a good start," said the blonde. "You can't keep cooped up there all by yourself. You need to get outside and enjoy yourself."

Angie conveyed her appreciation and recomposed. "Thanks, Rhonda. You're a good friend."

With the utmost politeness, Quinn leaned over at the girls and murmured: "Excuse me..."

Instantly, guarded posture and queer glares froze him out.

Painfully aware of his less-than-conventional exterior's ability to frighten the jumpy and offend the supercilious, he offered a gregarious smile and a cowboy nod in an attempt to expunge the tension. He kept his smile thin and tight-lipped, afraid to showcase his wonky, yellowed teeth.

"I couldn't help but notice that you seem a little upset," he remarked, meeting Angie's gaze. Her large eyeballs shimmered beneath tear gloss. Her puffed cheeks glowed a deep pink that momentarily camouflaged her blemishes. "I was wondering if you might let me buy you a shot to calm your nerves?"

The blonde returned an incredulous look at Quinn. "Actually, I have a dinner to get to. But *Angie* here would love some company. Wouldn't you, Angie?"

She shot Angie an overt and pressing glare. Angie protested her friend's encouragement with a helpless glance that the blonde willfully ignored.

"Sure," Angie reluctantly surrendered. Her eyes slipped kindly to Quinn, who was still leaning halfway off his stool in anticipation of a response. "Come on over."

The blonde left her friend with another exhortatory pat on the back and sashayed toward the door in four-inch heels.

Quinn clumsily seized his tumbler and coaster and shuffled over to the stool next to Angie. "Name's Harold," he said, offering his hand.

"Angie," she replied, accepting him gently. Her skin was softer than Quinn expected.

"So then, Angie...Care for a shot?"

"I can do vodka," she answered with a cramped amiability.

Quinn nodded. "Vodka it is."

He signaled the bartender and subsequently ordered their shots. The conversation stalled until the drinks returned. Quinn raised his glass ceremoniously. Angie mimicked the gesture with the slightest tell that she was enjoying herself.

"To silver linings," said Quinn.

Angie produced a doleful smile and joined Quinn in immediate consumption. The burn settling in his chest, Quinn hammered his empty glass on the bar. Angie did the same and smacked her lips with a resounding "Aaah..."

Quinn was pleasantly surprised. He also liked to smack his lips after shots.

"So, Angie...Why so glum?"

The question made her apprehensive. She looked away.

"I don't mean to pry," Quinn lied. "It's just that a pretty lady like yourself shouldn't be so sad."

Angie's expression lightened, and she began toying with the frizzy dead ends of her curls. "It's so embarrassing, really," she answered with a snorting laugh. Whether from the vodka or the compliment, her walls had started to come down. "And I'm not supposed to talk about it."

"Oh, nonsense. You can tell me. It's not like I'm the cops or nothing," Quinn lied doubly. "I'm actually a pretty good listener."

Angie continued to fiddle with her dead ends. Her gaze rolled upward, left, and to the bar screens. Finally, with a shake of her head and a twitch of her nose, she said: "Well, okay..."

Quinn put his elbow on the bar and rested his cheek in his palm.

"My husband...or at least who I *thought* was my husband, took off on our wedding night with all our wedding gifts and the Porsche my father had bought us. Disappeared with all our money. Poof. Gone. Isn't that the wildest thing you've ever heard? Like a TV show..."

Quinn's gasp and wide-eyed disbelief were authentic articles. If this Clyde character honestly had tried to steal from the supposed Tyrant, he was one dumb, dead duck.

"That *is* wild," he sighed. "Are you sure he took off? Something didn't, you know, *happen* to him?"

Angie reached for her apple martini next to the empty shot glass. "Pretty sure. I woke up in the chalet, and all the gifts were gone. So was he. He even took the engagement ring and wedding band from my finger."

She modeled her naked left hand for Quinn as she sipped from the martini's wide rim. She replaced the glass on the coaster and said: "Now my dad is away on business with my brother, and I'm all alone in the house. This was *not* how I was expecting to spend my honeymoon."

Quinn watched Angie curl on her bar stool. She looked cute—in a pathetic, shaved-panda sort of way.

"Well," said Quinn lightheartedly. "Maybe another shot will help."

Angie glanced upward sweetly from her rounded belly and smiled at Quinn. Her beaming eyes mirrored the bar lighting almost as vibrantly as her sweat glands. "I guess it couldn't hurt..."

They sat at the bamboo bar for another hour and chatted about nothing in particular. Quinn liked that she was easy to talk to. He often found himself nervous around pretty girls, but he did not have that problem with Angie. After a few more drinks and another round of shooters, Angie asked Quinn for a drive home. Not wanting her to see the unmarked squad car, Quinn explained that he had taken a taxi. She then asked if he'd like to split a fare to their respective destinations. Quinn said he would like that very much.

THE FOLLOWING MORNING, Quinn woke up with a pounding headache and a dry mouth. He lay in a large bed in the middle of a foreign room, boxed in by pink walls adorned with framed posters of Ed Sheeran and pop bands from the 1990s. He was naked down to his socks and boxers. Angie was asleep beside him, also naked and snoring lightly, her face buried in a pillow, curls sprung wildly outbound in a knotted mess. The forenoon light melted through the pink drapery over the windows and the overhead three-pane skylight. A zoo of colorful stuffed animals bordered the perimeter and gawked wordlessly at Quinn from behind beady button eyes.

Dawning a juvenile grin, Quinn basked proudly in the memory of his sexual conquest. He stealthily peeled the comforter obliquely across his robust belly and inched out of bed. His collared shirt, slacks, and dockers were waiting for him on the hardwood floor in the very same chaotic pile where they had been discarded hours earlier. As he quietly redressed, Quinn met the stare of a sizable purple stuffed elephant dangling off on one of Angie's wall shelves.

Enjoy the show last night? Quinn inquired impishly to the carnival prize voyeur.

Failing to receive a reply, he tip-toed out of the bedroom and found himself in the upstairs hallway. To his right was a large bathroom of modern decor and another bedroom. To his left, a paneled door gestured into an office containing a mahogany executive desk, bookshelves lined with thick, leather-bound editions, and a large window where sunlight poured onto the hardwood floor in pallid slices.

Frames of family photos checkered the long wall. A particular snapshot taken when Angie was only a little girl captured his attention. To his surprise, she was an average size for her age, a little husky but cute and wide-eyed. She wore her hair in pigtails, knotted with silk crimson ribbons. Her brother was a teenager, maybe twelve or thirteen. He wore braces and flourished a toothy smile as if someone had just told a funny joke. Sylvester Robertson dressed casually, his arm around the shoulder of his late wife. They looked healthy and happy. Behind them was a large in-ground pool, identical to the one in the backyard. A beach ball and a purple pool noodle floated languidly on the sparkling water. It was a sunny summer portrait of the ideal American family. Nothing about the photo alluded to anything related to the life of a criminal.

Quinn attended next to a picture frame higher up on the wall. Ostensibly, ten years had passed. Angie had inflated into a hot air balloon, her skin blemished and riddled with acne. The ribbons were gone. Her smile was genuine but pained. Sebastian was a young man dressed ornately and older than his age. His smile had flattened, on the verge of inversion. His stare was cold and shady under thick post-pubescent eyebrows. Robertson stood between his son and daughter, matured and succumbed to a wash of gray but dignified in both garb and spirit. The mother was gone. Behind them were a luxurious granite tombstone and many others of lesser size and worth.

Quinn was vehemently aware of the profits he could reap from his position behind enemy lines, the bounty he could uncover with only a little snooping throughout the manor. However, he decided that shagging the mobster's daughter was enough violation of his integrity as a law officer for one day and quietly descended the spiral staircase to the main floor, eager to escape from the mansion as quickly and as covertly as possible.

Downstairs, Quinn scudded into a spacious open-concept kitchen with ivory-tiled floors and equally colorless walls. Stainless steel pots and pans hung from a wide meandering ceiling rack. Sunlight beamed in from the French doors leading out to the pool area and galvanized the double doors on an industrial stainless-steel fridge. Next to the refrigerator was an eight-burner gas range and double-stacked stainless steel ovens. There was a small breakfast nook off to the side, where array of various fruits, the kitchen's only display of prismatic color, flourished from the ceramic bowl on the table.

Quinn exited the French doors into the pool area. Once outside, he took a breath and softly chuckled to himself. He used his phone to call for a taxi before following the sinuous paved walkway leading around the broad side of the estate where gnarly crawling vines ascended the drab gray stone. He basked in the sun's warmth, wearing the same goofy grin with which he had awoken in Angie's bed.

It had been years since he had felt so alive.

Some yards ahead, Quinn witnessed a throng of activity at the iron gate from the front drive into the backyard. The gardeners had arrived for their shift. As Quinn expected, Marvin was among the cluster of immigrants dressed in white. He did a double-take upon sighting an agent on the property.

Quinn cracked a conspiratorial grin. *That's right, Marvin, you dumb asshole. I porked Robertson's daughter. Believe it.*

Suddenly, Quinn grew aware of the fact that Marvin could, and very well might, disclose their run-in on his civilian informant report. McAllester would read the account and undoubtedly question Quinn as to why and how he entered the property.

Quinn unlatched the gate. The iron hinges let out a fine peal. He hurried down the four-car driveway, passing a lime-green Lamborghini and a black extended-cab Cadillac SUV. At the foot of the driveway, he saw a yellow cab approaching on the horizon.

He decided not to worry about McAllester. Having had sex for the first time in over a decade, Quinn felt too good to worry about anything. Besides, he had gotten McAllester what he wanted. He had solved the mystery of the absent groom.

And what a story it was...

Chapter Nine

Laura's voice was tinny and thin on the other end of the phone pinched between Mitch's shoulder and ear while he attended the stand-up mirror in his bedroom and buttoned up the collared shirt Laura had purchased for him during their shopping spree in Sandy Acres. He couldn't help but give his partner credit for how well she knew his body. The clothes she selected for him always fit impeccably and gave him the air of a real catch. At least the type of catch the *marks* would consider a catch. Laura's idea of a catch was something entirely different. Sometimes Mitch thought Laura's 'devil-may-care' affectation would better match John's personality than his own, not to say that he didn't enjoy their arrangement for what it was. They satisfied within each other a secular requisite, a primal hunger for nature's oldest habituation. No promises. No strings. No commitment. Their promise was to always be on their game. Their commitment was to the con.

"So, you got nothing else for me?"

Laura sighed heavily on the other end, clearly lacking enthusiasm. "I'm telling you, these people are machines: her and her father. I've been following them for three days, and each day it's the same thing. Off to work in the morning, stays in for lunch, stops by Dairy Queen on the way home. Every day, without fail. Then, she's straight back to the house. No visitors. No girls' night out. Judging by her Instagram, she's in there watching *Law and Order* and doing photo shoots with her cat Jenkins..."

Mitch chuckled. "That's our landlord's last name."

Laura joined him. "Woot! Woot! Conversation point."

"And what about the father?"

"The Sheriff is a dedicated man. Up at four-thirty every day, out of the house by six, at the office for six-thirty. First one to arrive, last one to leave. While he's on patrol, he likes to make face-time with the shop owners; everybody loves him. And around ten-thirty, he takes his lunch at—guess where?"

"Dairy Queen?"

She cackled on the other end. "We're way too good at this. Uh-huh. Yeah. Dairy Queen. The only problem I can see is his sidekick: a young, sprite chap I am assuming is the Deputy. He's with him all the time. Even goes into the mansion. He might be a problem."

In the mirror's reflection, Mitch saw Joey's head peek into the bedroom, followed by his wristwatch. He pointed to the time with raised eyebrows.

"We'll cross that bridge when we get to it. All right, I have to go. The guests will be here any second."

"Knock 'em dead, cowboy."

"Thanks...bye."

Not long thereafter, the first guest arrived. Joey made the introductions. "This beautiful lady is Tammy Eastwood," he said of the ginger-haired woman whom possessed both the portly figure and garish garb of an opera diva the likes of Deborah Voigt. If the frills on her yellow dress didn't catch Mitch's undivided attention, the orange eyeshadow below her drawn-in eyebrows was an infallible fail-safe. However, when she blushed at Joey's compliment, the cosmetic blended so seamlessly with her skin tone that one would not have even known it was there.

She presented a cling-wrapped bowl of what looked to be cobb salad. "Now, I'm on a diet," she said, revealing a Texan accent. "So, I brought some salad."

Mitch thanked Tammy kindly and carried the bowl to the backyard, joining it with the spread of potato chips and other salty finger snacks arranged in bowls on the picnic table next to the barbecue. He hadn't gotten back in the house before the doorbell rang a second time. The caller was an Asian man, presumably in his early to mid-thirties, of a slim build and dressed for the office. Joey introduced him as Robert Chiong.

"But you can call him Bobby," added Joey.

"I really prefer Robert," the young man clarified.

Before Joey could retract his unsanctioned liberty, the mark, Meryl Chestwick, appeared on the walkway.

"Meryl! You made it!" Joey cried as he ushered Robert with no subtle inelegance toward the orange-haired beacon waiting in the sitting room.

Meryl shrunk as if embarrassed to be singled out. "I did," she squeaked and tucked a few thin strands of dark hair behind her ear. In her other hand, she carried a pan covered in tinfoil.

Mitch stepped forward and retrieved the offering. His and Meryl's gazes locked for the first time.

"This is the roommate I told you about," said Joey.

Meryl smiled politely. She had a warm and earnest smile, wide and toothy. Her teeth were straight and well-maintained, and the slight dimples carved out on each side of her chubby cheeks were cute, if not charming.

She extended her hand. "Roy, right? Sean talks about you so much. I feel like I know everything about you."

No, Meryl, Mitch thought cleverly. *We know everything about* you.

Joey eyed the front walkway, where a teenager in an oversized white t-shirt and jeans approached. His shock of flaxen hair was an unstyled mess, and he sported a limping gait.

"You guys get to know each other," said Joey. "I'll take care of Chadwick, over here."

Mitch led Meryl to the other guests in the sitting room and heard Joey say to the kid: "No minors, little boy. There's alcohol in here."

"Don't be a dick, Sean," said the kid with a groan. "My Tinder date bailed on me."

The hypnotic aroma of burgers on the grill lured the party to the backyard, where the relentless sun beat down from an open cobalt sky. Considering her age, the widow Jenkins had done a commendable job maintaining her lawn. Still, her landscaping skills were no match for the late summer heat of the south, which left the grass surrounding the property wilted to a pale and sickly shade of yellow. Mitch and Meryl stood abreast, paper plates in hand, looking up at the second-floor window of the house, where the widow Jenkins watched the party contemptuously from behind thin lace curtains.

"Is that the landlord?" asked Meryl.

"Yeah. Miss Jenkins," said Mitch.

Meryl's face lightened. "Hey! That's my cat's name."

"Serious? That's a funny coincidence..."

"She doesn't look very pleasant..."

"Your cat?"

Meryl chortled and obstructed the view of her mouth with her hand. "No, your landlord."

"We invited her to join us. I get the feeling she doesn't trust us very much."

Meryl shrugged and turned her back on the widow's foul glare. "Small towns are like that. Everybody knows everybody. New faces scare them."

"Have you lived in Oak County your whole life?"

Meryl, chewing, nodded. "I have," she said once she had swallowed. What she said next was delivered less sturdily. "My dad is the Sheriff."

Mitch called no attention to her overt embarrassment. "Sheriff, wow..." he said, pushing up on his toes. "You must be a popular girl."

She produced a wry grin and rolled her eyes. "Oh yeah. If I ever get married, the whole town will be at my wedding."

"Do you have a boyfriend?"

Meryl shook her head, looking sorry. A silent moment lapsed. "What about you? Do you have a girlfriend?"

Mitch played coy. "No...not a lot of girls are into recovering alcoholics."

She surveyed Mitch's staunch anatomy. "You don't seem like such a bad guy."

Mitch allowed an awkward pause to fall between them. Stillness worked like a charm for cultivating romantic tension. He received the reaction for which he had set out. Her gaze, or the aversion of it, showed that she had become slightly bashful in his stay.

Administering perfect wing-man timing, Joey approached from the rear to cut the tension. "You two seem to be getting along okay," he casually remarked. "I told you she was a gem, Roy. Didn't I tell you?"

"What's up, Sean?" said Meryl, visually thankful for the distraction. "Thanks again for inviting all of us to your barbecue. Your place is wonderful."

"Hey, no worries," said Joey. "I wanted a chance to get to know my co-workers outside of the office. And nothing helps to get to know your co-workers like..."

He revealed a bottle of tequila previously cloaked behind his back. "Shots!"

The unexpected punchline garnered clipped laughter from the mark. "I thought you two didn't drink," she said with some confusion.

Joey grinned. "We don't. We're just good hosts."

She arched an eyebrow. "But you smoke weed?"

Joey froze. Mitch felt the pinch. "Uh, no. Not in a long time," said Joey with a half chuckle.

"But Chad told us all he smoked a joint with you."

Mitch hardened as his apprehensions were validated. *Fucking Joey*, he cursed inwardly, all the while acting aloof as if the idea of Joey consuming drugs was a laughable one.

Joey remained without expression for a space before raising a forefinger and saying: "Would you excuse me for just a quick moment?"

Meryl continued to Mitch as Joey scudded off: "It must be hard watching other people drink when you can't."

Mitch was half listening to Meryl and half watching Joey in his peripheries as he walked over to Chadwick, presently in the middle of a conversation with the smartly-dressed Asian man, and pulled him off to the side by the ear. Joey then proceeded to give the kid a solid albeit covert verbal lashing away from the guests.

Mitch returned his focus to Meryl.

"Not really," he replied. "Not when I think of the consequences."

That part wasn't a line. Though Mitch wasn't an alcoholic himself, he had seen the devastation of which liquor was capable through his father. The old man had drowned himself in an assortment of clear and brown bottles to wash away his self-loathing, only to find the stuff stuck to his soul more obstinately than grime to a drain pipe. In fact, the drinking made it worse. Much worse.

Mitch adjusted the medallion around his neck as Joey returned with the kid, who looked like he just had his nose rubbed in urine.

"Chad has something he would like to say to you," said Joey, clutching tightly on the kid's arm.

Eyes downcast, the kid muttered: "I didn't smoke a joint with Sean. I made it up."

"That's right. You made it up," coached Joey. "Tell them *why* you made it up."

Chad winced in protest. Joey squeezed his arm until his dopey eyes exploded in agony. Head bowed in defeat, the hostage added: "Because I wanted to sound cool. Because Sean is cool."

Joey let go of the kid's arm. A fingerprint sunburn remained on the pale flesh.

"That's understandable," said Joey. "Now, go tell everyone else."

He waited until Chad had puttered off toward the others before he turned back to Mitch and Meryl with a satisfied smirk. "Okay...Let's do some fucking *shots*."

Sometime later, the guests exchanged paper plates for Tequila-lined plastic party cups. The sun had fallen toward the western horizon, stretching long shadows obliquely across the prickly and sallow grass. The party had condensed around the picnic table, where leftover burgers and a half-empty bottle of Jose Quervo acted as a centerpiece. The charm of inebriation had started to work its magic on all in attendance, and jovial conversation flowed effortlessly around the circle. The vibrantly southern ginger, Tammy, had just finished telling a story about the time the town plumber, a hefty man in his fifties named Darren Moody, had propositioned her for a date and possibly more and how, fearing the awkwardness of crossing her eager suitor after her extended unreply, she endured a clogged kitchen sink pipe for over a month.

"I'll tell ya, I was doing everything I could to not see that man. I was washing dishes in the tub! Oh, lord. Nice man, though, Darren Moody. Very nice man."

A hearty rise of mirth proceeded the recount of her romantic blunder. When the laughter had settled, Joey nodded across the table and said: "What about you, Bobby? What do you get up to when you're not selling suck-and-blow robots?"

By now, Robert had given up on his request to be formally addressed, and, like the rest of his co-workers, the booze had knocked a few bricks out of his walls.

"Work a lot. Play with my cat. I like to go bike riding near the bluff. I used to dance, but it's been years."

"No way," said Meryl, next to Mitch. "You used to dance? I would have never thought."

Robert's smile, one with the purity of a fullhearted little boy, grew wider.

"What was it?" scoffed Chad. "Ballet? Tap dancing?"

"Break-dancing, actually."

Titters encircled the table. Joey spiked down an imaginary football. "No way," he said as he rose from the bench. "We gotta see this..."

"Where are you going?" Meryl called out to him as Joey marched toward the house.

Joey whirled and regarded the mark quizzically. "To clear the floor and put on some break-dancing music, *obviously*."

Inside, with the help of Chadwick, Joey moved aside the coffee table and the couch and rolled up the area rug, successfully producing a makeshift dance floor. Mitch went to the stereo and cued a hip-hop song from his workout mixtape that he thought would work well for the endeavor. It was a song from his adolescence and still one of his favorites: *'93 'Til Infinity by Souls of Mischief*. In high school, his friends Greg Sinclair and Matthew Roberts had poked fun at him for being a fan of *Souls of Mischief*, a curated studio band, instead of artists like *Big L* and *Jay Z*, who were, quote, 'real' gangster rappers. Mitch remained unashamed. And funny enough, his 'gangster' friends had grown up to be pretty vanilla types of guys; Greg worked in an office, and Matthew worked in landscaping. It was Mitch who turned out to be the hustler.

The smooth-riding bass line, siren sample, and dreamy Rhodes chord progression engrossed the apartment. The silky phonation of Tajai, the group's lead vocalist, poured out of the speakers:

"Yo whassup, this is Tajai of the mighty Souls of Mischief crew
I'm chillin with my man Phesto, my man A-Plus
And my man Op', you know he's dope (yo)
But right now y'know we just maxin in the studio
We hailin from East Oakland, California and, um
Sometimes it gets a little hectic out there
But right now, yo, we gonna up you on how we just chill"

The guests started to bob their heads and bounce their knees to the beat despite their overt alienism to the subculture, Chadwick excluded. Robert unshod his oxfords and stepped to the center of the rudimentary dance floor. Joey started to chant: "Ro-bert! Ro-bert!", and the others quickly conjoined, incorporating a synchronized clapping of their hands. For a moment, Robert gazed at his socks as if trying to recall the steps. Then, as if he had successfully retrieved the illusive memory, his legs parted wide and started to shuffle. The spectators, Mitch included, fell silent and watched on enchanted. Robert dropped to the floor and broke into a staple break-dancing trick known in the community as a 'windmill.' The bipedal move was a visually-appealing animation of the body that Mitch regrettably could never master in his short attempt at being a b-boy back in middle school. Robert's spaghetti-noodle legs flailed round and round like the blade of a blender set to frappe. At the same time, his tailbone spun furiously on the ceramic tile, rising and falling, rising and falling, all the while his face remaining strained and deadly focused.

Mitch was surprised to hear Meryl beside him rapping with the stereo as she rolled her head to the tempo. She was rapping all the lyrics correctly, and with comparable swagger.

"You like *Souls of Mischief*?" asked Mitch. The tail of his query inflected upward.

She ceased rhyming and continued to bob her head with the music. "Oh yeah," she smiled. "I don't care if they're a studio band; I think they're great."

She continued to recite the words under her breath.

A strange grin wriggled upward on Mitch's face.

Robert transitioned into another popular break-dancing move known as the 'worm,' where the dancer's objective is to undulate across the floor on his belly like a rubber pencil. Though Robert's form had lost its polish over the years, Mitch found his fervent attempt at such an esoteric repertoire fun to observe regardless.

When he at last rose to his feet, out of breath and forehead aglow, the whole party applauded his effort with cheers and whistles. Mitch celebrated with them. However, the smile on his face was for a different reason altogether.

Presently, Mitch's phone started to vibrate. He slipped the device from his pocket and adhered to the screen. It was a text from Laura.

Sheriff is heading your way.

Mitch glanced upward and zeroed in on Joey busy at the stereo, switching from the auxiliary setting to the local rock station he enjoyed. He turned up the volume on a crunching electric guitar riff and jammed with the song on air drums.

"Okay!" Joey shouted over the music. "More shots! Bobby, you get two, bud! I haven't seen break-dancing like that since...I've *never* seen break-dancing like that!"

Mitch broke from Meryl and gestured Joey to the kitchen. He relayed Laura's message quietly as Joey poured more tequila into fresh plastic cups.

Joey shrugged off Mitch's concern. "There's other houses this way. Who's to say he's coming here?"

As if to answer Joey's question, red and blue lights from the driveway flooded inside the apartment and strobed across the walls like a nightclub.

Chad raced to the front window for a better vantage point. "It's the fuzz!" he cried out.

Mitch and Joey froze. The bottle in Joey's hand continued to pour autonomously. Chad retreated from the window just as the front door thumped three times. Joey set the bottle on the counter and rushed to the stereo, killing the music. Mitch went for the door as the rest of the apartment held their breath.

Another three thumps rapped at the front door.

Mitch reached for the doorknob. His other hand pinched his lucky medallion in prayer. Upon opening the door, he met with two men in brown law enforcement uniforms. The officer at the forefront was the Sheriff. Even if Mitch hadn't recognized the man from the myriad recon photos and newspaper articles compiled during the research phase, the golden star over the lawman's heart and the shared surname of the mark on his nametag was a dead giveaway. The other officer, who was tall, scrawny, and half the age of the Sheriff, Mitch did not recognize. But his instinct told him that this was the Deputy about which Laura had warned.

"Is everything okay?" Mitch gently quandered.

"I don't know," the Sheriff drew out at length as he scrutinized Mitch narrowly from head to toe. Mitch remained rigid and allowed the Sheriff's gaze to wander, fearing the man could hear his clamoring heart. "We got a noise complaint from your landlord upstairs," continued the Sheriff when he was good and ready. "She says you all are boozing and getting out of control. Is everything all right in here?"

A concealed and relieved sigh seeped from Mitch's nostrils. Meryl appeared at his side and whimpered: "Dad! What are you doing here? So embarrassing..."

"Hello, honey," the Sheriff replied without sacrificing the slightest authority.

"Hey, Meryl," said the other officer.

Her face drooped blearily. "Hey, *Ronnie*."

Mitch pretended not to notice the exchange. "Yeah, we're fine. Me and my roommate are new in town, and we thought we would have a little barbecue for his new co-workers."

"Oh, I'm quite aware that you're new in town. I make it my business to know any new faces showing up in Oak County. May I come in?"

Mitch nudged the door open and motioned the two lawmen inside. Upon entering, the Sheriff removed his cattleman hat, revealing a thinning silver hairline, and held it at his chest while skimming the gathering's anxious attendance. He peered into the kitchen, where a legion of red plastic party cups surrounded the nearly-finished tequila bottle on the counter. He noticed the out-of-place couch, coffee table, and furled area rug. He absorbed the environment in its totality before he once again regarded Mitch and said: "So...you work at the hardware store."

A sharp nod returned. "Yes, sir."

"Glenn's a good man. He's owned that shop for years."

The other officer, Ronnie, wagged his head agreeably behind the Sheriff.

"Well, it's getting late," said the Sheriff, dawdling back toward the door. Ronnie followed suit, wedging his holster belt over his abnormally narrow hips. He advanced two strides, and the belt again slipped. "How 'bout you think about calling it a night. Let the widow Jenkins get some shut-eye."

Mitch nearly saluted. "No problem. We'll start packing it up."

The Sheriff replaced his cattleman and threw a shrewd glance at Mitch. "See that you do."

He regarded his daughter with intense brown eyes. "I'll see you at home."

Meryl huffed and tightly crossed her arms. "Can you just *go*?"

Officer Ronnie's gaze adhered to Meryl until the door had been closed in his face.

A moment elapsed before the guests released their breath. Robert appeared as if he was in the middle of a panic attack.

"What a party," Tammy chuckled.

"Small town cops suck," groaned Chad. "No offense, Meryl."

"No, Chad. For once, you're right. That was completely uncalled for."

Joey clasped his hand to his forehead as if gauging his temperature. "I can't believe that sweet old lady called the cops."

"Okay, guys," said Mitch. "I think it's time to call it a night."

The guests reluctantly acquiesced. As they started to embark from the house, Meryl stood back, as Mitch hoped she might. "Sorry again about my dad," she said. She looked as if she wanted to say more but struggled to find the words.

"Not a problem," said Mitch. "I really enjoyed talking to you. Would you like to get some lunch tomorrow?"

She winced. "I can't tomorrow. But Monday would work?"

"Monday sounds great."

They exchanged numbers and said goodbye. When the door closed behind her, Mitch nearly buckled at the knees.

He pouted at Joey. "There any of that tequila left?"

Joey scratched his head. "Uh, yeah. I think."

Mitch stretched out his hand wantingly. His protege released a soft, breathy chortle and turned for the kitchen.

Chapter Ten

McAllester flicked off the light switch in Jeanine's room and stood within the door frame, affectionately adoring his daughter and wondering how he had gotten so lucky. She had been very mature about letting go of her nightlight but preferred Dad to stand at the door until she settled. He remained at his post until his brave little girl closed her eyes, squeezed tightly on her teddy bear, and burrowed her tiny button nose into the toy's soft fur—safe and sound for another night.

He mutely stepped away from Jeanine's doorway and found Julia waiting in the hall. She leaned against the mustard drywall, arms folded across her sturdy Portuguese frame, the same raggedy t-shirt she had worn all day splotched with wetness from rinsing off dinner plates in the sink. Her sleepy brown eyes dazzled under the hallway chandelier and made her warm smile appear somewhat silly.

McAllester found her playful air contagious. "What is it?"

"Nothing," Julia whispered. "Just a nice sight to see, is all. Wish I could see more of it."

McAllester knew, at least he hoped, that there was no venom behind Julia's comment. Arguments over his domestic absence were not uncommon, and often they came with little to no warning. But Julia seemed unarmed, speaking more with coquetry than malicious insinuation.

McAllester pulled his wife close. Her hair was a little messy and smelled of dish soap. As he kissed her, he could feel the wetness of her shirt bleed through his button-down to the flat stomach beneath.

"I guess I could find another line of work," said McAllester in a soft murmur.

Julia pulled her head back slowly. Her eyelids slid open, and she let out a sigh that resembled a purr. "Mmm...We both know that isn't happening anytime soon."

She twirled and stepped toward the staircase. "At least with this promotion, you'll be off the task force and out of harm's way."

If I even get it, McAllester thought grimly. He had yet to tell Julia about the recent snag in his investigation.

He tapped her bum down the stairs, saying confidently: "It's going to be great for us, babe."

Halfway down the staircase, McAllester's phone started to vibrate. He slipped it from his pocket and glanced at the screen. It was Agent Quinn. Maybe there was news. *Good* news, hopefully. Although, when it came to Agent Quinn it was better to anchor one's hopes.

McAllester hurried down the stairs and hooked a quick right into the kitchen. He put the phone to his ear and, without any preliminary pleasantries, said: "What do you got?"

"You're not going to believe it," Quinn said on the other end. He sounded more zippy than usual.

"Try me."

"The groom was some sort of con artist. His whole wedding party, actually. Him and the best man disappeared with over two hundred thousand in gift checks and the Porsche. Stole the diamond right off her finger. The wedding was a sham. The Orthodox Protestant Church has no record of the union; they had a fake priest conduct the ceremony. Can you believe that? The goddamn priest was in on it, too."

"We got pictures of these people?" asked McAllester. Despite the grand nature of Quinn's intelligence, McAllester remained emotionally contained. He wanted to collect as many facts as possible while on the phone.

"Barely. A couple of Angie and the groom by the pool during regular surveillance. None of the wedding or with the priest. Robertson hired a private photographer who has not and will not be publishing the photos. Unless we get a warrant, we won't be seeing them."

McAllester was confident that ADD Martin would not be signing off on any warrants this late in the investigation. Still, he felt hope. "That's where Robertson went off to, I bet. He's out to avenge his daughter. If we find Clyde, we find Robertson. Okay...they're going to need to ditch the Porsche. But they're going to want to have it accessible. I doubt these guys are dumb enough to put an ad in the paper or leave a trail at car dealerships. Start looking into towns surrounding Cedar Falls. They didn't go too far. They'd want to get the car off the road ASAP. Look in storage units, junkyards. They're cooling it somewhere. Find out where."

"Got it," said Quinn.

McAllester busted into clipped laughter in an unusual moment of elated clarity. "Great job, Agent Quinn. How'd you find all this out?"

"Just good old-fashioned police work," said Quinn.

"Well, you did great," said McAllester. "I'll see you soon."

"See me?"

"Yes, sir," answered McAllester. "I'm on my way. I'll be on the first plane out of here."

McAllester hung up the phone. He was ripe with resilience. Sleep was no longer necessary. He needed coffee. He needed to get on a plane *tonight*.

He whirled on his heels and was caught off guard by the sight of his wife at the entrance to the kitchen. The warm smile from upstairs had flattened, and a challenging gaze fixed into his. There was no doubt she had overheard his conversation and was now in the mood for one of their long, drawn-out arguments.

Chapter Eleven

Mr. Robertson hated New York. The city was a cesspool of vice and sin. And although vice and sin had been longstanding contributors to his portfolio, the feelings he retained when intermingling with such embodiment of filth and decay were, at best, nausea and irritation. As he departed the convenience store on 33rd Street and clambered into the backseat of the Escalade, he yearned for the tranquility of Cedar Falls and the seclusion of his home office.

Sebastian was waiting in the driver seat and, from the reflection in the rearview mirror, called attention to the pack of cigarillos in his father's grip as the cellophane unwrapped. "Smoking? I haven't seen you smoke anything but a cigar since Mom died."

"It's this city," Robertson grumbled. "It brings out the worst in me."

He thumbed open the flap on the pack of cigarillos, removed one, and slipped its plastic tip between his lips. The fragrance of artificial grape flavoring permeated the SUV's interior.

He extended a wanting hand to the front seat. "Light?"

Sebastian, who had been texting on his phone, stopped what he was doing and scooped his lighter from the center console cupholder. He passed it over his shoulder into his father's awaiting hand. Robertson lit the cigarillo and took a long, satisfying draw off the strong tobacco. Tendrils of smoke plumed and sprawled a mask over his face. He returned the lighter to his son and opened his window halfway. The racket of late afternoon rush hour poured into the cab.

"Speaking of Mom..." Sebastian started up again. "I'm starting to think Angie should know how she really died. And not just that, but the truth about what we do, who we are. I think she's old enough to understand."

Sylvester Robertson gazed at his son through the rearview. He found it remarkable how much the boy looked like his father once had.

"What should I say?" he huffed. "'Honey, your mother didn't really die in a car accident. She was murdered by my friend and partner Eric Baldacci? Oh, and by the way, your brother knew this whole time, and we've both been lying to you?'

"Angie loved Eric. She called him 'Uncle'. You think I should tell her that her Uncle Eric murdered her mother?"

"That's how it happened, isn't it?"

Sebastian's gaze pierced into the reflection, and for a second, Mr. Robertson suspected that his son knew more than he should about his mother's demise. He quickly subdued the notion, for Robertson knew that if the boy had deduced the truth regarding his mother's untimely death, the confrontation would have no doubt been more volatile than a benignant inquiry.

Robertson took another slow haul off his cigarillo and savored the taste coiling down his throat.

"Start the car," he said.

Sebastian did as his father instructed.

They started along the road, and Robertson addressed the uncomfortable topic: "This life. What we do. It can be damaging. It can corrupt. To be successful in this business, one must turn his heart to stone. Granted, there are rewards to be reaped from such a sacrifice. But that is not the life that I want for my baby girl."

Sebastian focused on the weaving traffic, but Robertson knew the boy had digested every word. He ceased asking questions, and Mr. Robertson peacefully enjoyed his tobacco.

TREVOR WAITED ON THE corner of 6th Avenue and 53rd Street, clutching a manila envelope with one hand and anxiously sucking a cigarette with the other. He watched the evening traffic and looked for a black Escalade with tinted windows, the car in which Mr. Robertson said he would be arriving. Pedestrian foot traffic enveloped him as the march reached his end of the crosswalk. In their venture, most, if not all, of the throng made an effort to avoid jostling the towering and wide-shouldered Irishman. He knew this had less to do with their refined deportment than his daunting stature. Little did they know, at that moment, Trevor did not feel very daunting at all. He was terrified—a dwarf under the looming underfoot of an angry giant.

Nightmarish recurrences of the previous night's murders remained burned in his brain like branding on a cowhide. The image of Norman slung over the back of his chair; Robertson's son putting a pistol to the side of Clyde's head and pulling the trigger; Clyde's eyes going void and his body folding to the floor like a marionette; the screams, people scattering like roaches; Mr. Robertson and his soulless son standing on the other side of the table, smiling.

They were *smiling*.

Trevor knew that by giving up John, he was sealing his old business partner's fate, and he did feel guilty about that. But it was John or him. It wasn't his fault that John and his crew scammed a psychotic murderer who just so happened to be Trevor's boss' boss' boss. That was on them. Loyalty only goes so far.

Across the street, the Escalade pulled up to the curb. Trevor swallowed and tried to contain his acute panic. Small pellets of rain started to descend from the bleak silver sky and pitter-patter against the pavement as Trevor dodged an oncoming car to get across the road. The car honked its horn and zoomed by without slowing.

Trevor climbed into the vehicle's backseat and took a shallow breath as he settled inside the dry interior. He recognized the faint smell of synthetic grape and tobacco. Mr. Robertson accompanied him in the backseat. His son was at the wheel.

Trevor wasted no time in handing over the envelope.

"This everything?" grilled Mr. Robertson callously as he weighed the package in his hand.

"That's all I have," said Trevor. He was embarrassed of the slight but noticeable tremor in his voice. "They called me from a town called Sandy Acres, where they switched cars and phones. I don't know which town they're in now, but I bet it isn't too far off. They're running out of places to go. If you find those IDs, you'll find them. That's who the bandits are pretending to be right now."

The son scoffed in the front seat. Hand over the wheel, his Rolex shimmered under the soft cab light. "Bandits...so dramatic."

Mr. Robertson reached into the breast of his overcoat. Trevor clenched and held his breath. However, it was not a gun that Robertson withdrew but rather an envelope half the size of the one Trevor had surrendered. It was bulky in the rectangular shape of cash.

Oozing overt disdain, Robertson muttered: "For your troubles."

Trevor tried to steady his trembling hands as he took the payoff but failed. "Thank you, Mr. Robertson. And again, if I had known who you were...I never would have—"

Robertson looked away disgustedly. "Get the fuck out my car."

Trevor didn't argue. He clicked open the back door and was off into the rain as quickly as his legs could bound. After all, he still had to figure out what he was going to do with the three cold and grizzly cadavers waiting for him back at the spot.

Chapter Twelve

"For two?"

Behind the restaurant's entry podium, dual menus clutched at her chest, the young hostess's glare clawed at Mitch for a response while he acquainted himself with the framed cartoon portraits of rock 'n' roll legends on the wall behind her. The illustrator had cleverly exaggerated Mick Jagger's mouth into a gaping black hole and Elvis Presley's hair into a massive tidal wave of lube. Both had balloon heads three times their body size. Meryl, beside him, nudged gently to snap him out of his trance.

"Yes. A booth, please," Mitch stumbled and smiled awkwardly at the teenage redhead.

"Actually," Meryl interjected, "do you mind if we get a table instead?"

Mitch shrugged.

"Table it is," huffed the hostess, who looked as if she were exhausted from overwork despite the sparse patronage in the tiny dining area. After seating them at a two-seater near the back of the restaurant, the flustered young girl slapped the two menus down on the checkered tablecloth and bounded off toward the kitchen service entrance.

Mitch scanned the menu. It offered the typical small-town miscellany: Burger. Chicken Fingers. Club Sandwich. Steak or Veal dinner plates with baked potato or fries. The bare bones of culinary exploration put together in the kitchen the size of a closet with a retro deep fryer and a greasy flat top by a cook who looked like he had just crawled out of a dumpster. Every small town was the same, and it only intensified the further south they got. They were damn near Mexico now.

"If you don't mind me asking," said Mitch, breaking from the menu. "Why didn't you want to sit in the booth?"

Meryl started to cocoon. "Those booths don't offer much room for a big girl."

Letting out a marked breath, Mitch smiled and said: "You're not *that* big."

Meryl returned a thin half-smile, and a dimple appeared, but the reaction lacked authenticity. "You don't have to be nice," she said. "I know I'm fat."

Mitch nearly swallowed his tongue. Many of the past marks had been overweight, but none ever so candid about their situation. Her self-awareness caught him off guard, and floundering for a clever reply.

As if to free Mitch from the shackles of awkwardness, their waitress joined the table and jotted their drink order on a palm-sized notepad: A coffee for Mitch. Soda for Meryl.

After the waitress was out of earshot, Mitch said: "You know, there's *a lot* of sugar in soda pop. If you cut that out of your life, you might see some noticeable changes. But, just so you know, I think you're really pretty. And I'm not just saying that."

He *wasn't* just saying that. Besides being overweight, Meryl was an attractive woman. Inside and out.

She appeared uncomfortable but again offered a courteous half-smile. "Thanks, Roy. That's sweet of you to say."

A few seconds elapsed. This time it was Meryl who seemed to be at a loss for words.

"So," she said, rebooting, "what was it like growing up in the big city?"

"Noisy," Mitch answered. He hoped a joke and a charming grin would get things back on track. To his relief, she contrived a laugh. "It was okay," he went on with a shrug. "I mean, obviously, it ended with me getting into a lot of trouble. I think I'm safer out here."

Another courtesy laugh, softer and more contained than the first.

"What about you? What was it like growing up in Oak County?"

Meryl opened her mouth to speak. Before she could utter a word, the waitress returned with drinks, ready to take their order. Mitch got the burger. Meryl the same. When the waitress left for the kitchen, Meryl described pieces of her life before and after her family's inheritance. And, at the behest of a thoroughly intrigued lunch date, she continued talking even after the waitress returned with their meals, recounting the story of how her father rescued the oil tycoon, the celebrity it brought to her family, and how surprised they were to discover how much money had been left to them. Mitch listened fixedly as if he didn't already know.

"So, what do you do for fun?" he asked after the waitress returned and took their scraps.

"TV...I love *Law and Order: SVU*. And Netflix. Do you have Netflix?"

"With everything that has gone on in my life the last little while, I haven't really had too much time for TV. I've just been so busy," said Mitch.

"Must be nice," she said before taking the scraping final sip of her soda.

"What do you mean?"

Meryl shrugged. "I don't know...having places to go, people to see, errands to run...A life. A real life. Must be nice, is all."

"What's stopping you?"

She grew diffident as if ashamed of the answer.

"PLEASE, NO! PLEASE! Have mercy on me!"

It was too late.

Joey was hit with the dial tone, making it the fourth lead to hang up on him within the first ten seconds of the call. He slammed the receiver on the hook and fell back in his seat. He ran his fingers through his bangs and exhaled heavily. "Shit!" he cursed up at the ceiling tiles. "Why me, God?"

Presently on a call, Tammy turned in her seat and, under green eyeshadow, glared at him with a look that said: *Is that really necessary?*

Robert swiveled in his chair, twirling a pencil confidently between his fingers. "I'm top sales this month. I could give you some pointers."

"Screw off, Bobby," said Chad on Joey's right. "That just means you get hung up on a little less than the rest of us."

Robert's gaze narrowed. "My name is Robert, you drug addict. And at least *I* can pass a piss test."

"Calm down, boys," said Joey paternally. "I'll get it eventually. I always do."

The door to Joyce's office swung open. Her sharp, shrill cry inundated the room like a tidal wave: "Sean! My office! Now!"

Joey arched back his head and groaned louder.

Inside the office, Joyce sat crossed-legged behind her desk and tapped a pen against her keyboard in a hard and disagreeable fashion. She had harbored a tempestuous disposition all day, even for her, which had Joey walking on thin ice.

"Yes?" he asked softly as he perched on the seat across from her.

"How's the sales coming?" she demanded.

Joey bounced his head back and forth in casual cerebration. "I had some close ones. But no bites yet."

Joyce arched an eyebrow and displayed the faintest hint of a smirk. "Close ones? Really? You know I listen in on the new hire calls, right? I don't think I've heard you use the script once. I'm pretty sure you even yodeled at one lady."

Joey smiled in reflection. "It was early in the morning; I thought she'd appreciate it."

"Did she?"

"I don't know. She hung up on me pretty quick."

Joyce leaned forward and smacked her palm off the edge of the desk to emphasize each weighty word. "Stick. To. The. Script!"

Joey received his admonishment stiffly.

"We're coming up on the third quarter and we're the second-lowest selling branch in the country," she continued. "If we fall into last place, do you know what happens?"

Joey shook his head.

"We'll get shut down, Sean. We'll be out of a job. Now, I hired you because you have a lot of experience in sales. Start acting like it."

He felt as if he was getting yelled at by Mitch. Or Laura. Or John. Someone was *always* yelling at him.

"I'll do my best," he replied.

"Don't do your best. Just *do it*."

Joey stood and turned for the door.

"Oh!" Joyce abruptly exclaimed as his hand slipped over the knob. "And I heard you had a barbecue over the weekend for the staff. I don't get invited?"

"Who told you I had a barbecue?"

"Chad."

Joey clenched his fists. *That kid and his fucking mouth.*

"I didn't realize you wanted to come hang out with us phone jockeys. I can invite you next time if you'd like."

Her expression was anything but grateful. "I come where and when I *want* to come. And I don't need a *man* to tell me if it's okay."

Joey raised a hand in surrender. "Pardon me."

With a rigid finger aimed at the door, she curtly instructed him to get back on the phone and make a sale.

Joey slumped in his seat at his station, winded and uninspired.

"She chew you out?" asked Chad.

"Like a pit bull with a tennis ball."

Joey stooped over his desk and ran his hands through his hair. He stared coldly at the script in front of him as if challenging an adversary.

What do you want from me, you goddamn script?

The sacrosanct sheet of paper only mocked him with its unreply.

He slid the clipboard closer, picked it up in his hand, and read the text aloud. He tried to produce a similar upbeat affectation to the ones his co-workers used on their calls. Tammy was the worst. No one should ever be that perky at nine-thirty in the morning. "Hey there, is this the owner of the proprietorship I am speaking with? I'm calling from Vacuserve about a revolutionary new product that just came to market. It's a multi-use shop-vac that not only has solar charging capabilities but offers both a suck *and* blow option for all your cleaning needs."

Joey scoffed and shook his head. Reluctantly, he lifted the phone and dialed the following number on his list. As the ringtone pulsed in his ear, he inhaled and coached himself: "Focus. Be lame."

A teenager's voice appeared on the other end. "Hello?...I mean, Soobie's Auto, how may I help you?"

Joey cranked the pep: "Hey there! Is this the owner of the proprietorship I am speaking with?"

"The what?"

Joey rolled his eyes, instantly drained. "The shop?"

"Uh...no."

"Would I be able to speak with the manager on duty?"

"Yeah, one sec..."

The kid stepped away from the phone, replaced by a background soundtrack of whizzing air drills and the clanking of metal on metal. Joey glanced around the office, thought about lunch, and tapped his pen off the desk surface several times.

Presently, another voice appeared on the phone. Older. Grumpier. "Yeah?"

Joey's focus returned to the script. He straightened his posture and adopted a palsy, car-salesman-like cadence. "Hi there. This is Sean calling from Vacuserve. I'm calling you today to inform you about a revolutionary new product that just came to market. It's—"

"Look," said the man. His voice trailed off as he cursed someone in the background who had touched something that should not have been touched. "What was I saying? Oh yeah. I'm barely making overhead as it is. I had to hire my shithead nephew to beat the books. I don't have the money to be forking out on some new thing, you understand me?"

"I understand," said Joey. Another bitter defeat swallowed his motivation. *Why am I so bad at this?* he wondered. When it came to researching marks for the con, he was unstoppable. All it took was a couple of minutes on Google.

That's it! he thought in a sudden moment of clarity.

He minimized the software window on his monitor and clicked the Google icon on his desktop. With a rejuvenated spirit, Joey continued: "But what if I told you that this investment could *save* you money?"

"Oh yeah?" said the man, his curiosity still inferior to his disgruntlement. "How's that?"

While he explained, Joey simultaneously conducted a quick Google search of the prices for a regular shop vac and an air blower. "The product I'm offering today is a dual-purpose shop vac that acts as both a vacuum and air blower. It's equipped with solar power charge capabilities, which can save you money on your electric bill.

If you were looking to buy a vac and a blower separately, it would work out to about $250. This beauty is only $149.99 and comes with a five-year warranty."

"My leaf blower is off warranty and on its way out," muttered the man, more to himself than Joey.

Joey maximized the software on the monitor and referenced the shop's location. "And you guys get some leafy autumns out in Jersey. I bet the lot gets pretty cluttered."

"It's terrible," agreed the man. "I got my nephew out there with a broom every couple a hours."

Joey replied with a comradely chuckle. "Well, with this product, he'll be in and out, back inside the shop, and touching things he's not supposed to."

The shop manager rasped out a short chortle and a cough. "Okay, yeah. You said $150?"

"$149.99."

A sigh from the other end preceded a bout of silence, and then: "Okay, sign me up."

Elated, Joey took down the shop owner's credit information. With the phone back on the hook, he jumped from his chair and roared at the top of his lungs: "Suck my hairy balls! I just made a sale!"

The whole team, except for Meryl, out at lunch with Mitch, whirled in their seats with maddened expressions.

Robert slammed down his phone. "Well, congratulations, Sean! I just lost mine!"

"Me too," said Chad with a disgruntled exhale.

"Me too," said Tammy. She frowned and shook her head disapprovingly.

Coincidingly, Meryl returned from lunch and settled into her station. Joey inquired as to how her date panned out. She shook her head and looked apologetic. "I don't know if Roy is my type."

Joey had expected a more affirmatory response. "Are you going to see him again?"

She shook her head and scrunched her nose. "I don't think so."

Tammy placed a comforting hand on Meryl's shoulder. "Plenty of fish in the sea, Meryl. Well, I'm going to go get some chips from the vending machine. That salad I had at lunch just wasn't enough. Do you want me to get your after-lunch soda? A little sugar will do you good. Always helps me when I'm feeling down."

Meryl thought about it. "Maybe just a water."

MITCH RETURNED HOME from the hardware store just in time to tune in to *The Price is Right* with the widow Jenkins upstairs. He felt good about his first date with the mark and was keen to waste what remained of the day lounging on the couch with his feet up. However, his well-deserved afternoon of tranquility abruptly concluded when Joey returned just after six in a panic.

"What the hell, Mitch?" he demanded as he closed the front door.

Mitch swung his feet off the coffee table and clicked off the TV. "What? What are you talking about?"

Joey tilted his head. "*Uh*, I don't know. What happened on your date with Meryl?"

"Nothing. It was fine. We talked."

Joey threw his keys on the kitchen counter and went to the cupboard for a glass. "Well, you obviously talked wrong because she doesn't want to see you again."

Mitch pushed off the couch and twisted to face Joey. "She said that?"

"Said you *weren't her type*."

Joey turned on the tap and filled the glass with water. He swallowed a meager and anxious sip before setting it on the counter.

"How are you not her type? How did you *allow* yourself to not be her type?"

"Oh, no..." Mitch's stomach turned violently. He clutched his face in shame. "I know what this is about. She made a comment about her weight, and I suggested she give up soda. Because of all the sugar."

"Well, guess what? She did! But she also gave up *you*!" Joey rolled his eyes. "I mean, what were you thinking? You've been doing this for over a decade. You know how this works. You don't criticize the weak; it sends them running! You nurture them. You *love* them. You be the knight in shining armor they always *dreamed* would save them. You don't be a fucking fitness instructor, Mitch! Fucking Tony Robbins!"

Joey banged his palm off the counter to emphasize each weighty word. "Stick. To. The. Script!"

"Wait..." Mitch said. "She gave up soda pop?"

Joey nodded dramatically. "Yup! She used to get a pop every day after lunch. Today, after you, she gets a water. She even refused the donuts my supervisor bought after I made my first sale."

Mitch offered his congratulations; he knew Joey had been struggling at work.

"This isn't *about* me," shot Joey with a sharp finger at Mitch. "But thank you, I'm quite proud of myself."

He disarmed, approached peacefully, and sat on the couch beside his mentor. "You need to correct this."

Mitch knew his protege was right. "I'm sorry," he apologized. "I'll fix it."

"You better," said Joey. He rose to his feet and headed to his room. "*I* ain't going to be the one to marry this chick."

Feeling low, Mitch called Laura to see where things were on her end. Part of him just wanted to hear a friendly voice. She answered all his questions, but no routines had changed. She also mentioned that John was starting to go stir-crazy in the motel room and took the Charger out in a fuss. He didn't tell her where he was going. But even that was routine.

"What about you?" asked Laura afterward. "How's the love story?"

Mitch told her everything, from the date to Joey's lecture.

"Wow," she said afterward. "Never thought I'd live to see the day when Joey is the one giving *you* shit."

"The student becomes the master."

"Easy, Obi."

"But she did stop drinking soda pop. That has to mean something. I mean, people are told to quit smoking every day. They show pictures on the packs of tumors and little impotent cigarette penises, and people still smoke a pack a day. If she stopped drinking soda pop, it had to have at least crossed her mind before, the desire to lose weight. Maybe she does want to get fitter. Maybe it was just hard for her to hear at first."

"So you're thinking of doubling down?" Laura asked.

"I am."

"Whatever," Laura sighed. "But hurry up and work your magic, Romeo. Else I might have to send John over there to seduce her."

Mitch laughed under his breath at the mental imagery, surprised to find himself in better spirits. He hung up with Laura, heated a package of instant noodles on the stove top, and returned to his room to devise a plan for helping Meryl win her confidence back. And in turn, he hoped, he would win her heart.

Chapter Thirteen

John helmed the Charger doing eighty miles per hour down a long stretch of lonely highway. *The Rolling Stones* were on the radio, volume cranked. Rushing waves of fresh air poured through the open windows and circulated throughout the cab, washing the day's heat off the old man's restless skin and bones. It was a beautiful day, the kind of day that made John feel ten years younger.

His buckle-strapped boot applied pressure to the gas pedal. He watched the RPM needle rise before kicking the clutch and punching into third gear. The engine answered with a lively, guttural growl. The force of acceleration pressed him into the driver's seat. His tattered white t-shirt rippled across his narrow and crooked frame. He tightened his grip on the wheel.

This is what I needed, he thought with a deep, cleansing breath.

Hitting the open road had never been a problem for John. He relished the long drives, the solitude, and the timeless allure of an endless horizon. What *was* a problem, at least more than it had been in previous years, was being a prisoner in a small motel room and having to share the already confined space with wise-ass Joey or motormouth Laura. She sure liked to yap, that girl; always sharing an opinion no one asked her for. Mad at the world she was. For what, John didn't know. She hadn't worked an honest day in her entire pretty-girl life.

A lot had changed since he and Mitch started all those years ago. The crew had doubled, which John had thought would have taken away from his loneliness, but in reality, it only added to it. He felt outdated and alienated, ready to hang up his gloves and retire. He knew the team would get by fine without him. Back in New York, Trevor did most of the ID work, and Joey could handle the other responsibilities incurred from his departure. He was a whiz on that social media crap; John was certain the knucklehead could figure out how to toggle the phone. And, well, Mitch always figured out how to make it work. He would adapt and carry on.

Speeding past the 'Welcome to Sandy Acres' sign on the side of the highway, John considered making this job his last. Over the years, he had put away a nice chunk of his profits, even with the money he'd spent on whiskey and cocaine. Not to mention the girls; they weren't cheap. Well, some of them were. But now it was time to settle down and live out the rest of his days in a meager, quiet fashion. No stress, no fuss. Maybe he would get some part-time work to keep ahead, but that would be all.

John took the exit and geared down, slowing as he entered the rural neighborhood. The world became silent and serene. The breeze vanished. Both John and the car grew tortuously hot. He reminded himself to place fixing the broken air conditioner higher on his list of things to do. Thankfully, the Bed N' Bar was just down the road.

He was sure the team would have some harsh words for him if they knew he was returning to the buffer town to grab more coke, but, well...fuck 'em. If he was going to be subject to the endless and senseless jabbering of his beautiful blonde roommate, he needed something in his system to keep him entertained. And if they didn't like it, too goddamn bad.

If they ever found out, anyway.

He entered the motel property, parked the car in front of the Bed N' Bar, and grabbed his wallet off the baking passenger seat.

As he walked into the woebegone saloon, the smell of mold, tobacco, and urine tinged his nostrils. He blinked twice as his eyes adjusted to the dimness. The roughly varnished shutters on the windows were closed and forestalled enough daylight to make a vampire feel right at home. Sitting at a corner table near the bathrooms was the familiar bloated barfly that had sold John his coke during the team's initial pass-through. He was ostensibly younger than John, though not by a lot. If he had been much younger, he had done a very poor job maintaining himself. He was hunched over the table, mindlessly scrolling through a smartphone. The glow from the screen inked heavy shadows on the creases of his crow's feet and bulbous nose. His lips were droopy and wet from a recent gulp of ale. As John approached, the barfly raised his head like a curious dog and peered at the incomer cautiously. His hooded eyes widened in recognition, showing all smiles thereupon.

"Hey there, young fella," he said amicably. "Back again, I see."

"Yeah, yeah," grumbled John. "No need to tickle my ass hairs with that 'young fella' crap."

"Wouldn't dream of it," grinned the fly. He motioned to the opposing empty seat. "Sit down. What can I do ya for?"

As John perched, he noticed the bartender, practically a child, returning to the bar from the back with a box of lemons. He wore a loose-fitting t-shirt and had a baby face with wavy brown hair curtaining his brow like one of them half-girl Korean pop stars of the day. They shared a glance before the kid plopped the cardboard box onto the wood and began scooping out lemons one at a time, cutting wedges for cocktails.

John's focus shifted to the fly. "I was hoping you could help me out, same as last time."

"I think that's doable," the barfly returned enthusiastically. He coughed wetly into a closed fist. "How much were you looking for?"

"A quarter."

"Six-fifty, good sir."

John shifted his weight, reached behind him, and withdrew a thick envelope from his back pocket. He slid the package across the table. The barfly accepted and caressed it with dingy fingers. He peeled the flap and looked inside.

"Looks like a little more than six-fifty in here," he said as he thumbed through the bills.

"Well, there's something I wanted to ask of you," said John.

The fly paused and retreated slowly into his seat. A queer eye canvased his guest acutely. "And what's that?"

"Well, I'm up at Oak County at the moment, and without getting into too many specifics, it's a near impossibility for me to keep coming out here. I was hoping if I tagged a little extra onto the bottom line that you might see it in your heart to deliver it my ways. Saves me the trouble of having to sniff out another dealer, and it guarantees you a returning customer."

The fly let the request simmer while he scratched on his stubbly second chin. "Delivery, eh? Oak County? That's, what, 'bout an hour and a half drive?"

"More like two," John admitted.

The fly dug inside his ear with his pinky. "I don't know, fella. It's a bit out of the way."

"That's why I'd pay you extra. For time and gas."

"How much extra?"

"Two hundred per quarter."

"Make it three, and you got a driver."

"Two twenty-five."

"Two-fifty, then."

"Deal."

"*Deal.*"

"Great," said John. He produced his phone. "I'll text you the address. Number?"

They exchanged information, and the fly excused himself to the bathroom to fetch John's prize. John reclined in his chair and surveyed his surroundings. He glanced briefly at the bartender, head down, attending his lemons. To his left, a heavyset man wearing a trucker hat and pop bottle glasses ignored his half-eaten burger and cold fries as he apathetically followed the football game on the bar screen. John craned his neck for a broader look. An untenanted jukebox along the wood-paneled wall near the entrance glowed in dreamy technicolor. Beyond the dining area were a coin-operated pool table and a triad of dartboards where two middle-aged men threw game between sips of ale and sleepy conversation.

Yeah, thought John. *I could definitely retire here. This feels like home.*

Chapter Fourteen

The next day Mitch drove up to the grand iron gate isolating the baronial Chestwick property from the other comparatively drab and humble tenancies of Oak County. He buzzed up to the house using the intercom on the left of duo Corinthian-style pillars erected at the foot of the driveway. After a few rings, a lady's voice with a subtle Asian idiom and militant, though simultaneously innocuous, delivery appeared and addressed Mitch formally. He politely introduced himself as Roy Hawkins, calling for Meryl, and mentioned she would not expect him.

"One moment," said the woman.

Mitch waited. He savored the cool air-conditioning blowing munificently out of the dashboard vents. A sharp buzzing noise shot from the intercom, and the front gate inverted slowly. He throughed the parting wrought iron bars and started up the roundabout encircling the courtyard.

Fresh-cut grass sprawled evenly throughout the property ladened the air with a sweet, summery aroma. American Sycamore trees peppered the grounds and cast islands of shade under their wide-reaching crowns. At the center of the route towered a three-tiered stone fountain surrounded by a ring of virid artisan hedges. Sunlight dazzled off glassy water trickling from one bowl to the next, producing a dreamy bubbling percussion under a flitting flock of red-breasted robins' melodic twitters.

The estate itself was a stately display of colonial prestige. Flanking the imposing and ornate entrance to the manor, strategically situated between the portico's towering columns, were three gangling French windows displaying luxurious white silk drapery. The only furniture adorning the porch, very much out of place amid the opulence, was a single haggardly-crafted wooden rocking chair and, next to it, a rusty aluminum coffee can Mitch assumed was for cigarette butts or cigar entrails.

The strange juxtaposition of aristocrat and woodsman reminded Mitch of the old television show *Beverly Hillbillies.* He chuckled privately. That was the Chestwicks: just some regular old country folk who fell into a ton of cash and didn't let the money change them a wink.

He parked the Corolla and ascended the pooling staircase. He heard the door unlock as he reached the straw doormat, another adornment with the same worn homeliness of the rocking chair and cigarette can. The door opened. Meryl stood at the threshold with a confounded expression. Despite being early in the evening, she was already in her pajamas, face washed of makeup, and a pencil knotting her hair, Japanese style.

"Hey, Roy..." she said coyly. "What are you doing here?"

"Hey, Meryl," said Mitch with a brief and nonthreatening wave of the hand. "I was going to try my hand at the Oak Bluff hiking trail. I thought you might like to join me."

The perplexed expression on her face paired with a budding anxiousness. "Oh...um...I was just settling in for the night. My shows are on."

Inside the house, from down the hall, an illegible but passably Asian voice whispered something sternly at Meryl. Meryl bit her lip and glanced down at her slippers. "I mean, yeah, sure," she said. She regarded Mitch with a slightly less anxious smile. "Let me just change my clothes, okay?"

MITCH AND MERYL WALKED along a winding dirt trail bordered by gnarly brush and dry deadwood. Beyond, a dense forest of tall pines and lush foliage cut the sinking sun's orange-yellow light into thin, pallid slices. The air was quiet save for the occasional squirrel shaking a cluster of leaves or the light tweeting of a mother bird calling her chickadees back to the nest for the night.

"So, are you a big health guy?" Meryl asked as she idly observed the scenery.

Mitch shook his head and slipped his hands into his pockets. "Not really. I'm definitely healthier than I used to be, though. I was really falling apart for a little while."

Meryl offered a frown.

"Sorry," said Mitch. "I don't mean to be a downer."

She shrugged lethargically. "It's okay. I've been falling apart a bit myself lately."

Mitch kicked a stone and watched it tumble ahead on the trail. "Why is that?"

Meryl eyed him over. "Well, I wouldn't usually disclose this to someone I just met, but since we're being so *honest* and everything...I've just been kind of lost. Drifting. Emotionally, I mean. Geographically, I'm very, *very* stagnant...My best friend got married and moved out of state with her husband. She was the only friend I had left in Oak County. Now I'm the only one still here. Still living at home. Daughter of the Sheriff. Just drifting. Plus, things at work have been a little sketchy. I don't know if Sean talks to you about that sort of thing, but if our sales don't pick up, we could get shut down."

"Doesn't seem like you'd be too bad off even if they did. Do you even need to work?"

She grinned. "You're starting to sound like Ronnie."

"Ronnie?"

"The Deputy," she clarified. "He was the one who helped my dad break up your party."

"Oh. Him."

Meryl flicked her hair behind her shoulder. "Yes. *Him*. He thinks I'd be better off being a mother and a housewife."

"To him?"

She nodded.

"Not interested?"

Another shrug. "He never cared about me until after the inheritance. I think he just wants to get into the family. And since my *father's* taken..."

A genuine snort shot out Mitch's nasal passage, and he laughed. Meryl had some sour under all that sweet.

"But it's your *father's* money," he fished.

"True. But Ronnie knows about the deal."

"The deal?"

"When I get married, Dad is going to put the property in the name of my husband. My husband and me."

Bingo, thought Mitch.

He took a squirt from his water bottle. "How much is that big house worth?"

Meryl reached out for a sip. "Five million."

Mitch handed her the bottle.

Jackpot.

"FIVE MILLION."

Mitch held court at the head of John and Laura's motel room. John stood by the wall next to the nightstand. Laura was on the bed, back against the headboard. She was fresh from the shower and without makeup, wearing short shorts and a tank top sans bra. Joey sat at the vanity with his laptop open on the desk and his Red Sox cap pulled low on his head. Mitch watched them gape at his quote contentedly; however, the excitement was short-lived, replaced by collective uncertainty.

"I don't like it," said John. He stroked his chin thoughtfully. "It's not in our playbook."

"We know nothing about real estate," added Laura.

"We do now," said Joey. "I took a crash course on it when Mitch came home from his little hiking date, which, by the way, nice job on pulling that one around and getting her back on board. You truly are my mentor. I'm sorry I lost my cool. But I think this can really work. Hear me out..."

John slipped out a bulky gram baggie from the hip pocket of his slim-fitting jeans and proceeded to use the Charger key to scoop out a small clump of white powder. He brought it to his nostril and inhaled the cargo before passing off the bag and key chain to Laura, who repeated the same steps for herself before offering the bag to Mitch.

Mitch immediately realized where John had disappeared to the day he left without telling Laura where he was going.

"I'm good on that," said Mitch. "But I'm glad to see you two getting along so well."

Joey continued: "With Mitch's assumed identity, it's just a matter of getting the name switched over and then forging the mark's signature on the sale afterward. It's really not too difficult. Sure, it's not in our playbook, but fuck it, we need to *get* this in our playbook. Real estate fraud has become a booming market since the advent of the internet. We're missing out on big payoffs. On this scam alone, we would walk away with close to a mill each."

"That's retirement money," gasped John.

"That's the biggest take we've ever seen," said Laura. Her face had come alive. Whether it was the talk of money or the coke, Mitch couldn't tell.

"There's just one problem," said Mitch. "It might take a bit of time after the wedding to get the deed switched over."

"How much time?" asked John. He lit a cigarette and tossed the pack on the nightstand.

"Could be anywhere from a day to a month. Maybe more."

Expressions around the room deadened.

"That's insane," said Laura.

John hauled his cigarette while shaking his head disagreeably. "We leave night of. That's rules."

Mitch looked to Joey for validation. It was received, but hard won.

"It's a big payoff," explained Mitch. "Bigger than we've ever had. Laura, you said it yourself."

She took a deep breath and collected her thoughts. "I don't feel good about this. We're going way off book."

"I think we need to trust Mitch, guys," said Joey. Finally. "This is *his* hustle. He started this thing."

John narrowed his eyes contemptuously. "And a bunch of syphilis-infested, slave-owning bigots started America. It's called progression. It's called expansion. We all play a part in this, and we all go to the bin if things derail. We all have a say."

"Let's take a vote," said Laura. She restlessly slipped off the bed to her feet.

"Fine," Mitch conceded. "We'll vote. Who's against it?"

Laura and John raised their hands.

"And who's for it?"

Mitch and Joey raised theirs.

"Well, that was a colossal waste of time," John grumbled.

"Okay, we're tied," said Laura. "Now what?"

Mitch shook his head. "No, we're not tied. John's vote doesn't count. It's void."

"The hell it is," John shot back with a raised voice. "How you figure that?"

"Where'd you get that coke, John?" Mitch queried pointedly. "Because as far as I remember, you ran out before we left Sandy Acres, and as far as I know, you're not allowed to be buying drugs in the same town we're working, so...where did it come from?"

John returned a silent glower.

Mitch continued: "I'm going to put my money on the fact that you went back to the buffer town. Or you had one of your connections deliver. Either way, it's a massive breach of the rule book, and *that's* why your vote is void." Pressured exhales seeped out Mitch's nose. He hadn't wanted to admonish John in front of the team, as founding members they shared a certain respect, but John left him no choice. "You want to talk about going off book? About putting the whole team in danger? You returned to the scene of a crime to buy *drugs*. Either that, or you gave away our location. Again, for *drugs*."

John faltered under the evidence and swatted a dismissive hand at his accuser.

Without any further argument, the opposition yielded to their team leader. But not before Laura offered one final jab at the winning party. "I hope this has to do with money and not with feelings. You're not falling for this chick, are you?"

Mitch didn't flinch. "That's a ridiculous suggestion."

Chapter Fifteen

"Well, it's official. We're screwed."

Joey and the other telemarketers twisted in their chairs to face Joyce standing at the door to her office. Her transparent grief belied her sarcastic facade.

"What are you talking about?" Meryl asked.

"I just got a call from Head Office," Joyce explained in a heavy sigh. "They're shutting us down."

The team abruptly roused from their pre-lunch lull, Joey exceedingly so. For him, this announcement was ironically detrimental. He couldn't very well follow Meryl to another job. Laura would have to step in as his replacement, which, in turn, would mean his inevitable relegation to recon.

"That's not funny, boss," Joey informed his increasingly emotional supervisor.

Joyce ran a finger under each eye to collect moisture. She straightened her shoulders. "I wasn't joking, Sean."

"How can they do that to us?" Tammy demanded. She carefully removed her headset from her well-structured beehive and set it next to her computer.

"Yeah," Robert enforced.

"We're just not making enough sales," answered Joyce. "I thought that bringing in an experienced salesperson from the city would help our chances. I was wrong."

"How long do we have?" asked Joey.

"We'll carry out until the end of the month. You'll receive two weeks' severance pay and whatever vacation time you have accumulated. I'm so sorry, guys. I tried. I really did."

Joyce went back to her office and closed the door behind her. Those remaining sat silently and marinated in their defeat.

Joey couldn't help but feel partly to blame. After all, he had made very little attempt to take his job even the slightest bit seriously, never mind stepping up as any kind of leader. Foolish as it may have been, Joyce had been relying on him to spearhead the team to victory. She actually had *faith* in him.

And he was on the phone, yodeling to people.

"What am I going to do for work?" Tammy lamented.

"My car payments..." muttered Robert. He tensely massaged his brow.

Joey gave Chad a soft toe nudge in the shin. "What about you, kid? You going to be okay?"

He was busy scrolling through his cellphone and barely returned a glance. "I'll figure something out."

"Maybe you can get a job at Subway," Joey teased lightly. "Unlimited cookies."

Still staring at the phone in his palm, Chad raised his middle finger. He had been giving Joey the brush off all day.

"What about you, Sean?" asked Meryl. "What are *you* going to do?"

Joey whirled to face her. "I'll tell ya what I'm going to do, Meryl. I'm going to take everybody out to a bar after work today, and I am going to watch you guys get drunk. On me. I owe you that much."

"You don't owe us," said Meryl. "It's not like it's *your* fault."

"Yeah, Meryl. It is," said Joey. "It is my fault."

MITCH HAD JUST FINISHED saying goodbye to Mr. Willburrow from the barbershop, whom he had helped find the correct screws for a shelf he was installing in his backyard shed, when Glenn notified him of an order arrival in the backroom.

"Stock the aisles, face up the racks, then break for lunch," he instructed on his return to the checkout counter.

Mitch got on it right away. He felt a need, not just a front, but a real *need* to meet, if not exceed, Glenn's expectations. Glenn was a stern but hard-working and responsible man, the kind of blue-blooded American that made an honorable husband and a respected father. The kind of man that Mitch always yearned for his own father to be. The kind of man that Mitch himself dreamed of becoming one day. And even though, in reality, Mitch was a long way off from having the virtuous hallmarks of a man like Glenn, the charade wasn't any less fulfilling.

The front door opened with a chime, and two customers entered the store. From his vantage in the screwdriver aisle, all Mitch could make of them were the tops of their heads as they bobbed toward the front counter behind the racks. One of the heads wore a disturbingly familiar cattleman, and the other had a shock of cloud-white cotton candy hair. Mitch got a clearer view of the duo upon their arrival at the register.

His worrisome hunch had been correct.

It was the Sheriff underneath that cattleman.

Mitch's chest tightened moreover at the realization that the Sheriff's acquaintance was also a familiar face. He was the lot owner from the buffer town who had parked the Porsche. He dressed a little less casually than he had been at the junkyard, dawning a golf shirt and slacks instead of dusty, oil-stained overalls, but there was no mistaking the man's identity.

Mitch pinched his medallion and thanked the Lord that the Charger was with John at the motel, not parked in front of the store.

That would have been the end of it. However, the question persisted as to why these two men were together and if it had anything to do with Mitch or the Porsche.

Mitch eavesdropped as the Sheriff introduced the man to Glenn as an old alumni chum passing through Oak County to visit some family. Realizing this was all just a horrible coincidence helped mollify Mitch's disposition, and he continued his work. After some passive conversation, to which Mitch was only faintly listening, the Sheriff and the lot owner said their goodbyes to Glenn and turned for the exit. Mitch lowered his head and busied himself fondling merchandise, hoping to blend with the scenery and avoid recognition.

"Hey, fella! Long time to see," the lot owner called out pointedly to him.

Mitch's heart sunk into his gut and he swallowed. Summoning the full of his thespian talents, he whirled aloofly. "Excuse me?"

The lot owner's gaze latched. "You was the one driving that Porsche, ain't ya? I got it parked up in the yard still, collecting dust. It's a shame, really, a car like that..."

Mitch could feel the heat of the Sheriff's attentiveness as he waited for an answer.

"I'm sorry," said Mitch politely. "You must have me mistaken for someone else."

Now Glenn was watching from the register.

"I swore it was you," the lot owner humored. "With that candy of a girl. The blonde. Boy, I'll never forget her, longs I live!"

Two flannel-garbed perusers an aisle over turned their heads to the conversation. The whole store was waiting on Mitch.

"No," smiled Mitch, knees near quaking. "Wrong guy. Sorry."

"Roy, I'd like a word with you if I might," the Sheriff said dryly. He stepped forward, put a weighted hand on Mitch's arm, and guided him deeper down the aisle toward the storefront window.

Once away from prying eyes, he spoke covertly: "I *know* who you are, Roy."

Mitch held the Sheriff's dredging gaze steadily. Never before had his poker face been so rigorously put to the test. "I'm sorry, sir?"

"Your past, Roy. The drinking. The vagrancy. I know all about it. I had a friend do a check on you."

The weight on Mitch's shoulders unburdened itself. Time unfroze. Breathing resumed. *Oh.* That *past,* he thought as his yawning lungs filled with air.

"Don't look so surprised," smirked the Sheriff. "Did you really think I wasn't going to run the name of the new guy in town who's been spending time with my daughter? I'm not sure if you are aware of this, but my estate is worth quite a sum. It has a tendency to bring out all the crazies. Investors. Preachers. Crooks."

"Yes, sir. I'm aware. Not fully. But I know about the inheritance. I know about the estate."

"Have you told my daughter about your history?"

"I have, Sheriff."

The Sheriff's gaze searched Mitch's eyes intensely.

"Good," he replied, seemingly satisfied with his examination. "That's the respectable thing to do. She's taken a liking to you. She enjoys the time she spends with you. And I like that she's been getting out of the house more, experiencing life. It seems like you've been a positive addition to our lives all around. Glenn says good things of you. So, Roy, I would like to invite you over to the house for dinner. What do you say? This Friday? The Mrs. makes one hell of a roast chicken, let me tell you, boy."

Invited to dinner by the father, Mitch thought in lieu of a chuckle. *Unbelievable.*

"I'd like that very much, Sheriff," said Mitch. His augmented smile was nothing short of genuine. "Thank you."

The Sheriff left Mitch with a firm handshake from a callused palm. The lot owner quickly apologized for the mistaken identity and waved goodbye. When the two were back out in the parking lot, Mitch, dizzy from relief, said to Glenn: "I think it's about time for lunch, huh, Glenn?"

UPON JOYCE'S RECOMMENDATION, the team met after work to collectively drink away their sorrows at a bar called *Roger's*, located only a few blocks from the call center. It was a typical small-town bar, nothing too fancy or elaborate, the flashiest of auxiliaries being the Christmas lights running along the bar display and a neon Budweiser sign buzzing in one of the windows. Outside, the bronze sky was sinking under dusk's pale violet, and inside, the wonted thirsties filled the small establishment with a pally, albeit sleepy, ambiance.

Joey returned to the team's table from the bar with a jug of foamy domestic lager in each hand. Chad, behind him, transported two additional jugs. The kid had hurdled the dubious bartender with a well-crafted fake ID. It was *almost* as well-crafted as Joey's.

They spread the jugs across the table for everyone to share. Joey fell in a seat beside Joyce. Chad, a seat beside Joey. The kid's unusual behavior had endured the day without explanation. He had been withdrawn and uncommunicative. Sometimes he would glance at Joey as if he were about to unburden himself and then withhold and look away. Joey thought maybe the kid had developed a slight man-crush on him, which was understandable but unnecessary.

Thanksgivings from the office staff, Joyce included, circled the table as they gazed with animated graciousness over the multitude of foggy pitchers bestowed upon them. But there was no vitality in their activity. No *life*. The weight of disappointment and failure hung like a thick dark cloud over all in attendance.

"So, Sean," said Joyce with her elbow on the table. Her head rested on her palm, elongating her neck. "You don't drink?"

Joey winced. "Recovering alcoholic, unfortunately..."

Joyce blew a raspberry. "Nuts to that. Drinking is awesome. How else do you wash away the bitter taste of life's monotony?"

"Watch out, we got a poet here!" joked Joey. He jerked his thumb in Joyce's direction for the benefit of the others at the table.

Joyce recoiled with a sour face and pulled her drink closer.

"Hey, Meryl," said Tammy at the other end. "If I can't find another job and I lose my apartment, can I come stay at your mansion?"

Soft, polite laughter rounded the table.

"I wish I could house you all," Meryl said sweetly.

"If I don't find a job, they're going to re-posses my car," bemoaned Robert. He was hunched over his glass, tie dangling like a slacked noose around his neck.

"I have rent to pay, too, guys. It sucks, I know," lied Joey.

"So why you buying everybody beers, then?" said Chad, more as an accusation than a question.

"Don't hate the man for that!" said Meryl, raising her glass appreciatively. She took a hefty swig of the foamy golden lager and hardened the pint on her coaster before wiping her mouth with her forearm and displaying a look of shameless satisfaction.

The sight made Joey pull a face.

Meryl was a rager.

"I'll drink to that!" cheered Joyce. As if to compete with Meryl, she downed a sizable gulp of beer herself. Her glance returned to Joey as she wiped the excess moisture off her bottom lip with a thumb. She raised one shoulder and dropped the other in an attempt to beguile. "Miss it yet?"

Joey had to admit: the boss *did* look pretty good under the bar light. Maybe it was the hopeless, wild, 'just lost my job and my life is over' vibe she was putting out. Whatever it was, it was working for her.

"Yeah, I miss it every day," he responded.

Meryl swallowed another long wash, raised her glass, and said, "Tonight, we should just let all that bad stuff go and get as drunk as we can."

"Wasted!" followed Tammy, raising her glass to Meryl's.

Robert joined his teammates. "Wasted break-dancing!"

Two hours later, and another two jugs of beer deep, the office crowd had thrown in the towel. Joey had maintained a steady back and forth with Joyce, scooting closer to her each time he filled his glass. He found her rampant depression and depravity arousing. She had demons inside her that desperately needed exorcising; frustration she needed to grind away with savage force and friction.

Joey put out the bait, and she accepted his offer for a ride home. Meryl, Tammy, and Robert decided to split a cab. Chad had overheard Joey's invite to Joyce and asked to tag along. Joey was flabbergasted at the kid's naivety. Even so, he couldn't leave a drunk minor to his own devices.

At Joyce's house, Joey waited until she was out of the car and the passenger door was closed before he turned to Chad in the backseat and scolded him: "You stay here, you cock-blocking son-of-a-bitch!"

He left the kid in the car and joined Joyce at the foot of her driveway. "Nice place," he said, appraising her abode. It was a semi-detached, showing bay windows and a lovely stained-wood porch staging a swinging loveseat. "You own it?"

"Rent," she said. "You can come inside if you like."

Joey frowned. "The kid. Got to drop him off."

She stepped closer, tinging Joey's nostrils with wafts of stale beer and sweet perfume. "You could come back after."

Joey's eyes brightened. "Yeah?"

Joyce bit down on her lip, smiled, and nodded.

Joey started a slow backward pace for the car. "Okay, then. I...will be...right back."

He spun and whipped open the driver-side door. Moving in a blur, he had the keys turned in the ignition and his seatbelt buckled before Chad in the rear could complete his inquiry about moving to the passenger seat.

Screeching onto the road, Joey shouted: "There's no time, Chad!"

The Corolla braked hard in front of Chad's parents' modest townhouse. The porch light glowed in anticipation of their son's return. "Okay, Chad. Get out," commanded Joey.

Chad remained immobile; arms crossed over his chest. "There's something I need to talk to you about," he said.

Joey sighed. *Of all the times.* "What is it, Chad? You've been acting weird all day. Are you gay, Chad? Is that it? You're gay? It's okay if you are, I support that kind of thing, but do you think you could have your breakdown of self-discovery another time? I'm about to have 'sex with your boss' sex. Do you know about 'sex with your boss' sex, Chad? I'm assuming you don't. Otherwise, you wouldn't be *sitting here, in my car,* preventing me from having it!"

Chad aptly removed a cut-out newspaper article from his hip pocket and smoothed it with the stroke of his hand on the median center console. He then reclined on an obtuse angle, grinning wryly as if he had just laid down a royal flush at the final table in the World Series of Poker. The emboldened headline on the article read: 'VAGRANT ESCAPES!" Under, was a picture—mugshot—of Joey following his arrest for the bar fight back in Martydale. Below the picture, the caption read: *'Unknown suspect arrested in bar brawl broken out of county holding by three masked assailants.'*

Joey stared at the clipping in a trance.

"I know who you are," said Chad victoriously. "Not completely. But I know what you're about."

He revisited the same pocket and gently removed two more scissor-cropped articles, adding them to the first. Joey picked up the extractions and examined them one by one. The first story was from the *Auburn Hills Harold* about a groom who vanished in the night with all the couple's wedding gifts. The photo was a shot of the wedding party. Joey, the best man, stood next to Mitch, the groom. Holding the groom close was the beaming bride: a tall and spindly woman with a hunchback and a large mole on her chin. Judy Harris. Joey would never forget Judy or the exceedingly putrid flavor of her breath, which smelt like a small farm animal had rolled about liberally in its excrement before crawling into her mouth and dying.

The second article was from another small town local paper and bore a similar headline with a similar wedding photo. However, this bride, Tara Harper, was a great deal more attractive than her predecessor. She was slim yet figured in the back end, with a pretty face, full lips, and limpid blue eyes. She was also a raging psychopath brimming with a bad case of toxic feminism and an undeserved superiority complex, with an endless reservoir of pseudo-spiritual taglines about as deep as her bust size, which was not very deep at all. By the end of the con, the whole team was more than glad to be robbing her blind. On the night of their escape, they drove off in the Rolls Royce she and Mitch had chartered to the church service, singing: "Sayonara, Tara! Today and Tomorrah!" And they were still singing the same cheery tune a day later when they sold the Rolls Royce for parts at a buffer town chop shop.

"So, it's Meryl, right?" said Chad with a sadistic undertone. "You guys are going to rob her, aren't you?"

Joey didn't know whether to be furious, worried, or impressed. The kid had managed to do what in all the years hitherto only Joey himself had accomplished. He had unmasked the Wedding Bandits.

"How'd you figure this out?" asked Joey through the rearview mirror.

Chad had no qualms with revealing his methods. "Man! I knew something was off with you from the jump! I mean, you're supposed to be this experienced salesman and you can't make a sale to save your life. You say you're a recovering alcoholic, and you invite us all over for a *booze* party? The fuck? Come on. I could understand maybe some wine with some cheese and crackers, but you were shucking out tequila into plastic party cups. You tell me, what recovering alcoholic is smoking joints and having tequila parties? It doesn't make any sense. So I started looking into newspaper archives for nearby towns. And that's when I found these articles. You guys are leaving a trail. I'm not even that smart. Eventually, someone is going to find you."

Joey kissed his teeth. "Well, thanks, Miss Cleo. But why don't you let *us* worry about what we got going on? What does this mean? What do you want? *Money*?"

"I want you to quit fucking around at work. I want you to start trying. You're a con man, for Chrissake," shot Chad. "You're telling me you can't get a read on a line and hook them in? By the looks of it, you do it pretty well."

Joey was at a loss for words.

"Look," Chad continued with a startling measure of conviction. "If these people lose their jobs, their lives will be ruined. Meryl will be fine. You guys will be more than fine. But them? Me? We're the ones that will end up paying for it. Do you really want to do that to us?"

"I didn't realize you cared," said Joey.

"I am *not* working at fucking Subway sandwiches."

Joey let out a soft chuckle. "Fair enough."

"You do this, and I won't go to the Sheriff."

"Okay, fine," said Joey. The leather seat crunched as he twisted and offered Chad his hand. "Deal. If I can help save your jobs, I'll do my best to make that happen."

"Deal," said Chad. He slipped his palm into Joey's.

"Great," said Joey. "Now get out of the car, would ya?"

Chad obliged and jaunted backward across his parents' front lawn, extending an authoritarian finger at Joey until the black night swallowed his likeness.

As Joey started onto the road, he knew he had to inform Mitch of this new development immediately. There wasn't a moment to spare.

He braked at the cross in the road.

But then again, he thought. Joyce *was* waiting for him at her place.

Chapter Sixteen

Joey returned home the next morning at sunrise. The widow Jenkins was in the front yard watering her vivacious carnation beds. He offered her a wave as he loped up the walkway. Hose slack in her grip, the old lady fixed him a stern glare for his entire jaunt to the door.

Must be still upset about the house party, he thought, amazed that a woman so close to death could hold such an enduring grievance.

Upon entering the house, he spotted Mitch on the sofa, head against the backrest, staring vacantly at the ceiling. He rolled his neck idly to meet the arrival's gaze. Joey delivered the apology speech he had rehearsed three times on the drive from Joyce's place. He explained that he took the staff out for drinks and how it led to a night of passion with his surprisingly sexually adventurous supervisor. He conveniently omitted the part about Chad's revelation until he could get a broader handle on his teammate's disposition.

"Yeah, I know," said Mitch. "Meryl called me drunk last night from the bar. And then again when she got home. We talked through most of the night."

"That's great!" exclaimed Joey. He threw his hands in the air like a football referee declaring a field goal. "You got the late night drunk call. That's money shot. You're in. That's perfect. So, why are you up so early?"

Mitch rubbed his bleary eyes and yawned. "Couldn't sleep. Just kind of been sitting here...thinking."

Joey was starting to put the scene together. The stupid grin. Thinking. He didn't like what he was getting the scent of. "You're not...falling for this chick, are you?"

Mitch chuckled softly under his breath. "You're starting to sound like Laura. No. I'm not. But you have to admit she is pretty cool. Probably the coolest out of all of them." He ruminated another second. "Just like talking to her is all," he said, complimenting his nonchalance with a one-shouldered shrug.

Joey plopped down on the couch beside Mitch. "Tough when they're cool, huh?"

Mitch replied with a slow and thoughtful nod. "It sure is, bud. It sure is. I'm going there Friday for dinner, though. And we're going hiking again tomorrow."

Joey smiled and threw down a hard slap on Mitch's thigh. "That's my guy! You'll be slipping that ring on her finger in no time!" He stood up and stretched his arms to the ceiling, deciding to let Mitch enjoy his victory for a while before breaking the news about Chad. It was safer that way. John would want Chad, and maybe even Joey, wiped off the earth entirely if he were to find out the truth. "Alright, well, I'm going to grab a shower and get off to work. Don't want to be late. Joyce might spank me."

Joey grinned on the way to the bathroom. "On second thought..."

AGENT QUINN'S UNMARKED Ford pulled from the main road into the Sandy Acres junkyard. In the rearview mirror, the piloting agent watched his tires expel champagne clouds atop the parched landscape as they proceeded further along the narrow trail flanked by tall grass and dry crowns of bursage. The craggy terrain rocked the vehicle back and forth like a sailboat amid turbulent waters. Agent Quinn gripped the wheel. Normally, he might've found the present scene an opportunity to daydream he was a swashbuckling pirate or a fearless sea captain navigating through a perilous and tumultuous squall. However, he felt much less at home in his space now that Agent McAllester was riding shotgun. The two-hour drive from Cedar Falls to Sandy Acres with his task force leader had been a torturous affair at best. Since the pickup at the airport, it had been one gross infringement after the other.

No radio.

No smoking.

There were briefings and debriefings. McAllester vetted every detail from Quinn's reports and then reviewed the details again for confirmation. Thankfully, there had been no inquiry into Quinn's sexual encounter with the Robertson girl because Quinn had omitted that information in his accounting. Nevertheless, Quinn worried that his superior's hound-like instincts would eventually and inevitably sniff out the facts behind his highly unethical interrogation methods.

Passing the junkyard's 'welcome' sign, little more than a couple of plywood planks nailed to twin two-by-fours staked into hardened dirt, the property opened to divulge a cabin-sized work shed under a corrugated tin roof and a graveyard of abandoned and dilapidated vehicles from competing manufacturers that had not seen the stretch of the open road in quite some time.

Quinn and McAllester were only in the market for one particular make and model: A cherry red 911 Porsche convertible.

The owner of the lot, with whom McAllester had spoken on the phone shortly after he and Quinn had commenced their journey to Sandy Acres, was a tall and emaciated man that could have been anywhere in the age range of the late fifties to early seventies. His hair was as white as the stripe on a skunk's back, and he wore a set of loose, oil-stained overalls over a bedraggled white t-shirt. True to his word, he awaited their arrival by the tool-cluttered work area.

Quinn parked the car. He and McAllester exited and approached their man. The air was thick and smothering, sun glaring off the surplus of extant metal. McAllester adopted a formal smile and extended his hand as he neared the lot owner. "Mr. Ottoman? I'm Agent McAllester with the FBI. We spoke on the phone earlier."

"Very good," said the lot owner. He gripped McAllester's expecting hand and pumped twice. "Come. I'll show you the car."

They set off through the gangway of abandons. McAllester kept to his heels while Quinn trailed in the rear, gasping for breath, hands rotating systematically between adjusting his waistband over his gut and wiping clean the beads of sweat flowing profusely over his brow.

"They paid in cash for the year," said the lot owner as he strode. He spoke loudly and distinctly as if he were a tour guide. "I wrote them a receipt. It's the only record I have of the transaction. Only thing in the books. I suppose a credit card might have been more useful to you, but unfortunately, they paid in cash, like I said."

"How many of them were there?" asked McAllester.

Quinn in the back end baked vexatiously.

"Three," said the lot owner. "A girl and two men. The girl did all the talking. She went to the men when she needed money."

"Did you get a good look at them?" McAllester asked.

The lot owner glanced disagreeably at his dirt-caked boots. "The men? No. They were in the Porsche most of the time and wore hats low on their head. Made their faces hard to see. But the girl? Oh yeah. I seen her. Could probably sketch her from memory. A beautiful young lady. Blonde. Maybe twenty-four. No older than thirty. At least didn't look as such. She was absolutely stunning. Take a man's breath right out his mouth; she would. But don't quote me. I'm a married man, remember." The lot owner glanced over his shoulder and grinned at Quinn specifically. His crow's feet grew long and demarcated his narrow face. McAllester smiled politely, but Quinn knew the gesture was fraudulent; McAllester hated lewd remarks. Satisfied with his bawdy quip, the lot owner continued onward. "They bought a '69 Dodge Charger. Had some body issues, ran fine, though. They drove it on out of here. Paid cash for that, too. Do you know much about cars, gentlemen?"

"It's a classic," said Quinn from a distance, recalling his days as a boy watching *Dukes of Hazzard* on the couch with his father. He had always fantasized about owning one of those cars when he was older, but, like many of his childhood dreams, he had somehow failed to actualize the inclination.

"You bet," said the lot owner with a countenance somewhere between vindication and contentment. "Had plans of fixing her up myself, but they paid a fair dollar, so I was inclined to make the sale."

He stopped in his stride in front of a low-lying sports car draped in a thin white sheet and motioned with his hand. "This is her. Right here. A 911 Porsche convertible. Cherry red."

McAllester stepped toward the cloaked conformation. "May I?"

The lot owner nodded accommodatingly.

McAllester peeled back the sheet, revealing a wide black grill and a glossy cherry red paint job. The contours of the rounded hood gleamed in the daylight; the oval headlights dazzled like opals, and the famous hood ornament presented itself proudly above the license plate. McAllester continued to draw back the sheet, further revealing the automobile's sleek, soft-edged anatomy.

Quinn knew upon the cream leather seating's reveal that the Porsche present was the same Porsche parked outside the reception hall the night of Angie's wedding.

Suddenly, she appeared in his mind's eye: her head arched against her pillow as she lay under him on the bed. Her curly dead ends fell messily over her face while a river of sweat ran down her pale double chin. Quinn watched himself pumping in and out of her dewy form at a ferocious rate.

"Is this the one?" asked McAllester, his eyes on Quinn.

"Yeah, that's it," answered Quinn. The x-rated thought bubble floating over his head like a halo popped into oblivion. Still, a warmth lingered in his loins. "That's the one."

Though McAllester's expression remained deadpan, his eyes glowed triumphantly. He respectfully shook the lot owner's hand and thanked him for his assistance.

"No problem," said the lot owner. "Wish I could be of more help. I was sure I saw one of those fellows over in Oak County working at the hardware store, but I guess my eyes were playing tricks on me, as it goes. Fella had no idea who I was."

McAllester froze. "Did you say Oak County?"

The lot owner confirmed, and McAllester's triumphant gaze burned profoundly.

Inside the Crown Vic, McAllester opened the glove compartment. He withdrew a pile of blank civilian informant documents and tossed them haphazardly into the backseat, then wrenched out a road map and unfolded it over his lap until it had quintupled in size. His gaze wandered wildly over the paper's surface before zeroing in on something that halted his search.

"What is it?" asked Agent Quinn, less than impressed at the mess McAllester had made of his car.

Eyes glued to the map, McAllester said distantly: "Ever heard of Oak County?"

"Sounds familiar," said Quinn. Truthfully, he had no idea of its existence and even less of its relevance.

"Remember that oil tycoon who got kidnapped in the early nineties?"

Quinn vaguely recalled the story. He had been just a boy when it had happened. "Oh yeah. That's where they found him, right? Oak County? Some cop went into the bush alone, right? Saved him, yeah?"

"Exactly," said McAllester. "The kidnappers worked for the Tyrant."

"Robertson?"

"The same."

Quinn shook his head. "That's some coincidence."

He roused the engine and asked McAllester if they should start back to the motel.

McAllester yanked his seat belt over his lean frame and clicked it into place. "Get on the highway."

"Highway?"

"Oak County is only an hour or so out," said McAllester. "Let's go find us a '69 Dodge Charger."

Quinn was not in the mood for more long drives; they were far enough out of Cedar Falls as it was. "That's a long way to go for a hunch," he said, hoping McAllester would reconsider the order.

He didn't.

Chapter Seventeen

After a seven-hour first-class flight from JFK to Santa Ana, Robertson and his son arrived on the west coast, Escalade waiting for them in the underground park, gleaming under artificial light and concrete. They sorely clambered inside and, saying little on the trip, drove another three hours to the modest township of Sandy Acres. Following the direction of the mile marker on the side of the highway, Sebastian branched off at the exit, and minutes later, he pulled into the parking lot of the Sandy Acres Bed N' Bar.

His father handled the room booking while Sebastian waited outside the lobby and smoked a cigarette. The nicotine helped lighten his heavy head as he watched the night advance, daylight now only a thin pink line on the distant undulating horizon.

Inside the small, musky unit, Sebastian stretched out on the left of two twin beds and mindlessly ingested the week's sports highlights on the small box television. His father called home and checked in with Angie.

"She sounds a lot better," his father relayed after saying goodbye. "She went out for drinks with Rhonda. Said it really raised her spirits."

Still glued to ESPN, Sebastian replied: "Good. I'm glad to hear it."

His father unbuttoned the two top buttons on his collared shirt and disappeared into the bathroom. The door closed. Seconds later, shower water rushed and hissed behind the drywall.

Sebastian sat upright and watched if his father would again enter the room. When he was certain he was alone, he snatched the remote off the nightstand and raised the volume on the television.

He withdrew his phone from the pocket of his slacks and quickly skimmed through the contact directory until he found the name 'Gus.' He dialed the number and lifted the phone to his ear, gaze returning to the bathroom door.

The other end went live after a single ring. The voice on the line was toneless, with a slight inflection of the old country discernible in his cadence. "Hey, Sab..."

"Any updates?" Sebastian inquired. The roistering monologue of the distinguished sportscaster played over him.

"I'm waiting on my guy," said the voice on the other line. "What I know so far is that your mother was definitely having an affair with Eric Baldacci, there's no doubt. But that whole story your father gave you about her being killed because she discovered Eric was planning a betrayal is garbage. Besides the affair, Eric was as loyal to your father as anyone. I got my guy working on Eric's whereabouts the day of the murder. I'll know soon."

Sebastian's insides coiled, and a bitter taste coalesced in the back of his mouth. Rage compounded inside him, bubbling and boiling like a pot of burnt diner coffee. He wanted to strangle the feeling as if it were tangible. He wanted to seize the flickering nightstand lamp and smash it to shards against the peeling floral wallpaper. He wanted to flip the foul-smelling mattress and unload a full clip into the stuffings.

Until the room was raining feathers.

Sebastian maintained his composure. "Okay, Gus. Good work. Get back to me as soon as you can."

He ended the call, swallowed, and stared at the water-damaged stucco ceiling. From inside the bathroom, the shower's hiss persisted.

Snakes, he thought. The corners of his lips arched downward.

He turned off the television and closed his eyes, allowing a deep, cleansing breath. His heart rate slowed to a trot. The young Robertson was physically and mentally drained, yet he was confident he could not sleep. Not while knowing what he now knew.

He thought about his sister and how she had not been the only one in the family mortally betrayed by a person they loved. He thought about everything his father ever taught him about being a man, the rules and responsibilities accompanying such an honor. He thought about his mother and their little time together before her life was stolen. But most of all, he thought of vengeance and how he would soon deliver it upon everyone who dared to cross him.

Chapter Eighteen

Mitch and Meryl perched on the jut of the bluff, legs dangling off the mesa as they peered out to the blue-green expanse of water scintillating under the afternoon sun. Seven or eight stories down, the rushing tide broke against jagged rocks before thinning to suds on a pebbly beach. Mitch felt a dizzy tingle in his stomach.

"Are you sure this is safe?" he asked over a drifting breeze that cooled the sweat he had worked up on their hike. "Isn't this where people die taking a selfie?"

Meryl let out a braying laugh that concluded with a piggish snort. The sequence engendered Mitch's spurting levity.

"What's a matter?" she teased. "Don't trust me?"

"It's nature I don't trust."

"Fair enough. She is a cruel, cruel bitch."

"The worst," said Mitch.

Silence fell over the moment—an easy silence. Mitch squinted and watched two seagulls flapping in the distance, fighting over what looked to be someone's discarded pizza crust. The avian rivals squawked and threshed their limbs as their beaks tugged on each end of the abandoned sustenance like extremities struggling inside a Chinese finger trap. Other indiscernible warblers whistled sweet melodies from an intangible provenance.

The draft kissed Mitch's face. "So..." said Mitch, drawing out the vowel. "What's new in Meryl's world?"

Her eyes lit up as if she had just stubbed her toe on a sharp edge. "Remember that show *Bobby's World*?"

Mitch grinned. "Back when Howie Mandel had hair."

"Why do bald guys shave it to the skin like that? Seems a bit excessive."

Mitch shrugged. "You should find one and ask him."

"Maybe I will," said Meryl with conviction. "So, you want to know about Meryl's world, eh?...Well, Sean has been great on the phones the last two days. Someone lit a fire under his butt. We might even get to second worst by the end of the quarter. Which means I might get to keep my job. So, yah. Pretty happy about that. Go Sean."

She thought deeper, rolling her eyes left to right. "Oh! I joined a gym...well, *the* gym, the *only* gym."

Mitch raised his eyebrows. "Wow. Look at you."

She smiled proudly. "Yup. Even got me a personal trainer. His name is James. He's pretty cute, too."

"Uh-oh," said Mitch. "Should I be jealous?"

Meryl giggled, enjoying Mitch's moment of vulnerability. "I don't know. Should you?"

She playfully tilted her head and caught Mitch's eye. He met her mischievous gaze. At that moment, Mitch was no longer looking at a mark. He was only looking at a girl whose skin looked radiant under the summer sun. A girl whose green eyes, gleaming with flecks of gold, expressed something Mitch rarely ever got the chance to see in his line of work: purity. Without further contemplation, for further contemplation was unnecessary, Mitch succumbed to the magnetic draw, leaned closer, and pressed his lips softly on hers.

MR. ROBERTSON SHUT the door to the SUV and joined Sebastian at the hood. The sun glared off the chrome lining of the windshield, blinding him momentarily. Bronze specters drifted atop the cracked earth in a belated response to the dirt trail they had kicked up on the way into the property. Robertson's mouth was dry.

His black socks itched at his calves. It was a scorching afternoon, a day that he would have much instead spent poolside at his estate. However, a small part of him, a tiny fragment concealed deep inside his heart of hearts, was grateful to again be on the hunt. He had spent many years of his life on the hunt. He savored the hunt; he respected the hunt; the hunt is what had molded him into the man he was. Now, it was as if nature was again inviting him to sharpen his sword, reminding him that it was unwise for a beast as powerful as he to grow too complaisant.

Robertson sourly traversed the mustard clay path toward a moderately-sized workshop under a corrugated tin roof. Inside, a brittle old man wearing a pair of tattered overalls wrenched away on an engine block set upon his worktable over scrap newspaper. At the sight of the two Robertsons, the old man in the overalls set his wrench on the table and sauntered cordially toward them. He had very little meat on his bones for all his height, a narrow, horse-like face, and pronounced rounded cheekbones. Short, brittle hairs shot out from his slacked jaw like whiskers on a troll, and under a green John Deer cap low on his brow, ghost-white hair cupped upward.

"May I help you, gentlemen?" he inquired with all due courtesy.

"Are you the owner?" sniped Mr. Robertson churlishly. He did not intend to be so brusque, but the heat was taxing his patience.

The old man halted slightly and appraised the two Robertsons as if for the first time. His temperament abruptly annealed. "I am. And you might be?"

"We're looking for a 911 Porsche convertible that may have been brought here by some young men. Maybe they had a girl or an older gentleman with them."

Robertson cringed at his use of the word *gentleman*. But he saw that a light had flicked on in the old man's memory and knew they had come to the right place.

Presently, Sebastian's phone trilled a dainty melody. Robertson found this disturbance only slightly less infuriating than having to refer to that fake priest scam artist son-of-a-bitch in terms of endearment. He swiveled, adding to the itch of his collar, and glared at his son for an explanation. Sebastian pulled the phone from his pocket and checked the screen. He raised a forefinger, abutted the phone to his ear, and walked toward the SUV.

Robertson's jaw clenched the moment Sebastian turned his back. He couldn't fathom who might have been important enough to be on the other end of that phone at a time like this. Most likely, the culprit was one of Sebastian's many young, attention-starved girlfriends. The boy was a looker and a charmer, just like his old man had been and still was. The floozies flocked to him like bees to honey. Still, Robertson maintained that his son did too much for these girls. He gave them too much of himself. He needed to *focus* and leave the pussy at the door, sweet as it was.

Robertson swallowed his wrath and reconvened with the old man, who now appeared somewhat annoyed at his visitors.

"I'm not at liberty to divulge that kind of information," he replied while appraising Mr. Robertson with a wandering glance. "*Who* exactly are you, anyway?"

Robertson stepped closer, peered deep into the old man's wary eyes, and apprised him clearly: "I'm the owner of that vehicle. It was stolen from me. Now I'm going to ask you one more time...Did that car pass through your junkyard?"

The old man swallowed. His posture wilted. "Look, if this is a police matter, maybe it would be best if you called the authorities."

Sebastian returned from his phone call and rejoined his father's side. He was perceptibly distant. Hurt, even.

"No. We won't be notifying any authorities," Mr. Robertson assured the yard owner. He peered around the property for a sign of another prole, a wife, or anyone else that could make a break for a phone after witnessing what was about to happen. "But you *are* going to tell me where I can find that car," he continued. "Or my son here is going to put a lead bullet right between your googly fucking eyes."

The old man donned a wide-eyed look of horror. His mouth fell open like a freshman girl at a frat party. Robertson glanced at Sebastian. His heavyhearted pout had been wiped clean and replenished with the cold, calculated countenance befitting an executioner.

Robertson puckered a wry and haughty grin.

That's my boy.

Chapter Nineteen

Mitch came home just after seven, sore and famished from the hike. The kiss he shared with Meryl at Oak Bluff was fresh in his mind. The kiss she gave him when he dropped her off at the mansion was even fresher. It was longer. Deeper. He hated himself for being excited about something so trivial. He tried to convince himself that his emotions were only a somatic craving running its course.

To admit the alternative was unthinkable.

As he shut the apartment door, a shadowy form appeared in the corner of his eye. Someone was waiting for him in the house. Mitch whirled, fist-cocked, and ready to swing.

He came face to face with the intruder.

Laura.

She wore a tight black Zeppelin T-shirt and matching jeans. Red Chucks commanded attention. The clothes and the shoes were new, indicating Laura had been shopping recently. She had also trimmed her hair and applied platinum highlights.

Her lip gloss shimmered as a playful grin emerged. "Hey, stranger."

She stepped closer and pressed her thigh between Mitch's legs. He smelled gin and cigarettes on her warm breath. Her lips moved toward his and caressed his open mouth. Mitch retreated and gently positioned her at arm's length.

"What are you doing here?" he demanded. He grew increasingly furious as the words tumbled out but was careful not to alert the widow Jenkins upstairs. "How did you even get in?"

Laura flashed a wink. "Pluh-eese."

She stepped forward. In tandem, Mitch executed another evasive step. "You can't be here," he went on. "Do you realize how risky this is? How it can fuck everything up? Tell me you didn't drive here in the Charger."

Laura's playfulness dried up. The corners of her shimmering lips descended. Her forehead creased as an eyebrow arched offensively. "I took a cab. I wanted to surprise you. What's your problem?"

Mitch disarmed slightly. Most of his attention remained on the windows as he scanned for unfamiliar cars parked on the road. "Nothing. This is dangerous."

Her devilish grin reanimated. Her eyes swelled, wild and hungry. "That's what we do."

She came in for a kiss nimbly and caught Mitch off guard. He yielded to the advance as if some part of his subconscious wanted to compare Laura's kiss to Meryl's. With the slip of her tongue came a bitter numbness that tasted of gasoline. It was now clear why she had made the trip; the drugs had gotten the better of her.

She pulled away and whispered in his ear: "I wanna fuck."

A shiver ran up Mitch's spine, and the powerlessness of original sin consumed him, if only for an instant. What broke him from his trance, he could not discern—but it was something. He removed Laura's hand from his belt buckle and hardened his conviction. "No. All right? Stop it. I've been working, hiking, and I'm sore. I need a shower."

Her fingers crawled from his midriff to his chest. "I could come, too."

"No," said Mitch with finality. "You need to leave. Coming here was a bad idea."

She recoiled sharply. "What the hell is wrong with you lately? I think this girl is getting to your head. You don't know who you are anymore."

Mitch flipped the subject. "Did you know Meryl joined a gym?"

Laura kissed her teeth. "So?"

"Don't you think that is information my recon should be providing me?"

She rolled her eyes. "Okay, yeah, so, big deal. She stopped going to Dairy Queen every day, and she joined a gym. Fuckin' *wow*."

"She stopped going to Dairy Queen?"

Laura threw her hands in the air helplessly. "See? This is why I didn't tell you. I think you're sweet on this bitch, and I don't fucking like it. Don't forget, Mitch: you have a whole team that depends on you. It's not just about *you* anymore."

Her words packed more punch than he was ready for. "I know that," said Mitch, avoiding Laura's contemptuous glower. "Don't you think I know that?"

Laura turned away, sickened, and blew by Mitch on the way to the door. She gripped the knob and said: "I came in through the backyard sliding door, asshole. Those locks are shit."

She marched out of the house and slammed the door behind her.

The widow Jenkins is not going to like that, thought Mitch with a shake of his head.

He took a long breath and tried to shake off the last ten minutes. He went to the kitchen and poured himself a glass of water. On the counter was a note from Joey that read: 'Gone to bone my supervisor', with a crudely drawn smiley face at the bottom of the paper.

Well, at least someone is enjoying themselves.

WILLY DAWSON SLAPPED a ten-dollar bill on the bar and winked at the new day bartender Doug, Pat Newborn's kid, who had returned from college not a week ago and was putting his education to good use by working the afternoon shift at the Bed N' Bar until Blondie Becky came in at eight for the night rush. Willy liked Duggy. He wasn't as stuck up as many youths around Sandy Acres and had a vacuum of a nose, which was good for Willy's bottom line.

"Keep the change, college boy," said Willy as he slipped his stubby fingers into the handles of two frosty mugs and turned for his table by the window.

Willy placed the two mugs on the table, one on his coaster and the other in front of his trucker friend, Merv, who had come to see him that afternoon to purchase his monthly inventory of "wake-up medicine" used to get him through the long hauls on the interstate. During Willy's absence, Merv had opened the shutters and gazed out the window at the rays of red and violet blanketing the parking lot. The arrival of beer reclaimed his attention.

"Say, Willy," said Merv as Willy dropped in his chair. "Will you look at that there Porsche parked outside? Now what kinda person do you gather drives a car like that and stays at a place like this?"

Willy followed Merv's gesture and grunted as he transited his cumbersome flesh. He was shocked to see the same cherry-red Porsche convertible that belonged to the old timer out in Oak County parked along the curb, the same old timer who had returned to the bar not too long ago looking to have his packages delivered. Willy reckoned maybe his new client had thought twice about forking out the extra cash for door service.

Willy snickered. "Well, I'll be a monkey's nut. I think I know exactly what kind of person, Merv. They were in here just a few weeks back, came to see me like you're seeing me right now. Four of them. One of 'em was getting real friendly with Becky."

"You don't say," rejoined a stentorian voice from a booth near the entrance.

Willy jerked in his seat. With the exception of Duggy, he had assumed the bar to be empty. He reckoned someone must have walked in while he was putting together Merv's package in the bathroom. Whoever the new arrival was, they were not very polite, eavesdropping on respectable people's private conversations. Willy and Merv craned their necks and peered across the tavern to find the source of the interruption.

Two well-groomed businessmen types, one older and one younger, stood from a booth near the pool tables. Their steely gazes fixed on Willy as they steadily approached.

"Did I hear you say that someone was driving that Porsche a few weeks back?" said the elder of the two, a silver fox with wide shoulders and an enviable jawline. The younger, bringing up the rear, looked too similar to be unrelated; he possessed the same dark eyes and prominent chin, with a scowl as uninviting as his clothes were pretentious. Willy's instinct told him that these men were the law. He didn't like it. Both he and Merv had product on their person.

"Is that your car out there?" asked Merv in an amicable manner, unaware that he was all but certainly talking to the police.

"It sure is," said the silver fox. They were looming over Willy's table now. The silver fox drew a chair from the adjacent table and fit into it like a slipper. His demeanor adopted a hitherto unveiled gregariousness despite a hot gaze still burning under his thick, gray eyebrows. The younger one remained erect and militant. "I just got it back," continued the silver fox, speaking as if he and Willy were old chums. "It had been stolen from me. By *four* people, just like you said. Any chance you came into contact with these folks?"

Willy raised an eyebrow. "You ain't cops, is ya? You have to tell us if you are."

The question seemed to exhaust the silver fox but garnered no emotion from his junior. "No," said the fox. "No, we're not the police. And that assumption is untrue. The *cops* are more than fit to lie to the public."

Willy didn't appreciate the silver fox's crass attitude. No cocky out-of-towner was about to come into Willy's bar and start acting smart. He glanced at Duggy behind the wood, back at the two collar jockeys. He leaned forward on the table and glared at the silver fox with a haughty bug-eye. "Well, then why don't y'all get into your nice sports car and *get out of here*."

The silver fox bowed his head and laughed so softly that the sound was merely more than a whisper. Willy observed him guardedly and wondered what in the world was so funny.

Without forewarning, the silver fox propelled from his seat and lunged at Willy. His rough hand clutched Willy's throat and squeezed. Nose to nose, the silver fox's eyeballs bulged from his sockets. His words mowed down Willy with the force of a freight train: "Listen, you country bumpkin piece of shit! I'm through fucking around! I've been on the road for days, and I'm tired! Now, you're going to tell me what I want to know, or I am going to squeeze the life from your fat, hick neck. You got that?"

Willy's eyes darted to Merv for help. Regrettably, his client was catatonic in his seat and looked to be in the process of soiling himself. Frantically, Willy's gaze shot to the bar. Duggy gaped behind the wood, stiff as a fourteen-year-old's erection.

Do something, Duggy, prayed Willy. *Do something, and I swear I'll never short your bag again.*

As if to answer his prayers or to yield to Willy's desperate parlay, Duggy made a courageous break for the landline mounted on a support beam by the cash register. The young city boy withdrew a snub nose .22 from behind him and instantly squelched Willy's optimism. At sight of the weapon, Duggy skidded to a halt, sneakers squeaking against the sticky tile. He raised his hands over his head and floundered for words.

"Don't move," the city boy instructed flatly.

The command was redundant.

Willy's lungs expanded and filled as the silver fox released his Adam's apple. He hacked spurted coughs, adjusting to the returning flow of air. The silver fox rose. He produced a 9mm pistol and pressed the gun barrel against Willy's forehead. The steel was cold and hard on his brow as Willy whimpered through quivering lips: "Stop! Don't, okay? Just don't...I'll tell ya. I'll tell ya everything you wanna know."

The silver fox softened. He peaceably tucked his firearm into his waistband, dragged forward his seat, and rested himself. Willy struggled to remove his cell phone, hands quivering autonomously. The silver fox perched and waited patiently—for the moment.

Phone in hand, Willy speedily thumbed through his contacts and scrolled down to 'Skynyrd'. He slid the phone across the table to the silver fox.

"They were in here boozin'," he sputtered. "One of them, the older one, grabbed some blow from me. He came back a second time a few days later. Not in the Porsche, though. In a Charger. A '69 Charger. Like *Dukes of Hazzard*. Charcoal paint job. Said his partner was giving him heat. He wanted me to deliver. The address is on the phone. It's in Oak County, 'bout an hour out."

The silver fox picked up the phone and rubbed his sweeping jaw. "Oak County...That's where that kidnapped oil exec was found some years back, no?"

"I don't know," shivered Willy. "Maybe."

Willy checked on Merv, whose trembling gaze manically attended his pint.

"You mind if I take this with me?" the silver fox asked Willy. He lifted the phone to the side of his face and modeled it like a television commercial.

Willy nodded a slow up and down, blinked, gasped, and finally wagged his head furiously. "I mean, no. No, I don't mind."

"Great..." The silver fox opened and showed teeth. Willy expected to see blood-soaked fangs like that of a white wolf or some other prowling predator of the night. Instead, he saw an immaculately polished grill fit for a politician. He glanced sedately at his young partner and said: "I think we're done here."

The snub nose aimed at Duggy sparked and let out a deafening blast that ricocheted off the tavern walls. The spent bullet ripped through Duggy's chest and burned a frayed hole in his shirt. He crashed against the liquor shelf and dropped behind the bar. Bottles wobbled and clanked. Forties of Tanqueray and Johnny Walker Black fell off the display and smashed onto the tile. The gunman swung and aimed at Merv. He fired a shot into Merv's throat above his clavicle. The bullet came out the other side and broke clean through the window pane. Webbed cracks sprouted from the point of exit. Merv choked and gurgled and clawed at the wound. Between gaps in his fingers, red-black blood trickled down his knobby knuckles. The gunman fired a third shot into Merv's forehead and sent him home.

The silver fox rose from his chair and seized the 9mm from his waistband. He aimed the barrel point-blank between Willy's furrowed eyebrows.

Willy closed his eyes and prayed to God.

Chapter Twenty

Joey was the first to arrive at work in the morning, as was routine since Chad presented his unexpected ultimatum. He settled at his workstation and booted his PC. The computer whistled and hummed to life, the dated processor's internal fan working overtime to cool the ancient circuit board. The number sixteen, the number of sales needed in the next week to keep their jobs, weighed heavy on his mind. Despite achieving the title of lead sales since his promise to commit a valid effort, he felt, even more than the pride of his laurels, the weight of responsibility in leading his team to victory.

Meryl and Tammy were next to arrive. Tammy commented on how good Meryl looked lately. Naturally, Joey's attention whirled to Meryl as she sat down at her workstation. Tammy was right—Meryl was glowing. Her clothes were smart. Her skin beamed healthily. Her eyes, framed by coquettishly-styled hair, were bright and teeming with life. In addition to all this, she had shed noticeable inches off her midsection. Joey wondered why he hadn't noticed these modifications until now and realized that for the first time in his adult life, he had been more focused on his duties at work than on the women in his periphery.

Meryl thanked Tammy for the compliment and modestly tucked a few strands of hair behind her ear. After booting her PC, she swiveled in her seat and waved to Joey a small hello. Joey returned a singular nod. He might have flirted a little if she hadn't been the mark.

As loudly as her baby blue eyeshadow and pylon orange formal wear was bright, Tammy exclaimed: “No! I mean it! Are you on some kind of new diet? Kito? Or is it Kayto?...Kooto?”

Meryl smirked bashfully and shook her head. “Nope. Just exercising every day. I got a gym membership, and I’ve been going on a lot of hikes at Oak Bluff with Roy. I’ve noticed a big difference in my energy levels. I stopped eating takeout, and I don’t snack very much; I haven’t had the time lately. So maybe that is to blame. And I don’t drink soda anymore—too much sugar. I pretty much stick to water. Water with lemon if I’m feeling adventurous.”

Chin resting on her palm, Tammy’s head bobbed vigorously.

Robert and Chad trickled in. Robert narrowed his eyes at Joey as he crossed. “It’s on today, Sean. I’m outselling you. Period.”

“Bring it on, Bobby,” said Joey, edging him on.

Chad took his usual seat next to Joey, leaned in closer than expected, and whispered: “Damn. Meryl’s looking finer and finer these days.”

Joey grinned. “Eyes on the phones, kid. She’s taken.”

Joyce was last to arrive. Thermos of instant joe in hand, she said her usual drab and drowsy good morning to everyone on her way to her office and paid Joey no special attention. As of yet, their little fling had gone unnoticed around the phone room by everyone except for Chad. However, to Joey’s current knowledge, the kid had managed to keep his mouth shut regarding this particular. For once in his life, Chad had kept his big mouth shut. Joey reckoned that he might not have been the only one who had matured over the last little while.

The team got on the phones with intention, and there was little chatter between calls. Erelong, marked sales gradually appeared on the whiteboard. By lunch, they had sold seven units; four of those sales under Robert. The energy in the room was so palpable, the goal so within reach, that the team ate at their desks, and returned to the phones long before the culmination of the allotted thirty minutes.

Robert knocked down a sale. Meryl followed with two more on the board. Tammy confirmed a sale after that. Robert put up another two in a row. Chad and Joey each made a sale about an hour later.

With thirty minutes left of the workday, Chad crossed off the sixteenth sale, selling a deluxe unit to Jasper Mechanical in Connecticut. Joey nearly fell off his chair when, amid the usual hemming and hawing one receives from an ambivalent prospect, he heard the kid say: "I hear ya, Sal. I have two kids myself. It's a tight economy we're in. Small business is a tough ship to steer. But the ones who survive in this economic climate are the ones who adapt and evolve. All my other clients have had nothing but great things to say about this investment. In fact, Sal...Are you listening, Sal? I want to tell you something. These people are *saving* money. The solar battery charger is a godsend, they say. Sent from God, Sal. I mean, dual function *and* free energy? That's a win-win in my books, Sal. And the warranty and guarantee make sure of it. I stand behind this product like I stand behind my kids, Sal."

Joey screwed his face. *Economic climate? Tough ship to steer?* Who did this kid think he was?

After recording Sal's banking information, Chad slammed the receiver back on the phone with a force that shook the desk. He jumped from his seat, punched his fist into the air, and shouted: "Yee! That's how it's done! Thug life, bitches!"

The team laughed, cheered, and stood in ovation.

Joyce promptly appeared from her office, gaped and eyes aglow. "Does this thug-life announcement mean what I think it means?"

"We did it!" cried Tammy. She continued to clap long after the others had stopped.

"Lord, I don't believe it!" gasped Meryl.

Robert beamed at Joey and pointed to the whiteboard triumphantly, his name marked in cursive above Sean's. He bounced his eyebrows in jest at the defeated. Joey bowed his head respectfully and honored the redeemed top seller.

Joyce punched a fist into an open palm. "Fantastic! Great news, you guys! I'm going to get Head Office on the phone right now and tell them. Drinks on me after work!" She cast an electric glance over her shoulder at Joey as she heeled back to her office and closed the door.

The team reposed at their stations. Their cumulative elation had time seemingly moving at half its usual speed. The final twenty minutes passed as if hours until finally, it was time to punch out.

"You coming out for drinks, Meryl?" asked Chad with a sideways grin at the mark.

"Can't, squirt," Meryl answered as she loaded her bag. "I have a dinner date with Roy."

Whether from being called a squirt or from being rejected by his newly-formed crush, Chad curled like a prawn in his chair and muttered under his breath: "Yeah, I'm sure *that's* going to end well."

Joey could have smacked the kid right where he sat.

After punching out, the team, minus Meryl, headed back to Roger's for a round of drinks, only this time around, they were celebrating keeping their jobs rather than mourning their loss. There was no denying the poetry of toasting victory in the same place they once wallowed in defeat. However, it was a short retreat for most. Exhausted from the day's excitement, all but Joyce and Joey stayed for a quick pint before departing for their respective abodes. Joey said goodbye to Tammy and Robert, and as Chad passed, Joey smacked him on the arm.

"What do you say, kid? A deal's a deal."

Chad nodded. "We're square."

Joey smiled. "Alright. Way to make that last sale. See you at work."

Upon Chad's departure, Joyce raised her shot glass filled with the whiskey ordered from the top shelf in honor of the special occasion. Joey tapped it with his can of non-alcoholic beer, and they swallowed.

"Thanks for the drinks, boss," said Joey. He leaned back in his seat, shoulders deflated.

Joyce placed her shot glass on the puddled bar next to her martini. "If that is what you wish to call it. No alcohol...*pssh*. What are you even doing in life?"

Joey wanted to apprise her that he could drink her under the table in a heartbeat, but *Sean* just put on a humored half-smile as if being teased for his sobriety was commonplace. "Still," he said. "Thank you."

Joyce rolled her eyes lazily and ran a hand through her short hair. "Thanks for the dicking."

Joey gasped and laughed. "Excuse me?"

With heavy eyelids, Joyce smiled childishly. She put her elbow on the bar's edge and rested her cheek in her palm. "It's how Chad so eloquently refers to sex."

Joey did recall Chad saying something of the sort. "It's no problem," he told her. "I'm always here to help a damsel in distress."

Joyce sighed. "I don't know what I'm going to do with you...I feel like I'm going to wake up one day, and this will all just be a dream."

Joey gulped his can. "What makes you say that?"

She shrugged one shoulder. "It's been a while since I met someone I liked. I don't like a lot of people. I mean, I'm not a bitch or anything like that." She paused to appraise her statement. "Well, yeah," she corrected. "I'm kind of a bitch. I may have some trust issues, but who knows?"

"Did you always want to be a supervisor in a call center?"

Joyce sat upright, her sly eyes shifting sidelong in his direction. "*Yeah*, since I was a little girl."

Joey looked up at the bar television, amused.

"No," Joyce went on. "I did have other ambitions in life. I really wanted to be an archeologist when I was younger. You know...dinosaur bones and stuff?"

"What stopped you?"

She took a sip from her martini, thought about it, and shrugged. "Myself, I guess...I started working at Vacuserve to pay for my car. Then I started dating this guy. I thought we were serious. He didn't. By the time we broke up five years later, I had the supervisor position, I had my place, and I was...comfortable. I guess."

Joey digested her response. "So, you're happy?"

Joyce laughed at the question. "Things have been okay lately." Her face twisted some. "But there's always that little piece of me that wants to just take off to a new city and start a new life. Be a completely different person." She sat with a thoughtful expression, then shifted her face to Joey and searched his eyes. "Does that make any sense to you?"

Joey hunched over the bar with his arms crossed. "Yeah, Joyce. It does."

Chapter Twenty One

Mitch arrived at the Chestwick estate shortly before six and was greeted at the door by the housemaid. Hitherto, he had only interacted with the woman through their exchanges on the intercom. He would learn later that the immigrant from China was in her early fifties, but at a glance, Mitch assumed her to be much younger. Her skin shared the tautness of a woman in her thirties and had a natural glow most noticeable on the contours of her high cheekbones. She wore an unremarkable black blouse and a conservative manila skirt that ran long past her knees. A heart-shaped face, oil-drop eyes, and a head of long, silky black hair showing maiden signs of gray crowned the diminutive stature off which her ceremonious garb loosely draped. Upon their introduction, she said no words; her deep-reaching gaze was sufficient to lead Mitch where she intended.

Lassoed by her masterful energy, he stepped into the main foyer, whereupon he gaped wondrously at the artful marble flooring that dazzled under a massive and exceedingly opulent crystal chandelier bombing down on him from the precipitous arched ceiling.

A carpeted sitting room with a lowered ceiling was directly to Mitch's right. The walls, furniture, carpet, drapes, and pottery were invariably albescent, and hung neatly on the walls was an array of abstract art illustrating powerful shapes and colors that broke up the monochromatic motif and added to the space's prevailing air of modernism.

Next to the 'White Room,' which Mitch decided the segment should henceforth be titled, stretched an expansive mahogany spiral staircase ascending to the second floor.

To the left of the capacious hallway leading at length to the distal kitchen and backyard, closed off by twin mahogany French doors, was what looked to be, from the little Mitch could discern through the embossed cubic panes, a library or an office. Rows of hardcover books lined the shelves of lofty bookcases along each wall. A gilded lamp hooded with a green lampshade surmounted a side table next to a maroon couch. Also on the side table was a heavy leather-bound book Mitch suspected to be the Bible.

Mitch digested the regal panorama and smiled warmly. The five million Meryl had quoted as the home's value seemed right on the money.

And he was only in the lobby.

The housemaid beckoned sharply to the second floor. Her voice was just as hawkish in person as it was over the intercom. Promptly, Meryl appeared at the head of the stairs. Her flowing hair curtained her face as she peered interrogatively over the railing. She and Mitch shared an impish salutation.

As she descended the staircase, Mitch noticed the gold Rolex on her wrist and the matching heart-shaped locket sloping under the fold in her oversized cashmere turtleneck. The lordliness of the gold, and consequently its inhabitant, rekindled in Mitch unwanted memories of marks past. It was not a recollection he suffered lightly.

Presently, his most recent quarry reached the foot of the stairs, and the housemaid returned to the kitchen.

"Hey, stranger," Meryl beamed. Her gaze was hopeful and earnest, unaware of Mitch's rolling inner turmoil.

She opened her arms for a hug that, in his detachment, he returned primarily out of reflex.

Once recalibrated, he said with an unwitting shiver: "You look great."

She smiled thinly at his approval.

"I feel like I should have brought something."

"Oh, no," she assured with a tiny hand swat. "The fact that you're brave enough to step into the lion's den is more than enough. Come, I'll give you the grand tour."

The circuit's first stopover was the study. Upon first stepping through the yawning French doors, Mitch was overwhelmed with the equally pleasant and abrasive scent of old paper and pipe tobacco. His feet fell soft upon felt carpeting while his authentically awestruck gaze swept the plurality of hard-shelled books and volumes of encyclopedias enveloping the walls. Rubbernecking the theatrical homage to higher learning and spellbound by the prevailing musky and nutty aromas, Mitch asked: "So, whose idea was this?"

Meryl grinned devilishly. "This was actually my request...I *really* like *Beauty and the Beast*."

Mitch wrinkled his brow, curiously nonplussed. The former's augmenting grin bared pearls. "Originally, Dad wanted a poker room with a pool table. But Mom was dead set against it. I suggested the library half-jokingly, but Mom just latched onto it, and Dad let it happen. So, yeah."

"Have you read any of them?"

She shook her head with apparent compunction. "No. They're huge. I play chess sometimes when Dad smokes his pipe."

Mitch crept along the bookshelves, carefully scanning titles that spanned from law and science to Dickens' and Shakespeare's complete works to an impressive collection of *Sports Illustrated* and *National Geographic* magazines dating back to each publication's inception. He paused at a small glass-cased display between a set of bookcases at the far end of the room. Contained inside was a vintage nineteenth-century nickel-plated six-shooter resting in a purple velvet mold next to six gold bullets. The purple backdrop once again inspired unwanted memories of marks past.

After the con, they're gone, he privately reminded himself.

He caught Meryl's eye and gestured to the six-shooter. "What's this?"

"That was the original 'thank you' gift from the oil tycoon Dad saved. *Before* the millions of dollars. It's nice, huh?"

An older woman entered the study, with whom Mitch shared a genial glance. He was sure the smartly-dressed stranger was Mrs. Chestwick, the lady of the house. While under Meryl a foot and of a leaner build, the two's eyes, nose, and hair were unmistakably related. Her face was healthy, though sun-worn and coriaceous, and there was an eagerness and a vibrancy about her character that Mitch found immediately disarming.

"Mom, we were just talking about you," said Meryl across the room. "About how Dad wanted to put the pool table in the library."

Mrs. Chestwick nodded wistfully. "Could you imagine? We'd have the whole Sheriff's department in here smoking cigars and playing cards until all hours of the morning. The library is a much better idea. Thank you, sweetie."

"This is Roy," said Meryl, gesturing to Mitch.

Mrs. Chestwick politely acknowledged her guest from where she stood. "I've heard so much about you," she said pleasantly. "Can I offer you a drink? A soda? Beer?"

"*Mom*," stressed Meryl. Her eyes widened as her head jerked toward Mitch. "Remember?"

Mrs. Chestwick adapted seamlessly. "Oh, yes. That's right."

"A water would be great, thank you," Mitch politely acquiesced.

"Great," said Mrs. Chestwick, proffering another mannerly and passive smile. "I'll be back in a jiff."

In what felt like no time, Mrs. Chestwick returned with a slender glass filled with ice water, and a napkin. Mitch thanked her and sipped casually as he fell into the familiar routine of parent pleasing. The key, Mitch found, was to be engaging and affable in responding to inquiries while at the same time providing a clear sense that you were there to please their daughter and not her parents. This approach tends to be translated poorly during the initial introductory phase, especially by the father, but it was all part of a bigger plan...

As a potential suitor, you *want* the father to distrust you initially because then you get to *earn* his trust. And if he, through fastidious deliberation, comes to find you an honorable suitor for his daughter, he would have a much harder time believing any nasty rumors of your ill character because, remember, he too had thought of you poorly at one time and, through myriad examples to the contrary, had found such dubiety unwarranted.

Mitch had been all around the country, and when it came to fathers, unanimously, they would much prefer their daughters to settle down with an imperfect man of confidence and stick-to-itiveness over an obsequious bootlicker who reeked of insincerity and obscure intentions.

As for the mothers, they are a slightly more capricious breed. Sometimes they want nothing to do with you; they are just happy that their daughter is happy. They will accept you into the family but will respectfully remain emotionally and often physically distant. Other times, they will test you for no reason other than to keep you on your toes. This venture can be bothersome but successfully curtailed with frequent public displays of affection toward their daughter and minimal discord in the bedroom that might eventually find its way to the ears of the matron hen. However, more often than not, Mitch found, was the case where you needed to flirt with the mothers occasionally to satiate their feminine ego and help them feel young again. Witnessing a young and virile man regularly shower their daughter with such gentle whispers of romance when their spouse had long retired such coquettish expressions can often lead to subconscious or even conscious feelings of jealousy and resentment. Thankfully, with moms, unless your offense on their invention is irrevocably grand, they will preserve their slanderous remarks for conversations transpiring in your absence to save you the embarrassment of their candor.

Following a few questions about Mitch's childhood and handing out helpful hints of advice for a new townie, Mrs. Chestwick returned to the kitchen to check on dinner, whereupon Meryl and Mitch continued the house tour.

She led Mitch upstairs, where the circuit started and finished in her bedroom. She gently shut the door and, like a ballerina, twirled on the balls of her feet to face Mitch. She touched his cheek, pushed up on her toes, and pressed her lips to his.

"Sorry," she said as her eyelids peeled open. "Really wanted to do that."

"Apology accepted," he murmured before returning to her lips.

Her heels hit the floor, and she widened the space between them to present her capacious quarters. "So, what do you think?" she asked spiritedly.

Like her mother's attire, the room's decor portrayed a conservative elegance. The walls were painted the same pale pastel purple as the thin curtains framing bay windows at each end of the far wall. A throng of stuffed animals and richly embroidered pillows populated each nook.

Again, Mitch cringed at the presence of purple, and the sense of foreboding it aroused within him.

The wall art was bland and impersonal, looking as if curated by a contracted decorator and never replaced with something more musing to Meryl's tastes. To Mitch's right was a queen-sized bed crowned with embellished pillows varying in color and size along an arched gilded spindle headboard pressing the wall. The comforter, which looked like it had migrated from the 'White Room' downstairs, appeared like a marshmallow melting over a gram cracker bed frame. The wall nearest Mitch mounted an imposing flat-screen television. And at the far end of the room was a luxury bathroom next to a prodigious walk-in closet. The sliding door opened halfway, exposing Meryl's extensive collection of clothes. Many of them were in a pile on the floor.

"Thought there'd be more *Beauty and the Beast* posters..." grinned Mitch.

Meryl didn't miss a beat: "Well, I already got the library."

"True...Is that where the *Law and Order* happens?" he asked, pointing to the flat screen.

"It is. Though, I haven't watched much TV lately. I guess you're to blame for that. We can have a special screening after dinner if you'd like."

Her searching gaze connected. Mitch allowed it to roam.

"You sure I'll get it if I haven't seen the other episodes?" he joked.

She looked away, smirking. "Yeah, shut up. You watch *Law and Order*."

Her eyes suddenly widened. "Oh. I forgot to tell you. We're second worst!"

"No way. You get to keep working the phones?"

"Like a stripper works the pole."

"That's great."

She nodded exaltedly. "Yup. If we can hold out until the end of the week, we're home-free. At least for another year. Sean didn't tell you?"

"Haven't seen much of Sean lately. He's been spending a lot of time with your supervisor."

Her eyebrows raised like a gossip radar antenna. "*No*. Them?"

Mitch chuckled softly. "Yup."

From downstairs, the housemaid's resounding dinner announcement penetrated the bedroom door and startled Mitch.

He grinned. "She's a loud one, isn't she?"

Meryl reacted impassively. "Yeah. Gloria's a champ. You know when it's dinner time."

The two descended to the ground floor and joined Mrs. Chestwick in the dining room as Gloria deftly arranged the appetizers in succession across the center of the elegantly set table.

This section of the manor was equally impressive as the other quadrants. An ornate row of icicle chandeliers in the dining room suffused pools of dim light along the navy-colored walls. A brawny china cabinet proudly displayed a collection of antique plates and gleaming silverware deep-set in blood-red velvet display cases. An imposing oil painting of stampeding horses exhausted the majority of the partition opposite.

Mitch nibbled his appetizers sporadically, though his plate invariably brimmed with the offerings available. He had crossed enough gentry mothers to know that little else pleased them greater than finding their nourishment well-received. And even though Mitch was all but certain that Mrs. Chestwick hadn't herself slaved over a hot stove to produce tonight's bounty, he believed his keen attention to her efforts remained appropriate nonetheless.

It was evident to Mitch from the atmospheric gaiety that he was a welcomed addition to the table. He imagined that there may have been dinners in the past where Meryl's loneliness had caused her to be far less vibrant than she was tonight. He envisioned her slumped over her plate, silently stabbing at her mashed potatoes, her mother and father wishing they could say something to brighten her disposition but knowing they could not. It's a sight no parent likes to see in their children, nor one a child likes to see in their parents. Mitch remembered shortly before his mother packed her things and left Mitch and his father to rot, how she would sit at the dinner table, a smaller, much less exquisite version of the one he sat at now, and say not more than three words for the entire meal. From there, she would be off to bed to sleep away her unhappiness or, more likely, set out for the remainder of the evening to contrive new happiness with a novel and attentive escort, only to return at sunrise, if at all. Mitch's father was invariably too besotted to notice these hard realities. But Mitch noticed. And it tore him apart.

Mrs. Chestwick held a glass of Merlot loosely between her fingers and conducted a few more short inquiries into Mitch's—or Roy's—life in New York. Mitch returned safe, vague replies he had long since memorized. These false histories were so ingrained in his character that it took nearly no thought at all to recite them. And, as neither Mrs. Chestwick nor Meryl was familiar with the trappings of the fabled Big Apple, his fabrications were accepted as truth and promptly disregarded.

The mother's apparent lack of misgivings toward his backstory was a relief, of course, but it also filled Mitch with a certain measure of self-reproach. Being a Wedding Bandit, you don't just rob the bride. You rob the parents' hope to see their daughter have a happy ending, their hope for grandchildren, their dignity and trust in people, and, yes, lots and lots of their money. Knowing all this and refusing to be detracted requires a certain degree of heartlessness in the caper's perpetrator. However, over the years, Mitch had successfully trained himself to stow these feelings of guilt and remorse deep within a dark, secret corner of the soul where they needed never resurrect.

He returned Mrs. Chestwick's polite smile and loaded his plate with more chilled shrimp and crispy spring rolls.

Soon, the Sheriff arrived home. He had brought with him a dinner guest: Ronnie, the deputy.

Gloria readied the new addition at the table. Her skillful execution reminded Mitch of a stagehand, switching set pieces during a performance blackout. Ronnie slipped into his seat when her campaign concluded and did not acknowledge the help. The Chestwicks seemed to be unstirred by Ronnie's company, which led Mitch to believe the deputy's inclusion at the table was a semi-regular, if not regular, occurrence.

"So, *Roy*," Ronnie said as he tucked the seat of his chair under tan slacks. His gaze burned over the table's breadth. "Why would a city dweller like yourself want to move to a quiet place like Oak County? It must be rather boring for you, no?"

Laura was right, thought Mitch. *This guy might be a problem.*

"A small town like this is exactly why I moved out here," Mitch answered cordially. "The city is noisy, faceless, and it can be ugly. These days I like my life to be filled with a little more peace..." He looked to Meryl. "A little more beauty..."

Mrs. Chestwick and the Sheriff softened like warm butter in their chairs. Ronnie appeared stung, but he filled his plate without rebuttal.

Gloria began serving roast chicken, mashed potatoes, and green beans. This time, Ronnie greeted her by name, cementing Mitch's hunch that the deputy was more than an occasional house guest. Once she had distributed each plate respectively and set the piping-hot gravy at the center of the table, the Sheriff paused to say grace. Mitch mirrored the custom when Ronnie and the Chestwicks closed their eyes and bowed their heads. As the Sheriff recited his prayer, Mitch felt the tenderness of Meryl's palm slip into his under the table. Their fingers interlocked. After the prayer, the two shared a short and private regard.

The Sheriff hungrily seized his fork. "So," he started, glancing between Mitch and his meal. "Are you a man of faith, Roy?"

Mitch lifted the smallest of three forks beside his plate and advanced on a bean. "Yes, sir. Very much so."

Ronnie let out a sonorous chortle that filled the room, gawking at Mitch rudely. "That's a dessert fork! Oh, Lord! I thought you city folk were supposed to be civilized!"

The Sheriff placed an assuasive palm on Ronnie's forearm. "Now, Ronnie..."

Under the table, Meryl unfettered her hand. She pointed to the tallest pronged utensil while shooting Ronnie a nasty glare.

"Oh.." said Mitch, feigning amusement at his ignorance. In truth, he had been well aware of the intended uses for his cutlery, but also knew Ronnie's haughty reaction would result in the remaining diner's adulation of his working-class humility.

Mitch retrieved the appropriate fork and again approached a bean. "To answer your question, Sheriff: I'm a practicing Orthodox Protestant. The church became my rock when I got sober."

Ronnie rolled his eyes deep into the back of his head. The Chestwicks' gazes widened with captivated expressions. Time seemed to stop, and the room hung in silence.

"Well...imagine that!" laughed Mrs. Chestwick heartily.

The Sheriff wagged his head incredulously while chuckling to himself. He pointed to Meryl. "Sweetie, I think you picked a winner."

Mitch looked to Meryl for an explanation. Which, to his horror, he readily received. "We're Orthodox Protestant, too," she averred warmly, sharing her parents' pleasant astonishment at this discovery.

Mitch beamed. "That is great."

But in reality, it was not great. Mitch was in deep shit. Orthodox Protestantism had always been the default religion for the con because it provided a valid explanation as to why he couldn't have sex before the wedding night and because no one, ever, is a practicing Orthodox Protestant. A recondite faith allowed Mitch to bring in John as his sham priest and conduct a sham ceremony without anyone knowing enough about the proceedings to repugn their validity.

Mitch suddenly grew aware of the tiny golden crucifix on Mrs. Chestwick's necklace and the more prominent crucifix nailed above the entrance to the dining room. His stomach turned sourly. He knew nowhere near enough about the faith to hold up under questioning.

"There's a church right here in Oak County," said Mrs. Chestwick aidfully. "You should join us for worship this Sunday."

Mitch stuffed a forkful of roast chicken into his mouth, smiled agreeably, and nodded as he chewed.

"So, guess what, Dad?" diverted Meryl in the nick of time. "The call center broke our sales quota. We get to keep our jobs! You should have seen us today; we were on fire."

The Sheriff nodded and swallowed his mashed potatoes. "Glad to hear it, sweetie."

"You know, I just don't get it," said Ronnie. He swirled and whiffed the Merlot in his chalice pensively and at length before proceeding. "You would make such a good mother. You're loving. You have the hips for it. Any man would be lucky to have you. And yet you still work, and worse yet, at such a trivial job. It's so beneath you. It's just strange to me."

It was evident Ronnie's comment had flattered Meryl, despite her attempt at squelching such effects. "I happen to enjoy what I do," she replied, playfully coy. "I love the people I work with. There's no rule that says if you're a mother, you have to stay at home."

"Well, not on a hardware store salary," said Ronnie. His words tapered off so that they were virtually inaudible. Despite the theatrical attempt to curtail his invective, all heard the comment.

Meryl dropped her fork loudly on her plate. Mrs. Chestwick grinned and reclined in her chair as if to respectfully bow out of the 'boys will be boys' tussle. The Sheriff glared at Ronnie and shook his head disapprovingly.

Mitch knew the deputy had challenged him, as cowardly as it was to do during dinner, surrounded by Meryl and her family, a guest in their home. Mitch also knew the only way to respond in this situation properly was with good humor, even though most of him wanted to ask the scraggy brat to step outside so they could settle the quarrel like men.

"Well, I enjoy getting to help people. I'm sure you can understand that," said Mitch, referring to the silver badge over Ronnie's heart. "And if something better comes along in the future, I'm okay with that, too."

"That's a good attitude," said the Sheriff.

"Trust in the Lord, and he shall provide," added the lady of the house.

Ronnie accepted Mitch's retort, though his resentment toward Oak County's newest edition continued to hover over the table like a foggy dew in a graveyard on Halloween.

After the main course, as Gloria apportioned cake and coffee, Mitch asked the Sheriff if he would tell the story of the oil tycoon and the bandits. Excited gazes beamed around the table at the legend's mention. The Sheriff flustered slightly as if the request had caught him unprepared, but Mitch could tell by the childish gleam in his eye that the man had no qualms with holding court.

"Well, I suppose that would be okay, Roy...At that time, I was just a patrolman. There was a ribbon-cutting ceremony out of state for a pipeline that would bring U.S. oil into Mexico. Now, the Mexican cartels down south were against the pipeline, thought it would feed too much money to the local government and strengthen the fight on the drug war. The cartel's business partner up here, the Tyrant, I believe they call him, sent over some goons to kidnap this oil tycoon. And that's exactly what they did. Took the man right off the street in front of his building. It was front-page news all across the country. He was gone for about a week before these bandits contacted the FBI with their demands. They wanted that pipeline shut down, and if it wasn't, they were going to kill this tycoon dead.

"Well...One day I was off duty, sitting in my car, parked on the side of the road, listening to the radio, and I saw someone I had never seen before coming out of the market with some groceries. As I'm sure you've learned by now, Oak County is a small place, and it was even smaller in those days. There was something about this man that just seemed wrong. He was about your age, give or take...He was nervous. Edgy. Looked like he hadn't slept right in a while. Stood out immediately. I followed him when he drove away, figuring maybe he was just passing through and picking up some supplies as travelers sometimes do. He ended up over at Oak Bluff, which I'm sure you've become familiar with on your hikes with Meryl. There's a mess of woodland there, trails and such. I watched the man get out of his car—*with* his groceries, mind you—and head for the bush. It didn't seem right. I waited there and watched, but he never came back.

"As the sun was starting to set, I got out the car and headed toward the bush. I took my firearm, but I kept it hidden under my shirt. Like I said, I was off duty, so I looked like a civilian. I walked along the trail for some time, and that's when I saw them through the trees. They were sitting on a couple rocks with the oil tycoon, having a little picnic in the forest. I guess they thought no one would recognize them in the sticks. Maybe they thought we were a bunch of rednecks with no TVs or something of the sort."

"So, what did you do?" asked Mitch, genuinely enraptured by the story and the campfire manner in which the narration unfurled.

"Well, I didn't want to take the chance of leaving and having them escape, but I had no communication with the Sheriff's Office. That so, I decided I'd have to do something right then and there. I approached as if I were just a hiker until I got close enough. Then, I withdrew my firearm and announced myself. They started shooting. I shot back. I dropped one of them. I took a bullet in the leg before I dropped the other.

"Long story short, the oil tycoon made it out of that bush alive, and the pipeline went through without a hitch. The Mexicans got their oil. Then, years later, after I had been promoted to Sheriff, to my surprise—"

"To *all* our surprises," tittered Meryl softly.

The Sheriff's lip twitched slightly upward. "Well, I think you know the rest of the story. I'd show you the bullet scar on my leg, but it would be poor table manners."

"Wow," said Mitch. He fell back in his chair, bewitched. "That is heroic."

"It was duty," said the Sheriff. "A man can't neglect his duty." His gaze held on Mitch and penetrated deeper than the beneficiary would have liked.

Meryl excused herself and her guest from the table. They returned to her bedroom. She closed the door gently. She put on an episode of *Law and Order* and, supine on her marshmallow comforter, they conversed while the program dramatized quietly in the background.

"I hope my family didn't scare you off," she said in jest.

"No, not at all. They're nice," said Mitch.

"Don't mind Ronnie. He's just protective of me."

Mitch grinned and, curious about how Joey's research and Laura's recon overlooked the major detail of Meryl's family's faith, said craftily: "So, you're an Orthodox Protestant..."

Her expression blated. "What a coincidence, huh? And don't worry about coming to church. We don't go. Mom was just messing with you. Dad says religion is something for the household, not for the public. Especially for a law-enforcing family. He doesn't want people to think he holds any prejudices. So we don't talk about it."

"That's a good way to be," said Mitch. Inside, he surfed a rolling wave of alleviation.

Meryl glanced aimlessly around the room. "So..." she said at length. "Do you believe in all that no sex before marriage stuff?"

Mitch's phone started to vibrate. He withdrew it from his pocket and viewed the Caller Id. It was Laura. He swiped 'Decline' and returned the phone to his pocket. His gaze returned to Meryl. "Do you?"

She giggled like a child playing a game of peekaboo. "I asked you first."

Mitch sat up and propped himself against the headboard. "I don't know...I mean, I don't think that sex is something that should be just thrown around."

Meryl crawled a little closer. "But if it was someone you cared about?"

"If it was someone you cared about, I could see..."

Meryl canted her head and approached Mitch's neck. She touched her lips softly on his skin, her breath slow and heavy, teasing him. The type of teasing of the senses that makes the hairs stand up on the back of a man's collar and sends goosebumps running across the length of his shoulders. He opened up for her, elongating the neck. She kissed it once softly. When she kissed it again, her tongue slid warm saliva under his jaw.

"I could see..." Mitch tried again, losing focus.

Her head rose. She kissed his chin, his mouth. Mitch parted his lips and let her in. She breathed heavily through her nose as he pulled her closer. He couldn't fight it. He didn't want to. He allowed her leg to stretch over him. He allowed her hand to explore under his shirt before her fingertips found their way to his belt buckle and pulled loose the strap. He allowed her to unbutton his jeans and for her hand to slip warmly under his briefs.

His phone started to vibrate. But it was too late. Mitch had wholly given in.

When it was over, Meryl went to the closet and changed into pajama bottoms and a loose-fitting t-shirt. She climbed back into bed with Mitch, naked to his underwear, and rested her head in the groove between his shoulder and chest. She let out a soft sigh that sounded more like a purr. Her hand reached for the medallion around his neck. She pinched it between her fingers and examined it. "You're always wearing this," she said quietly.

"I didn't realize you noticed," said Mitch. He stroked her hair patiently.

"What is it?"

"It belonged to my father. Now it's mine."

"Is he back in New York?"

"No. He's not around."

"I'm sorry," she said in a babyish cadence. "Were you close?"

"At one point, we were, but...alcohol changed that."

She sighed, and her breath trailed across Mitch's chest. "If he could see how far you've come, I bet he'd be proud. It's never too late to start over."

Her words resonated within him. They pierced his fictitious persona and landed in the shadowy, dark realm where the genuine Mitch hid from the world. Not Mitch presently, but Mitch who had run away from home all those years ago. Was it too late for him? Could he start again? Like Roy. Like Meryl. Like his father never could. Like Laura never would. He took a long, deep breath and closed his eyes. Meryl put her arm across him and squeezed.

MITCH AWAKENED TO AN empty bed and the sound of Meryl's shower running. He couldn't recall the last time he had opened his eyes so refreshed. His muscles oozed with warmth. His head tingled lightly. Daylight beamed through the gauzy curtains and sent a pallid glow into the room that glinted off specks of dust floating in the air like rising snowflakes. It was early morning. He and Meryl must have fallen asleep watching *Law and Order* and slept through the entire night.

He sat up against the headboard and rubbed his eyes. When he opened them, he saw a black hairy mound with two large yellow eyes glaring at him from the edge of the bed. Behind this whiskered quadruped, a prickly tail slithered gracefully upon the marshmallow comforter. If Mitch remembered correctly, the curious and nimble animal before him was non-other than Jenkins, the family cat. Their gazes locked, each waiting for the other to make their first move. Amid the stillness, Mitch felt this feline was wiser than he and fully aware of his ill intentions for Meryl. An instant later, as if somehow assured by Mitch's wordless trepidation, the feline erected on its forequarters, leaped off the bed with a snap of its shiny tail, and hurried out of the bedroom through a narrow aperture in the door.

Mitch exhaled and settled against his pillow languidly. His thoughts regrouped, and Laura's call the night before beckoned his heed. He clambered out of bed and lurched for his jeans curled up on the hardwood. The floor was cold under his naked heels, and his whole body inadvertently shivered. He blearily wrestled the cell phone from his pants pocket, perched on the edge of the bed, and dialed his voicemail.

He had half-expected to find an apology message waiting for him now that Laura had sobered up and realized how out of line she had been sneaking into the apartment. He was not expecting the message he received. Laura was sobbing. It was hard to hear her clearly under the din of commotion swelling nebulously behind her. "I don't know where you are or why you're not picking up, but Mitch, I need you to come get me ASAP. We have a major problem.

It's John. Somebody shot him...He's dead. John is dead, Mitch. He's dead."

Chapter Twenty Two

Mitch was out of the car the moment it swerved into Miss Jenkins' front drive, up the walkway seconds after that. He dashed unthinkingly through the front door. The apartment was quiet and inert. He called out for Joey and received no answer. He hastened from room to room, throwing open doors, analyzing emptiness, and moving onward to the next fruitless search. Upon his return to the sitting area, he noticed something he had overlooked on his initial run through the apartment: the sliding door to the backyard was lifted off its rail and slightly ajar.

Laura's dig swept through his head. *Those locks are shit.*

Across the room, he spotted a small piece of paper on the kitchen counter.

Maybe he slept at the supervisor's, reasoned Mitch in a paroxysm of desperate negotiation.

He scrambled to the counter and retrieved what he now identified as an awaiting note. The penmanship was hauntingly familiar, recognized before Mitch had read but a word.

All in one moment everything made clear, terrible sense. John's murder. Joey's disappearance. The dignified longhand staring back at Mitch confirmed his worst fears.

Hey, Clyde!...Or is it Roy?...How about MITCH? It's your
father-in-law! Hope you haven't forgot about me already.
I haven't forgotten about you. :)
We have your best man. Sorry about your priest :(
Be calling you soon. Pick up.

P.S. Don't try to leave with the Porsche. We got that back, too.

Mr. Robertson. Angie's father.

He had found them.

OBSCURED IN THE PARKING lot outside John and Laura's motel room, Mitch waited for his partner anxiously in the Corolla. The engine idled. A trembling hand grasped the wheel for reassurance. The thumbnail on his free hand yielded to nervous mastication. Sparsely a cuticle abided. The brim of his baseball cap angled steeply on his face, secreting his fixed and maniacal watch on the oblique ribbons of yellow police tape barricading the entrance to the room-turned-crime scene. The local cops, squad cars, and an emblazoned news van had since cleared the property.

John was dead.

How long would it be before Joey faced the same fate?

Mitch's thoughts returned to the days, years ago, before Joey was a bandit and the two worked together at a bar in Minnesota during Mitch's job on Mary Collins: the shy, introverted daughter of a lottery winner. Mitch's car 'broke down' in front of the library where she worked, and he approached her with a hat in hand and a helpless smile as she loped through the courtyard toward her car. She let him use her phone to call for a tow and waited with him until John showed up in a stolen truck and uniform. They chatted for a while. Mitch offered to buy her a drink if she ever found herself at the bar where he worked. Not long after that, she popped in, hoping to take Mitch up on his offer. If Mitch wasn't so busy working on Mary, he might have noticed how closely his bar-back had been watching him. But Mitch didn't give the kid a second thought...not until one particular night as he and Joey were cashing out at the bar after closing, and Joey said covertly between them: "I know what you're doing, man. It's smart."

Mitch faltered and quickly recovered with a countenance of infantile ignorance. "What do you mean?"

His aversion only provoked the kid. "Come on," said the young Joey. "I mean, you're supposed to be this experienced bartender, and you can't mix a drink to save your life. You don't even know which drinks get limes and which get lemons. That's day one shit."

Mitch remained aloof, though he was impressed at the youngster's skills of deduction.

"You tell me," the kid pressed on. "What kind of recovering alcoholic is shucking drinks at a dive bar? It doesn't make any sense."

Mitch sipped his water and pretended to watch the baseball highlights on the bar screen.

"You know, I followed you the other day," Joey said at his apex of self-satisfaction. "I saw you ditch the tow truck. Your car didn't break down. That was a setup. So you could bag the lottery winner's daughter."

Mitch couldn't help but crack an indictable grin.

From then on, well...it had been a good run. Joey had earned his right to play with the big boys. His indecorous humor and dauntless charm were a welcome addition to the team, and his handsome looks were an asset to the schematics. But it wasn't just his looks that made him worth keeping. He was highly apt regarding the newly established computer technology that John had been far too old and Mitch far too poor to grasp. This new skill set allowed the team to expand their reach in the lonely heart community and opened up a world of possibilities previously repudiated, if only through ignorance.

But now John was dead.

Mitch couldn't lose Joey.

He *wouldn't.*

The nostalgia cloud disintegrated as he saw Laura lumbering through the parking lot toward the Corolla. Hair enmeshed her face.

Egg-shaped sunglasses covered her eyes. She wore the same Zeppelin t-shirt she had worn the day she had broken into the house. Both the shirt and Laura looked run-down and in need of a wash. She didn't acknowledge Mitch until she was in the car with the door closed, and even then, she resisted his gaze. As they began to drive, Mitch asked if she was okay.

"A little shaken up," she replied.

She sounded calmer than she had on the message.

When he asked her what happened, she told him how she returned to the room after killing some time at the resident bar and found the door half open and John sprawled face down on the carpet with a bullet hole in the back of his head.

"Then what?" Mitch prodded.

She released a helpless sigh. "I grabbed the keys to the Charger and went back to the bar. I picked up some random and spent the night in his room with the cops three doors down."

Mitch let out a heavy breath. He wanted to console his shaken teammate, but there was no time. "Alright...Listen. I have some bad news. Joey's been taken."

A shapely eyebrow raised above Laura's capacious shades. "Taken? What do you mean? Arrested?"

"Kidnapped," said Mitch. "By Angie's dad. He's the one who shot John."

Her mouth shot open like Mitch had poured a bucket of ice water over her head. "Her *dad*?"

"Maybe the brother, too. I'm guessing. He broke into the house, left me a note."

Laura sat back in the seat and clasped her forehead. "This is fucked."

"Super fucked."

"So? What do we do?"

Mitch swept the parking lot with his gaze. "Head back to my place. He's not turning us in. He wants to meet. Said he'd call."

Laura lurched forward with expostulation. "You're not going to meet him, are you?"

"I can't let him kill another one of us," said Mitch. "I started this. It's my responsibility."

Another lengthy and lamenting sigh escaped the remaining bandit. "Well. If you think it's best, then...Okay. Let's do this. I'm in."

AGENT QUINN STOOD ABREAST of the Crown Vic and inhaled a long, self-indulgent drag off his cigarette. He let the nebulous toxins marinate in his lungs before exhausting two billowy streams from his gaping nostrils. Across the motel parking lot, he noticed one of the end units boarded off with police tape.

An overdose, maybe?

A murder?

Quinn grunted to himself over McAllester's miserly lodging choices, recalling their previous night at a subpar Holiday Inn halfway between Sandy Acres and Oak County. The ice machine was out of order, and Quinn was forced to put down warm rum and cokes all night. Now they were settling in Oak County, and Quinn's fearless leader was booking them a room in the goddamn hotel from Psycho.

Agent McAllester returned from the lobby just as Quinn was sucking out the last rapid draws from his butt. Squinting up at the young morning sun, the task force leader handed Quinn a plastic swipe card. "Room 21," he instructed.

Quinn reluctantly received his alms. At the same time, he noticed, as he usually did, a trim young blonde bounding gracefully through the parking lot. It was her red Converse shoes that first commanded his attention. That and the Zeppelin t-shirt stuck to her undulating figure. Her head stooped as if to shut out the world, and big Jackie-O sunglasses camouflaged half her face. Even so, Quinn was surprised to find that he knew this girl.

"Get in the car," he urged McAllester in a stage whisper, hoping his adjoined glare, bulging and aggressive, would translate the urgency of the request to the receiving party. McAllester, as he did so often, raised a wary brow at his subordinate, preferring dubiety over heed. Quinn discarded his cigarette into the webbed twigs and foliage of an adjacent hedge and repeated the instruction as he hastened into the car. McAllester entered the vehicle much less spiritedly and looked at Quinn strangely as he pointed beyond the dusty windshield splattered with fly guts to the young blonde woman dressed in black. She appeared headed for a sedan parked in the middle of the lot—a Corolla. Inside the vehicle, a man with a baseball cap low on his head sat in the driver's seat, waiting.

"She's one of them," said Quinn excitedly.

"Who?" queried McAllester, looking somewhat annoyed. "The blonde?"

Agent Quinn's head bobbed furiously. "She was at the Robertson wedding. I saw her come out to check out the Porsche with Robertson and the groom."

"You sure?"

"Positive," said Quinn. "Doesn't she fit the description the old man at the lot gave us?"

Squinting through begrimed glass, McAllester appraised the subject and came to the silent agreement that the woman was indeed congruous with the lot owner's description.

They watched her get into the Corolla. Quinn lifted the set of binoculars resting in the center console. He peered through the magnified lenses. A glance at the driver caused his heart to clench and churn in his chest. He ejaculated an incredulous chortle at the sheer coincidence before him.

"That's him," he announced. "That's Clyde Morrison."

"You're shittin' me," said McAllester.

"I shit you not," Quinn replied assertively. His amazement had morphed into something palpably darker.

Quinn voyeured Clyde and the blonde's conversation for nearly a minute before Clyde started the engine, and the Corolla crept forward. He frantically tossed the binoculars into the center console and jerked to start the car.

McAllester reached over and blocked the keys from the ignition.

"Wait," he ordered.

Quinn's cheeks burned hotly. "What? No way! We have to follow them!"

McAllester pointed over Quinn's shoulder, out the driver-side window. "Let them go," said McAllester. "We stay with the Charger."

Frustrated, Quinn followed McAllester's gesticulation and peered out his driver-side window.

There, in the corner of the lot, he saw the vehicle. The frame was matte charcoal and dappled with grainy oxidation.

Body issues.

Just like the old man from the junkyard had said.

Chapter Twenty Three

The abrasive potato sack over Joey's head had been itching at his nose since he and Joyce had been abducted at the apartment, handcuffed, and thrown into the backseat of Mr. Robertson's Escalade. Initially, he had tried to relieve himself with a vigorous head shake. The type of shake that makes one's brains rattle inside the skull. This strategy was unsuccessful and rather disorienting for a spell. Next, he had attempted jutting his nose forward and sliding it up and down against the inner skin of the sack. Still, the itch endured with a vengeance. Finally, as the SUV ventured over a stretch of jagged gravel, the vehicle rocked side to side, causing the sack to scrub across the tip of Joey's nose at just the right angle and grant alleviation so euphoric that it bordered on sexual fulfillment. However, his newly invigorated spirit was evanescent at best and promptly overwhelmed by much bigger problems on the itinerary.

The lengthy mystery drive concluded suddenly. Joey heard the Escalade's front doors click open and gravel crunch under heavy feet. The back doors opened. A rough hand grabbed Joey by the arm and pulled him from the vehicle. Joyce yelped as someone on the other side of the SUV did the same.

This is it, thought Joey. *The gig is most definitely up...is it jig or gig?*

His one regret was that Joyce had to be alongside him when karma arrived to collect its due penance. She was innocent. She didn't deserve what Joey feared was about to come. But there was nothing he could do now. He had tried pleading with Sebastian once to let her go when the young Robertson and his father initially ambushed him at the house. It was clear that the two were not interested in negotiating the matter. After all, Angie was innocent, too. Look what happened there.

A heavy hand shoved Joey along in a blind march, the scraggy gravel loud under his sneakers. An omnipresent generator thrummed loudly and trembled the air. Presently, the rocks beneath Joey's feet turned into smooth concrete. The same heavy hand grabbed Joey's arm and sat him down on a cold block of cement. Joey's tailbone hit the hard surface, and pain shot up his spine like a rocket. His captor yanked the sack off his head, unveiling his location.

He was on a construction site, surrounded by blinding spotlights inside a looming grid of steel beams. In the distance, cement blocks propped up a single-wide trailer with a dusty sign on the corrugated frontage identifying itself as the Health & Safety trailer. Strewn sporadically between mounds of excavated dirt were stacks of wooden skids tied down with blue tarp. The low orange sun and bright white halogens backlit his kidnappers, cloaking them in silhouette.

Joey turned his head away, eyes adjusting to the burning spaceship lights and neon pink sky. He saw Joyce beside him, sitting on the same block of cement an arm's length away, the potato sack still over her head. Sebastian reached and plucked it off. She recoiled, blinked twice, squinted, and confoundedly surveyed her new surroundings. Mascara was smeared under her eyes from tears that had since dried. Her lips arched in a frown, quivering. She sniffled and sobbed lightly. Sebastian drank her fear with sadistic delight. Mr. Robertson stood behind his son and calmly adjusted the cuffs on his pinstripe suit.

"Don't you think this is a little dramatic?" asked Joey. His undertone was intentionally glib.

Sebastian advanced two steps and drove his bouldery knuckles through the side of Joey's face, ringing Joey's skull like a school bell.

Mr. Robertson crouched down, glared into Joey's eyes, and, in almost a growl, said: "Let's get one thing straight, you soggy cunt scam artist. *I* ask the questions now. You got that, *Sean*?"

"Please," sobbed Joyce. "Whoever you are, just let us go. We won't go to the police. You won't go to jail, I promise."

New tears streamed down her milky cheeks, arousing Mr. Robertson and his mental case of a son.

"Oh, honey," said Mr. Robertson with a *tsk* and a head wag. "I've been importing kilos of cocaine into this country for over forty years. If I was worried about being arrested, it wouldn't be for kidnapping a bunch of fraudsters and giving them what they deserve. Besides, I own construction sites all over this state. All it takes is a hole and some cement, and you're forgotten forever."

Joyce broke and started to bawl. Joey's stomach twisted into a double knot. For once in his life, he was at a loss for words. Until now, he had thought Mr. Robertson was just an angry father trying to act like a gangster in the movies to intimidate the people who broke his daughter's heart. But he wasn't trying to *act* like a gangster. He *was* a gangster.

This exponentially raised the stakes and the possibility of their inevitable demise.

"Let her go," Joey demanded, embarrassed at the desperate shiver in his voice. "She doesn't know anything about this. She doesn't know who we are or what we do."

Joyce lifted her head and sniffled the wet snot dribbling from her nostrils. "Sean, what are you talking about? Who are these people?"

"I'm not who you think I am," he confessed to her softly, temporarily disregarding his captors. "I've been lying to you."

Mr. Robertson's expression lightened as he watched the emotional exchange. He placed a finger on his mentum and said: "So...She isn't one of the gang, then?"

Joey glowered at him with fire in his eyes.

Robertson let out a sharp "Ha!" from the bowels of his gut. He took a bold step toward Joyce and examined her closely, slowly, like a bear sniffing a petrified hiker lost in the deep woods. Joyce held her breath and shut her eyes. Robertson turned to Joey and, with the utmost exuberance, inquired: "She's not the one, is she? The target you plan on duping?"

Joey shook his head, teeth clenched. Had he been unshackled, he would have leaped up from the concrete block where he sat, ripped the old man's black heart from his chest, and shoved it up Sebastian's ass.

Joyce tried to reason with their kidnappers once more: "Dupe *who*? What are you *talking* about?"

Mr. Robertson didn't reply. Her imploring eyes went next to Sebastian. The son was evenly withholding. Finally, exhausted from panic, she turned to Joey.

"This man is a terrible man," said Mr. Robertson with his finger in Joey's face. "He and his 'bandit' consorts go from town to town, preying on women, fooling them into thinking they've found the man of their dreams, and then marrying them, only to take off in the middle of the night with every dollar and gift given to the newlyweds by honest, hardworking people! They're cowards, the lot of them. Nothing but *spineless* cowards."

Joyce's expression paled as though the words had knocked the wind out of her. Joey watched her eyes calculate and fit the puzzle pieces together. She canted her head at him, narrowed her gaze, and gasped: "Meryl?"

Joey's deficiency of denial confirmed her suspicion. And his failure to defend himself only engendered her increasing enmity.

"His name isn't Sean Harris," continued Mr. Robertson with no subtle air of vindication. "It's Joey Blanche. He's not from New York; he's not a recovering alcoholic; he's not a salesman...He grew up in a small town in Minnesota and spent his young adulthood committing small crimes like stealing cars and B & E's, preparing himself for his role as a serial fraudster. He left without saying goodbye to anyone, not even his own mother."

A scabbed wound from Joey's distant past peeled open, unleashing an outpour of unsettled guilt and sorrow, a pain that stung even worse than Sebastian's right cross. He looked to Joyce for a hint of compassion and found nothing waiting. Mr. Robertson turned to Sebastian and said: "I have a meeting. Make the call. I want that son-of-a-bitch here *tonight*. We can settle this once and for all."

MITCH AND LAURA SAT at opposite ends of the couch in his sitting room and watched their reflections in the black mirror of the television screen. The two had exchanged few words since they arrived at the house save Mitch's inquiry into whether or not Laura wanted milk in her coffee. Black was fine. Mitch's phone rested on the sitting room table next to some loose bullets and the pistol he had unearthed from the bedroom closet. The last time Mitch needed to arm himself was when the team had to break Joey out of holding in Martydale. There was tragic humor in knowing the gun was again out for Joey. But this time, Joey had been apprehended by people much more dangerous than the local police, and the rescue team was one bandit short.

Mitch said a prayer in his head for John and kissed his medallion.

Laura's expression soured as she watched him. "Not the time for that superstitious bull-crap, Mitch," she admonished coldly.

More silence prevailed.

It was ten after seven when the phone started to vibrate on the table. Bullets jostled over the trembling wooden surface. Mitch retrieved the phone and checked the ID.

It was Joey.

Mitch swiped his finger across the screen and abutted the phone to his ear.

"Be at 932 Orwell Street at ten o'clock. If you bring the cops, he dies like your priest."

The line went dead, followed by a flat tone.

Mitch rose from the couch and anxiously slipped the phone into his pocket.

"What did he say?" asked Laura.

"That was Sebastian. Ten o'clock."

Laura taciturnly absorbed the information.

"Think the daughter knows?" asked Mitch, wondering aloud. He imagined arriving at the meetup point and seeing Angie waiting for him with a gun in her hand and a vindicated smirk on her face.

Presently, there came a rap at the door. Laura and Mitch jolted at the ready. They watched the door, motionless.

Another knock, louder this time.

Mitch seized the pistol from the table and went for the door. He cautiously peered through the peephole and sighed heavily upon seeing Meryl on the step. Part of him was relieved she had come. Now more than ever, he craved her unwavering tenderness. Conversely, the bandit in him knew that her presence would further complicate matters. He tucked the gun into his waistband and covered it with his shirt. He took one last deep breath and opened the door enough for his head to squeeze out.

He forced an innoxious smile. "Hey."

Her green eyes brightened as she met his glance. "Hey."

Instantly, the pressure on Mitch's shoulders spread wings and fluttered skyward. "Good to see you," he said amicably. "What's going on?"

Meryl shrugged. "Just wanted to see how you were. You left kind of quick this morning. I got out of the shower, and you were gone."

"Yeah," said Mitch. He drew out the syllable to buy himself time while he conjured a proper excuse. Ideas came; nothing stuck. "Had a little bit of an emergency," he coughed up furtively.

"Is everything okay?" she asked.

"Yeah. No. Things are okay. I'm just a little busy right now. Not really the best time, you know?"

Mitch glanced across the front lawn to the street. A blue sedan parked along the curb behind Meryl's car. Inside it were the other employees from the call center. Mitch remembered their faces from the party. The kid, Chad, was riding shotgun. The ginger, Tammy or Sammy, was at the wheel, and the Asian, who didn't like when people called him Bobby, was in the backseat. Each beamed intensely in his direction.

"Brought the whole crew, I see."

Meryl glanced over her shoulder at her company. "Yeah... That's the other reason I'm here. Sean and Joyce didn't show up for work today. We all are working really hard to keep up our sales, but without Sean, we're screwed. Chad was adamant that we stop by to see if everything was okay. I told him they were probably just having sex, which still is pretty irresponsible, what, with our jobs on the line and everything, but..."

Mitch felt a force yawning the door from behind him.

Laura.

Meryl's eyes widened as Mitch's teammate revealed herself in the doorway. Mitch remained inert, struggling to process the consequences of Laura's irrevocable error in real-time.

Meryl's kindly smile persevered, but the lights in her eyes noticeably dimmed. She faltered momentarily, then quickly recomposed. "I'm sorry," she said. "I didn't realize you had company. I'll be on my way, then."

From the corner of his eye, Mitch watched Laura curl a crooked and malignant smirk as Meryl started down the walkway for her car. Mitch chased after her, too furious with his teammate to stick around and try to explain to her the severity of her actions.

"Meryl! Wait!"

He reached for her hand, grazing her skin before she pulled away.

"It's not what it looks like," he pleaded.

Meryl whirled, tears welling under a dubious gaze.

She was waiting.

A mental Rolodex of on-the-spot justifications spun furiously through Mitch's weary mind, yet every excuse he could muster felt cheap and shopworn. He knew that the only sufficient explanation was the truth. The whole truth, and nothing but the truth. Anything else, and he would lose. Not the five-million-dollar house; he'd lost that anyway. He'd lose her. And the thought of that burned him up inside hotter than hellfire.

His impromptu words spilled out with the repentance of a thousand apologies: "Meryl, I'm a liar. A really, really big liar."

Meryl wiped the tears from her eyes. "So, I guess that's your wife, then? You're married? Was she on a business trip or something?"

Mitch stared at his feet like an ashamed child. "No. No, I'm not married. But marriage has something to do with it."

In all his years on the con, Mitch had never needed to explain himself, his real self, to anyone. And it wasn't until now that he was in its throws that he realized how ugly the truth truly was. He pressed on: "I'm a con man. A drifter. Meryl, my name isn't Roy. It's Mitch. Sean, he's a con man, too. His name is Joey. He got the job at the call center to keep tabs on you and to introduce us." Enduring the ever-throbbing numbness in his throat, Mitch pointed to Laura, still framed in the doorway with her arms laced proudly. "That girl is part of it, too. She's been following you and your father since we got here."

Meryl appeared spun in a hundred circles. "I don't understand...Who were you conning?"

Mitch let out a breath and, hard as it was, forced himself to meet Meryl's glossy, bloodshot gaze. "Girls like you. Girls who have money. Girls who are lonely. We marry them...*I* marry them. Then we leave with the money, gifts, whatever we can get. It's... it's usually a lot. But someone took Joey, and they killed my other partner. If I don't do something, Joey will die, too."

He watched Meryl's heart shatter into a million tiny pieces before him.

"I'm so sorry, Meryl. I never thought I would care about you the way I did. I really felt something. Something real."

She forced a desperate laugh. By now, the tears had stopped falling. "Real, huh? Real enough to lie to me? Real enough to manipulate me? Make me fall for you? Then *steal* from me?" The more she spoke, the more maddened she grew. "Who are you? Some thief? Some asshole? You just come here, feed me a bunch of lies and bullshit, and steal from me? From my family?"

She started for her car, sniffled, and said behind her: "I hope you find your friend; I really do. But the both of you can burn in hell...Fucker."

Meryl glanced at Laura, turned, and disappeared into her car. Coincidingly, Mitch noticed the blue sedan as if for the first time and realized that, in his haste, he had mistakenly confessed his true identity to a larger audience than intended. The ginger and Bobby gawked at Mitch with pitiable, dewy-eyed expressions. Not Chad, though. His disposition remained unchanged.

As Meryl burned rubber down the street, Chad exited the blue sedan and loped across the lawn to meet Mitch where he stood.

"Sean's not here, is he?"

Mitch shook his head.

"He's in trouble, then?"

Mitch nodded.

"And Joyce is with him?"

"Your supervisor?"

Chad nodded.

"Could be," said Mitch.

"I know about you guys," said Chad. "I don't know if Sean, or whatever his real name is, told you. But I know. And I want to help." The kid gestured to the sedan. The ginger and Bobby continued to watch Mitch like a good soap opera. "We all do."

Mitch might have laughed if his spirit wasn't in such a state of disrepair. "I don't think you understand what's waiting out there, kid."

"It's *Chad*," the boy asserted tersely.

Mitch raised a contrite right hand. "Chad, sorry...Look, I might not make it back. And I do this for a living. People could die. *You* could die."

Chad's gaze gleamed. "Yeah...but what a story to tell. And besides, I live in Oak County; I ain't exactly living."

Mitch felt like he was back in that restaurant in Minnesota, Joey asking for a spot on the team. Despite the millions of reservations Mitch had about bringing any more people into the mess he created, he went against his better judgment and, as he had for Joey all those years ago, gave Chad the chance for which he was asking. The two shook hands before Mitch invited him and the other two misty-eyed spectators inside to forge their strategy. No matter the outcome, one thing was certain: after tonight, the Wedding Bandits would be no more.

Chapter Twenty Four

Inside the Crown Vic, Agent McAllester and Agent Quinn watched the Charger under the shroud of night from an inconspicuous distance. The smell of fried potatoes and onions had promptly consumed the cab upon Quinn's return with their takeout. The brown bag from Dairy Queen rested warmly on McAllester's lap as he picked at his fries sparingly. Agent Quinn was much less diplomatic in his consumption. After ferociously unwrapping the outer grease-drenched paper, he brought the sandwich to his face as if to tease and heighten his anticipation. He sensually closed his eyes before a generous, if not greedy, first bite. Panicked breaths and wet lips clapping followed. McAllester couldn't help but observe his partner in a mix of amusement and repulsion as Quinn swallowed the mouthful of beef and heaved a sigh of satisfaction.

"I'll tell ya," said Agent Quinn, exhibiting a satiated afterglow. "I don't know what to make of all this." He slurped his soda at length and swallowed before letting out a crisp, resounding *Aaah*... "I mean, what kind of people are these? Going around and breaking girls' hearts? Stealing from them? Especially Angie. She didn't hurt anybody. She's a sweet girl."

McAllester found Quinn's perspective curious. "Sylvester Robertson, Agent Quinn. He's the one we're after. He's the bad guy here. Besides the laundry list of felonies he's got under him, he's also suspected of murdering his wife and business partner. Why are you worried about some small-time scammers?"

Quinn inhaled a clump of crispy golden fries and washed it down with another long draw of soft drink. Upon resurfacing for air, he said: "Robertson kills criminals. Guys that signed up for that life. Angie, she's just an innocent girl."

"A civilian," McAllester emended.

"Exactly. I almost hope Robertson snuffs these guys out before we bring him in. The world will be better for it."

McAllester reclined in his seat and reflected on Quinn's words. For the most part, he did not disagree. Whoever these conmen were, they were on the wrong side of the law; that was no question. But McAllester's promotion to Assistant Deputy Director wasn't riding on the apprehension of some small-time thieves. It was riding on Robertson. It was riding on bringing down the Tyrant.

"Have you ever heard of Thomas Blood?" asked McAllester.

Quinn, grinding beef and onions in his mouth, unaware of the mustard blotch on the corner of his bottom lip, curtly shook his head. "No. Should I have?"

McAllester nestled into his seat a little tighter. "He was a thief. In 1671, he infiltrated the Tower of London and stole the Crown Jewels."

Quinn grumbled: "Fucking Brits..."

"He was Irish, actually," corrected McAllester.

Quinn wiped his mouth with a red-and-yellow-blotched napkin. "Figures..."

"Anyway, Blood didn't have an army. He didn't use violence to get what he was after. Didn't need to. He got into the castle by pretending to be a clergyman. Once inside, he befriended the man in charge of protecting the king's priceless artifacts, a man by the name of Talbert Edwards.

"Now, Talbert had a daughter that he wished to be married, and Blood mentioned that he had a very well-off nephew that was also looking to wed, so Talbert invited both Blood and his nephew to the castle to speak on the union and also, as a way to sweeten the deal, get a look at the famed Crown Jewels. Blood accepted the invitation and enlisted his son to act the part of the nephew. The two of them went to the castle and allowed Talbert to lead them to where the jewels were kept. Once in the room, they assaulted him and made off with the jewels."

"Did they get away with it?"

"With the jewels? No. The king's guards caught up to them as they fled and took them into custody."

"Good," said Quinn with an air of self-satisfaction. "Justice served."

"But that's not the weirdest part," said McAllester.

Quinn, foraging for fries at the bottom of his paper bag, noted yonderly: "This whole story is pretty weird."

McAllester persisted, undeterred. "When Blood was caught and asked how he managed to steal the Crown Jewels, he insisted that he wouldn't talk to anybody but the king. King Charles, surprisingly, opted to grant Blood his wish and met with him. No one knows what was said in that meeting, but when it was over, Blood and his son were granted a full pardon."

Quinn's forehead creased with perplexity. "Okay. So? What's the point of the story?"

"Before Blood turned to crime, he had been a loyal soldier in the uprising against the Royalist Monarchy. He even was awarded land for his military service. It wasn't until King Charles' eldest, Charles II, took power that Blood's land was confiscated, leaving him in financial ruin and forcing him to plan his caper. So, I guess what I'm trying to say is: sometimes admirable men are forced to commit less than admirable deeds. And if you're clever enough, you just might get away with it."

Quinn scoffed. "You sound like you're rooting for these guys."

Sinking into his recline, McAllester stared abstractly at the headliner and let out a long, sleepy breath through his nose. "Just a story, Quinn."

Quinn leaned forward in his seat and pointed out the windshield to the headlights pulling into the motel parking lot. A Toyota Corolla, the same model and color as the one in which the suspects earlier departed, crept like a jungle panther through the rows of cars before slowing to a stop in front of the Dodge Charger.

"That's our guy," said Quinn.

"THAT'S OUR GUY," SAID Laura at the helm of the Corolla as the bandits, old and new, prowled the motel parking lot. She pointed to the Charger, gleaming under the moonlight.

Mitch, in the passenger seat, exhaled laboriously. Under the low brim of his baseball cap, he turned to face Chad behind him. "Okay, Chad. We'll grab the car and then make our way to Sandy Acres. You sure you're comfortable with driving stick?"

A wicked grin stretched across Chad's face as he leered at the classic through his window. "Oh yeah. We're good."

"Great."

Mitch regarded Robert and Tammy beside Chad. "You guys good?"

The two of them affirmed, albeit queasily.

Lastly, Mitch turned to Laura.

"I'm good," she answered preemptively. Her tone was taut and slightly aggressive. "Let's get going."

Mitch reached for the door handle. "Okay. Let's get it done."

Mitch and Chad exited the vehicle and, proceeding a short stretch and yawn, headed for the Charger. The night air was toasty; heat radiated off the pavement. Mitch tossed Chad the keys, and Chad opened the driver-side door. He bent inside, reached the passenger-side door, and unlocked it. Mitch promptly clambered in and shut the door, mildly entertained at Chad's beguiled expression while examining his new toy. Though equipped with a subtle musky odor deeply embedded in the leather seats, the Charger's interior held much of the splendor that had since deteriorated from the outer shell.

"This is so badass," Chad whispered as his electric gaze wandered the dashboard.

"Glad you approve," said Mitch.

Outside, the Corolla circled and headed for the street.

JOLTING ALIVE IN HIS seat, McAllester grabbed the binoculars from the center console. Vantage magnified, he watched a kid in his early twenties of slim build and dark hair get out of the Corolla's backseat, stretch, yawn, and move for the Charger's driver's side. The runaway groom, Clyde Morrison, exited the car next. He wore a low baseball cap on his face, casting his chiseled features in shadow. He approached the Charger's passenger side. Still inside the Corolla was the blonde from earlier, currently at the wheel, wearing a stoical expression. In the backseat were two new faces: a pasty, heavy-set ginger woman and a slim-faced, thin-necked Asian man, presumably in their thirties. The pair appeared incredibly nervous and guilty. The Corolla rounded back out to the street. Red taillights disappeared around the corner. Clyde and the unknown were inside the Charger. The headlights illuminated. The V8 engine came to life with a growl.

CHAD INSERTED THE KEYS into the ignition. The Charger's body, and Chad's with it, shook with the engine's arousal. Chad's grin augmented exponentially. He geared into drive and crept toward the road.

Mitch's apprehension in allowing the kid to drive subsided upon witnessing the smoothness of his clutch work changing in and out of gears. The kid hadn't been lying about his abilities behind the wheel. What wasn't so settling for Mitch was the other car that had pulled out behind them, still visible in his rearview.

"Not too fast, okay?" Mitch warned. "We're trying to stay low-key, remember?"

"Got it," confirmed Chad, eyes wide and bright.

As they approached the highway exit, Mitch glanced in the rearview. The car from the parking lot was still behind them. "Hold on," said Mitch cautiously. He pointed to a narrow side road branching off from the main street. "Turn down this road. I want to see something."

Chad's voice raised in pitch: "No highway?"

"No. Go around the block. We'll circle around."

Chad changed lanes and made a short left onto the side street. Mitch kept close on their rear as they cruised down the narrow, shadow-choked artery. His chest tightened as he saw the headlights of their tail turn down the same road.

"Dammit..." Mitch muttered to himself.

"What is it?" asked Chad. His eyes broke from the road briefly to witness the concern on Mitch's face.

"We're being followed."

Chad's gaze shifted to the rearview. The headlights behind reflected off the mirror and cast a rectangular strip of luminance across his otherwise gray-washed face. He frowned.

"Remember when I told you to go slow?" said Mitch.

"Yeah?"

Mitch reached for his seat belt. "Scratch that. Go fast. Go *real* fucking fast. Lose these guys, will ya?"

Chad's goofy countenance resurfaced. "With pleasure."

His knuckles tightened white around the steering wheel. His sneaker sunk the gas pedal. The V8 roared like a proud lion as the car propelled. Chad's right knee jumped, the left foot punched the clutch. His right hand hammered into third gear. The lion roared louder, angrier—gravitational force thrust Mitch and Chad deep into their seats.

Mitch spun and looked out the back windshield.

The pursuer's headlights shrank smaller and smaller.

"WHY'D THEY TURN LEFT?" asked McAllester. He leaned forward in his seat and watched the Charger turn down a side road.

Quinn eased off the gas. "Maybe they made us."

"Stay on them," said McAllester.

Even if the target was aware, the risk of losing their only connection to Sylvester Robertson was too great to fall back. McAllester knew if he had traveled all this way and returned without the Tyrant in handcuffs, he could kiss the ADD position goodbye.

Quinn followed orders and turned left behind the Charger. He maintained a steady, inconspicuous distance. Tiny pebbles on the pavement crackled outside the car and popped under heavy tread.

A quick screech shot out into the night. The Charger's engine bellowed. Their target pulled away at a startling rate.

"They're going," Quinn pointed out. It was a statement McAllester found painfully obvious and irritating.

"Stay on them!" McAllester barked.

Quinn stomped on the gas. His hairy-knuckled fists choked the wheel. A hardened resoluteness stiffened his beefy face.

Suddenly, the night was electric. McAllester sat back and embraced the exhilaration derived from the hunt. The subsequent pulsating adrenalin was something that had brought him great joy during his short stint as a field agent. As they raced down the dark side street with the Charger in their sights, he forestalled the edges of his lips from curling upward.

It was good to be on the hunt again.

Without the warning of brake lights, the Charger made a hard left onto a residential street. The suspects vanished around the bend. Quinn slammed on the brakes and almost overshot the turn entirely. The time spent correcting course reestablished much of the whittled distance between their target.

McAllester tensed. The fever of nostalgia cooled. He was starting to regret not being behind the wheel. "Move it!" he yelled at Quinn, glowering fixedly at the neon taillights pulling away.

Quinn floored the gas. The RPM needle raised steadily.

MITCH LAUGHED OUT LOUD, body stuck against the passenger door from the force of Chad's quick and unannounced left turn onto the residential straightaway. Chad straightened course, punched the stick into third, and stomped on the gas. The engine responded with a demonic growl and launched them headlong. Mitch whirled in his seat and peered through the back windshield. The pursuer's headlights were nowhere to be found. A second later, the headlights appeared. Gaining. Fast. Mitch faced forward, exhibiting a veneer of confidence for the benefit of his young assailant. "Okay," he said with fragile equanimity. "We're not out of the woods yet. What else you got up your sleeve?"

Chad's eyebrows trampolined. "I *got* shit," he assured. "Put on the music."

The balls of this kid, thought Mitch. "No. No way. We're not about to..."

Chad popped the clutch, slammed into second gear, and careened left onto another residential street. The car fishtailed and straightened. Chad's foot thumped on the clutch and shifted to third as he screamed: "Tunes! Put. On. The. Tuuuuunes!"

The exhilaration on the kid's face paired with contagious manic laughter were enough to make Mitch, for the merest of measures, think about how much fun it would be to have a son. To have a family of his own.

Fuck it, he thought. He turned on the radio. *Let the kid have his tunes. Better off dying to a soundtrack.*

Instantly, the low drone of the V8 amalgamated with the famous whiny vocals and crunching electric guitar of Neil Young's *'Rockin' in the Free World.'* Mitch reckoned that John must have been the last person in the Charger. For a moment, the music welled a stir of unwelcome emotions in him, memories of an era he would never relive. He considered changing the station until he saw Chad bobbing his head to the snare clap, gleaning a swelling conviction.

Mitch left the dial where it was.

"There's one more kid that'll never go to school
Never get to fall in love, never get to be cool
Keep on rockin' in the free world."

Mitch spun in his seat and looked out the back windshield. The pursuers completed the turn and were gaining steadily. The headlights remained on the Charger's heels, bright and haunting.

"Gonna have to hit 'em with something better than that," said Mitch, facing forward.

As if offended by the insinuation, Chad ceased head-bobbing and punched into fourth gear. The Charger blasted down the straightaway at furious speed.

"LEFT! LEFT!" MCALLESTER yelled sharply.

Quinn flinched and scowled, eyes dead ahead. He wouldn't waste time explaining to McAllester that he had seen the turn and anticipated the Charger's move. These clowns might have made a fool of Angie, but they would not make a fool out of him. The Crown Vic swerved left, following the suspect onto another residential street. As the Crown Vic straightened out, the Charger accelerated, pulling away. Quinn reacted in tandem and smashed the gas. The speed gauge rose to fifty miles per hour.

"Ram his side," ordered McAllester. "Spin him out."

Not a bad idea, thought Quinn. *Too bad I was already thinking about doing exactly that.*

Precision Immobilization Technique was the technical term for the maneuver McAllester was suggesting. PIT for short. But Quinn guessed McAllester didn't have much need for technical terminology while he sat cozy behind a desk at the field office. The move required pulling alongside the fleeing vehicle and gently steering into its tail, which, if properly executed, caused the suspect vehicle to swing in on itself and lose control. Quinn drifted slightly to the left and aligned with the Charger's backside. Both his hands steadied the wheel as he calculated the appropriate timing and velocity.

It's time to take these crooks down once and for all, he vowed privately. *For Angie.*

"OH, NO..." GROANED Chad. He cast a worried glance at the rearview as the pursuer's headlights drifted out of his eye line into his blind spot. His focus returned to the road, chewing his nether lip as if trouble weighed heavily on his mind.

Mitch absorbed his chauffeur's uncertainty. "What is it?"

"He's setting up for something," said Chad. His glance pivoted to his side mirror. "Either they're going to try to pass us or..." He continued to chew his lip. His attention pendulated between the road and the driver's side mirror.

"Or what?" snapped Mitch.

Chad's head twitched sideways. He frowned. "If it's what I'm thinking, these guys are cops, man. They're about to ram us."

Mitch watched the rear windshield, the pursuer near enough now that he could identify the car's hood ornament from the fiery glow of the Charger's taillight. The kid was right. It was a Crown Vic. A V8. A fed car. The relief of knowing it wasn't Mr. Robertson or Sebastian gnawing at their haunches evolved into trepidation over why the FBI might be on his tail. Had they found him? After all this time, had they finally tracked him down? If so, Laura and the rest of the call center folks would be waiting longer than expected at the meetup point. Much longer. It also meant Joey wouldn't be coming back alive.

"Anything you can do to get us out of this?"

A slow but assuring smile split the kid's face. He nodded and glanced at the driver's side mirror. His right hand gingerly released the steering wheel and floated toward the stick. His vivacious countenance matured into one of steely determination. "Hold on to your balls. Here we go..."

Chad stomped on the brake like the first panicked boot thrust of a hermetic old man discovering a burning bag of dog shit on his doorstep. The Charger's momentum screeched to a halt. White smoke engulfed the vehicle's exterior as if a Vegas stage magician had pledged its disappearance. Mitch's belt strap chomped hard and deep into his shoulder, scratching at bone. Clouds of chalky smoke diminished to reveal a motionless world. Addressees above the semi-detached garages sharpened and identified themselves in rusted bronze. Painted eyes on garish garden gnomes watched the unfolding events with inert gazes. Directly outside the passenger window, Mitch witnessed the Crown Vic rip by like a tumbling comet barreling across the planet's surface. Chad geared down and spun left as hard as he could. The Charger careened into a one-lane access road between two brick-and-mortar commercial buildings.

Twenty yards ahead appeared the germinal street converging onto the highway. In another dizzying whip, Chad navigated a stark right. The Charger fishtailed into a shallow alleyway amassed in an inescapable blackness that convinced Mitch Chad had piloted a nosedive into the edifice. Movement came to a quiescent conclusion. Chad switched off the engine, shut off the lights, and raised a finger to his lips.

Mitch stole a deep, slow breath through his nose and exhaled through pursed lips. If the Crown Vic were to traverse the throughway shining a spotlight, the two were as good as collared. He pinched the medallion around his neck. There was nothing left to do now but wait and see.

Ten to fifteen seconds later, a space that felt more like ten to fifteen minutes, they watched through the rearview as the Crown Vic, moving too fast to have seen them, too fast to have even looked, raced through the alley toward the main street.

Chad and Mitch let out a simultaneous sigh.

"Okay," Mitch murmured weakly. "Chill here for a minute, then get us on the fucking highway."

Chapter Twenty Five

Joyce chortled exasperatedly. The sound bloomed across the dark, deserted construction site. It was her first sign of life since Sebastian departed to take a phone call from a caller he wished to remain anonymous. Of all the noises she might have exerted, Joey was least expecting to hear laughter. He lifted his hanging head. "What? What's so funny?"

The moonlight gilded her skin porcelain. She shook her head with the slightest of grins. "My father used to say, 'Joy-joy, you have the absolute worst taste in men.' It really pissed me off, you know? That he would think that. But I guess he was right. Couldn't even see the guy I liked was a con artist."

"Hey, that's not fair," objected Joey. "Liking you was never part of the con. It just happened. It wasn't acting. I really enjoyed spending time with you. I mean, you put on this hardened feminist exterior, but inside you're just a big softy. I love it."

She scowled superficially. "I'm not a softy."

Joey couldn't help but return a provocative smile. "Good. Because if we're going to get out of this alive, we're going to need to harden the fuck up."

Joyce let out a hopeless cackle. "And how are we going to survive this? We're handcuffed. No one knows where we are. *We* don't even know where we are."

Joey's face hardened with gravitas. "The team will come through. They always do."

"Your criminal buddies?"

"Yeah, my *criminal buddies*. They're not as bad as you think. In fact, they're a lot better people than I am. I'm always fucking up, and it's always been them who end up pulling me out of the shit. They're loyal. Maybe you don't see that, but they are. You know there was one time when I got arrested and they risked their freedom, maybe even their lives, to save me?"

Joyce raised an interested eyebrow. "Yeah?"

"Fuck yeah. I was an idiot and went out after a job to get drunk. We were supposed to leave town that night, but, as usual, I thought my responsibilities could wait. I ended up getting in a bar fight, and the cops arrested me, put me in the county lockup. The whole time I was in that cell, I was blaming the guy who hit me, the bartender for calling the cops, and the police for arresting me. And to be honest, when the team came and broke me out, it was like I *expected* it. Like I would have been furious with them if they didn't..." He took a deep breath. "It's my fault you're here, Joyce. So if you're going to hate someone, don't hate my criminal buddies. They don't deserve it. I do."

A quiet ensued beneath the long-suffering thrum of the generator.

"You're not that bad of a guy, you know," Joyce said eventually. She preserved a half-grin until Joey leveled her gaze.

Slow, echoing applause wrenched Joey's attention and sullied the tender moment. He and Joyce swiveled to the gloomy staircase Mr. Robertson ascended. Sebastian followed close behind his father.

"What a beautiful sentiment," the elder Robertson remarked. He towered over Joyce and grimaced down on her. Joey's fists, unfairly inhibited by steel, balled behind his back. "It's too bad this love won't get a chance to unfurl," Robertson lamented theatrically. "It would have been so magical. But the fact is: you broke my daughter's heart. You played me for a fool. And no one, *no one*, fucks with the Robertsons, you understand me?" Mr. Robertson acknowledged

Sebastian. "Don't you see, son? It's people like this who killed your mother. People who want to steal everything we worked so hard to build. They have no honor. No loyalty. If it wasn't for bastards like this, she would still be alive. So get rid of him. Rid the planet of these thieving bastards. Do it for your mother."

On command, Sebastian stepped forward and withdrew the pistol tucked in his crotch like he was trying to compensate for something. He extended his arm and aimed at Joey.

Joyce wailed: "No!"

Mr. Robertson sneered at Joey, practically salivating. "Time to pay the piper, you son-of-a-bitch!"

With a twitch of Sebastian's thumb, the pistol's safety disarmed. Sebastian stepped closer. Death stared Joey in the face, and he was ready to receive it. But as the doomed supposed his last breath, Sebastian suddenly pivoted and targeted his father. He pressed the muzzle into Mr. Robertson's fleshy temple and pulled the trigger.

AFTER A LONG AND PARANOID drive, Mitch and Chad arrived at the meetup point Sebastian dictated on the phone. It was a fenced-off construction site on the edge of town, near the Sandy Acres Bed N' Bar. Mitch beamed at the sight of Laura in the Corolla across the street. For a space during his car chase, he worried he might never get to see her again. And even though he still harbored resentment toward her for revealing herself to Meryl in the way she had, he had learned that his capacity for forgiveness remained resolute for the souls he would not want to live or die without in the face of certain demise.

Robert and Tammy were in the backseat, looking like they were in the middle of serious regrets. A retro boom-box stereo sat on Robert's lap. Tammy nervously gripped an aluminum baseball bat.

Both cars emptied, and the five convened in a circle in the middle of the street. Robert held the stereo by the bulky plastic handle at his side. Tammy brought the baseball bat and a large flattened cardboard box that she handed Chad. The workmates shared a mimed but consolidative reunion. Mitch beckoned Laura's gaze. She lacked expression and looked as if she was running on empty. He wondered if she was as happy to see him as he was to see her.

"Okay, guys," said Mitch to the new team members. "If we do like we practiced, things should go smoothly."

"*Should?*" squeaked Tammy. "That's not very settling."

"Unfortunately, it's the best I got," said Mitch. "If anyone wants to back out, now is the time."

Tammy and Robert declined the offer, and Mitch had no doubts that Chad was all in. "Okay," said Mitch. "Let's go." He placed a gentle hand on Laura's hip. "You good?"

"Yeah," she said. "Yeah, I'm good."

Her gaze attempted to slip, but he found it and assured her he would return soon with their fellow bandit.

He carefully crossed the construction site's front gate, pistol at arm's length, finger poised on the trigger. The crunching gravel under his heels alarmed him. He faltered and signaled to the gawking bandits with a forefinger to his lips. The team returned anxious gesticulations evincing their understanding.

Mitch continued ever cautious of his weight distribution on the bed of jagged stones beneath his feet. Nearby, a powerful generator roused to life. The initial rumble and proceeding electrical hum startled the three new bandits into a paroxysm of trepidation. All team members, Mitch included, halted their positions with expressions that betrayed the anticipation of an imminent ambush. When the blitz did not arrive, the generator's rattle was ultimately more of a blessing than a curse, allowing the party to tread forward on the gravel with fewer stipulations.

Mitch dashed behind the Health & Safety trailer that, reminiscent of his mobile-home-park youth, floated on four equally-spaced rows of cinder blocks. He signaled his tail to remain by the front gate. The trio nervously, Chad less so comparatively, obliged.

Mitch peeked around the corner and surveyed the perimeter. An Escalade SUV was parked abreast of heat and frost insulation boxes. Beyond, erected on an elevated concrete stage, loomed a stout steel beam skeleton of what would eventually become some species of distribution office. Halogen lights affixed to tripods illumined the architectural bones like a movie set that allowed Mitch an easy view of Joey and the short-haired woman, who Mitch concluded was Joey's lover and supervisor, sitting on a massive concrete block near the center region of the building-to-be. Presently, Mr. Robertson strolled toward them, clapping facetiously into their helpless faces. Sebastian followed his father, as was the routine.

Mitch stepped from behind the trailer and scrambled toward Robertson's SUV, where he took cover at the boot. Waving to the entrance, he signaled the team to trace his initial route and take cover behind the trailer. He poised his pistol at the Robertson men until each bandit had safely completed the feat.

Next, Mitch stooped nearly ninety degrees and made a beeline for a tarped stack of pallets ahead and to the right. Robertson was busy barking gospel at Sebastian, and the move went undetected.

Mitch was close enough now to hear what Robertson was saying: "Don't you see, son? It's people like this who killed your mother. People who want to steal everything we worked so hard to build. They have no honor. No loyalty. If it wasn't for bastards like this, she would still be alive. So get rid of him. Rid the planet of these thieving bastards. Do it for your mother."

On command, Sebastian stepped forward and withdrew a steely pistol from his waistband. He outstretched the firearm at Joey.

Joyce wailed: "No!"

Mitch set aim at the back of Sebastian's head. His finger hugged the trigger but did not yet pull.

Mr. Robertson glowered maniacally at Joey, screaming: "Time to pay the piper, you son-of-a-bitch!"

Joey glared back at him, jaw clenched, unflinching.

As Mitch prepared to shoot, Sebastian stepped out of the line of fire. Before Mitch could recalibrate his aim, Sebastian turned his gun on his father, pressed it against his temple, and fired a shot. The gun exhumed a belching pop and flash of fire. The bullet went through Robertson's skull and splashed out the other side. Mr. Robertson folded to the ground like a wet towel. A yellow-brown plume of dust mushroomed into the air as his body smashed the concrete. The cloud descended patiently and buried Robertson's pinstriped suit in a thin layer of filth. Mitch thanked God the blast was as loud as it was; otherwise, Sebastian might have heard Tammy when, upon witnessing the unsuspected murder from behind the trailer, she reactively yelped into the open night. Mitch and Chad whirled and threw her a scolding glare before Mitch reestablished his crosshairs on Sebastian.

Sebastian lowered his weapon. With tears in his eyes, he screamed at his father's contorted cadaver: "No honor? No loyalty? It was you who murdered my mother, you piece of shit!" Sebastian double-pumped the trigger and spent two bullets into his father's lifeless chest.

Mitch signaled the team to break for the SUV. From the trailer, the three dashed headlong toward the vehicle accordingly. Tammy ran with her eyes puckered shut the entire time.

Sebastian continued to harangue his predecessor's corpse: "Thought you could lie to me? To Angie? Use mom's memory to manipulate us so I would help you knock off the competition? You make me sick!" He spat on Mr. Robertson's shocked and statuesque expression and watched with sadness and antipathy the saliva change from white to brown as it traversed his father's dusty cheek. He raised his head to Joey. "That prick had it coming, believe me. But don't you worry. For what you did to my sister, you're heading to the same place. And when your partner gets here, he'll be joining you. My dad may have been a lying scumbag, but he was right about one thing: no one fucks with the Robertsons!"

Mitch signaled the others to get into position while Sebastian thundered forth his tirade: "You see, for my whole life, I lived in that bastard's shadow. And for a long time, I idolized him. It wasn't until I did some backpedaling of my own into my mother's murder that I realized the story he told us didn't add up. And like the way we found you, I followed a trail of blood that led right back to the motherfucker. He killed my mother for finding love with another man. For that, he had to pay. And wouldn't you know it? Tonight he was murdered by the bandits who defrauded his daughter. Luckily, I survived the gun battle."

A self-satisfied grin stretched across Sebastian's face. His temper cooled. His posture evened. He forgot about the fresh corpse resting at his waxed oxfords. "It's my time now," he declared with conviction. "Too bad you have to die. You guys are clever. I almost want to offer *all* of you a job. Oh well..."

He raised his pistol at the supervisor. She turned away and leaned into Joey's heart.

Mitch signaled Robert.

Robert pressed play on the boom box.

The generator's hum faltered to the sudden supernova of hip-hop music consuming the construction site; more specifically, the unmistakable 90s smash hit *'93 till Infinity* from the rap group Souls of Mischief.

Sebastian, Joey, and the supervisor combined whirled to locate the source of the sound.

"Yo whassup, this is Tajai of the mighty Souls of Mischief crew
I'm chillin with my man Phesto, my man A-Plus
And my man Op', you know he's dope (yo)
But right now y'know we just maxin in the studio
We hailin from East Oakland, California and, um
Sometimes it gets a little hectic out there
But right now, yo, we gonna up you on how we just chill"

The smooth-riding breakbeat engaged, and frontman, Tajai, commenced his iconic verse.

Sebastian spotted Robert and Chad below. They stood around a stereo on a piece of flattened cardboard over the gravel beside his Escalade, bobbing their heads. At first, the former was shocked, startled even. His nonplussed expression promptly matured to one of violence.

"Hey!" he shouted at the interlopers through the darkness. A discernible pulsing vein bulged from his beefy neck.

Seemingly deaf to Sebastian's attention, Robert stepped onto the cardboard and, in the fashion emblematic of a true badass B-Boy, began to shuffle his feet and flap his outstretched arms like a hungry seagull at war over a discarded pizza crust. Chad stood beside the stereo, nodding to the rhythm.

The fact that the two had neglected his brazen bark further infuriated the junior Robertson. He hurried down the concrete steps and stomped through the dirt and gravel toward the insolent breakdancers. His gun followed tentatively at his side.

"Hey, assholes!" he bawled. "You trespassed on the wrong property, you dumb shits!"

He raised his pistol, unaware that directly behind him, Tammy had revealed herself from the cover of the SUV, aluminum baseball bat cocked and gripped tightly. With a mighty wallop, Tammy cracked the instrument across Sebastian's crown. He folded, tumbled, and rolled into a supine position. Tammy raised the bat above her head and swung down powerfully on the gunman's face. With a sound not unlike the crunch of gravel, blood spurted from Sebastian's beefy nose like paintball splatter. He went limp, out like a light.

"Wow," gasped Chad. He stooped and cut the stereo. The omnipresent hum of the generator returned to fill the space.

"Tammy's a gangster," uttered Robert, paralyzed with revolt and wonderment.

Tammy giggled softly, pleased with her work.

Once Mitch was sure Sebastian was unconscious, he raced to Joey and the supervisor. They howled and cheered at the sight of their liberator and stood as Mitch approached. Mitch stepped over Mr. Robertson's lifeless body and quickly released the captives from their containment with a bullet through each chain.

Joey wasted no time in throwing his arms around Mitch and squeezing tightly. "You're my fucking hero, dude! Over and over!"

Mitch returned the embrace, then recomposed. "We're not out of the woods yet. We need to get moving." He regarded the supervisor and offered warmth in his gaze and smile. There was no time for introductions.

She returned the gesture wistfully. "...thank you," she whispered. Her eyes welled with gracious tears.

Tammy, Robert, and Chad inched forward and made themselves known. Joey's eyes brightened wide at the sight of his coworkers. "Look at you guys!" he hollered. "I did not expect to see you coming to my rescue."

Tammy blushed. "Well, you did save our jobs. Thought it would be kind to return the favor. Southern hospitality and all..."

Joey and Chad shared a high-five and a hug. Robert was breathless and squeezed Mitch's arm. "He almost shot us," he gasped. "We could have died."

"I had my gun on him the whole time," Mitch assured, though he knew the young man wasn't wrong.

"You did great, Bobby!" exclaimed Joey. He regarded Mitch quizzically. "Where's the guys?"

"Laura's in the car," said Mitch. His gaze fell downcast. "John...he didn't make it."

Joey's celebration sharply halted. He appeared winded and off-balance as he ingested the poignant news.

Mitch placed a solemn hand on his shoulder. "I know...We can't stick around and talk about it now. I need you to get these guys back to Oak County, then meet Laura and me at the bluff. We'll leave from there."

Mitch extended his palm to Chad. "Going to need those Charger keys, bud."

"Aw, *man*," Chad whined. He reluctantly surrendered the key chain.

Mitch patted him on the shoulder encouragingly. "You did great. Would have made a hell of a bandit."

The six of them started toward the yawning fence gate. "Final stretch, Jo," said Mitch. He burrowed his pistol into his waistband behind him. "Let's finish this."

"For John," said Joey.

"For John," said Mitch.

Chapter Twenty Six

The Charger approached a slow park at the entrance to Oak Bluff, headlights casting twin pallid beams against the log gate and hiking map. Beyond was a void of blackness under a star-studded panorama. Mitch killed the engine, and the lights went out. He and Laura exited the vehicle. The closing doors echoed across the landscape over stridulating crickets and softly crashing waves far below the mountain's edge. Mitch invited nature's soundtrack. During the drive from Sandy Acres, the radio had been a distraction, and he and Laura had been far too tangled in respective meditations to have any semblance of a conversation. Laura's elbow rested on the window ledge; head canted in her palm as she watched the white lines zip past. Mitch had one hand on the wheel, the other on his pistol, and spent more time glancing at the rearview than paying attention to the stretch of road ahead. His eyelids dragged, and he was afraid to shut them, even for a blink. Each time they closed, he saw Meryl's face bearing the same tearful expression.

Mitch would have never dreamed in a million years that being called a 'Fucker' would cut him so deeply.

His impromptu dissolution with the Sheriff's daughter felt wrong, tearing at his insides and making the idea of the midnight getaway, something that should have brought him peace, feel selfish and irrational.

"I'm going to give Joey a call," Mitch apprised Laura in impotent susurration.

Laura nodded with a mirrored want of intensity. Whatever anxieties had milled inside her head during the car ride seemed to remain at the forefront of her concerns. She leaned against the hood of the car with a sole on the fender and lit a cigarette. Gray-blue tendrils floated off the glowing red ember and streamed upward to the endless canopy of constellations. She bent her head, gazed at the moon, and exhaled a narrow stream.

Mitch tucked his pistol and walked ten paces along the dirt path toward the distant shadows. When he was out of earshot, he dialed Meryl's number, whispering a prayer and pinching his medallion.

The line rang once.

Twice.

Meryl's voice, cloying and courteous, appeared. Mitch's breath caught in his throat, heart aflutter. A moment later, to his folly, he realized what he was listening to was her prerecorded voicemail greeting. Meryl kindly instructed the caller to leave a message and have a nice day. After a shrill concluding beep, Mitch acquiesced, though he could not envision a future where the rest of his day, or days for that matter, would be any sort of *nice*. Not with knowing what he had done to Meryl's heart.

And what Meryl had done to his.

As he spoke, he spared nothing, letting each word fall from his lips like disconsolate souls diving off the ledge of a skyscraper to a ready and inevitable demise. And when he said his last goodbye, much like the jumpers, he found himself a little more dead inside. He pressed 'End', swallowed his emotions, and slipped the phone into his pocket.

"Okay," said Mitch once returned to Laura and the Charger. "Now we wait."

She had pulled her hair into a ponytail during his leave and was anxiously biting her lower lip. "Think we could take a walk? I don't feel so good."

Mitch agreed. He pointed to the narrow trail leading to the brush ahead, a path he and Meryl had taken together many times. He sluggishly embarked. Laura followed his lead.

"Everything okay?" asked Mitch tenderly. Small twigs crunched and snapped under their heels. The crickets' throaty ballad intensified. "You've been real quiet."

"Nothing is okay, Mitch," she said weakly, almost to herself. "This job has been a disaster. No score. John's dead. What are we going to do for IDs now? How can we go on?" She spoke slowly, exhausted, like the questions had haunted her for a lifetime. Mitch knew they were valid questions to which Laura deserved to know the answer, even if the truth was disagreeable to her ears. Mitch met her expectant gaze and remembered all those years ago when he first saw her in that decrepit midwestern pool hall, bending over the table in a low-cut shirt, staring down the length of her cue with a cherry smirk on her face, hustling some poor young sap who had thought he had bagged himself a real trophy. By the end of the night, all Romeo had bagged up was the contents of his wallet.

Laura was a con artist long before she ever became a bandit. And even in the harsh contrast of the pool hall lighting, she was a breathtaking sight. She had the devil's gaze, a goddess' body, and an effortless grace that was impossible to ignore. Mitch drew to her like the proverbial moth to flame.

Maybe that's exactly how she planned it.

When Mitch intimated the idea of bringing her along to the next town, Joey had some choice words prepared for his mentor. He told Mitch he was getting played like an Asian girl plays the piano: *really* fucking good. Without John's majority vote, she might have remained in that little town. Maybe for the better.

"It might be time to rethink what we're doing," said Mitch as they breached the woods' leafy density. Crooked branches outstretched overhead, swallowing the dazzle aloft. Rooty outgrowth abreast their ankles reached out from the stony dirt like the morbid hands of the undead emerging from their graves for a moonlight promenade.

"Like what?" Laura asked with a twisted face.

Mitch returned a brushed shrug. "I don't know...maybe being ourselves. Being regular people, you know? Just boring, regular people." He smiled at her, hoping for a similar return.

Laura shook her head and laughed feebly under her breath. "I thought you might say something like that."

Mitch stepped forward. His shoe tightened against his toes, causing him to falter and lurch. He glanced peevishly at his feet and discovered a loose shoelace wormed under his dirt-crusted heel. He withdrew the pistol from his waistband and handed it to Laura, saying: "Here, hold this a sec.."

He crouched down and quickly re-tied the insurgent string. Over a passing breeze soughing through the thicket, he heard the click of his pistol's safety, followed by the sensation of cold metal on his nape.

He froze in his kneeling position.

"Get up," said Laura. Her voice was as frigid as the steel against his skin.

Mitch's heartbeat quickened, his brain refusing to accept what his body already knew. He cautiously rose, hands outstretched at his side, praying this was Laura's twisted idea of a kinky joke.

"What's going on, Laura?" he asked with a slight tremor in his throat. "You're not serious right now, are you?"

He couldn't see her face to get a read on her.

"No, Mitch," she said tonelessly. "I think I am the only one who *is* serious."

She pressed the muzzle into his back and ordered him to walk. Mitch did as commanded and continued along the trail, compliant until he could figure out a way to escape this situation with both parties intact. But a burning question occupied his brain that needed answering before anything further could be done. "Did you do it? Did you kill John?"

The gun pressed deeper into his back. He heard her digging through pockets. After a lingering silence, she spoke, but not to Mitch. "Hello? Sebastian, it's me. I have him. We're at the bluff in Oak County."

Any pieces that remained of Mitch's heart crumbled to dust inside his chest. His brow stooped low. His throat throbbed under the weight of betrayal.

"Okay, babe," sang Laura into her phone with a well-known facile coquetry. "See you soon."

More shuffling as she returned her phone. Above, the moon peeked through arthritic boughs and circled Mitch's dizzy head.

"Why are you doing this, Laura?" he asked despite the open wound of her treason. "How can you betray the team like this?"

Her tone was sodden with resentment when she replied after a moment's contemplation. "This is your fault, Mitch. You and Joey, parading around, treating the con like an episode of *Temptation Island*. You lost sight of what's important. I'm not going back to hustling horny college kids in the pool hall. I'm too old for that. I need something long-term. I need security. Sebastian can provide that. It's *his* time now. He just needs the right woman beside him. Killing John and Robertson was *my* idea, Mitch. They had tracked us down. It was only a matter of time before they got to us. And it was clear I was losing you to that chunky monkey you're so drawn to." She huffed under her breath. "Look where *that* got you..."

"You're the one holding the gun," uttered Mitch. His hope for reconciliation withered and expired.

"You forced my hand," said Laura decidedly.

Mitch exhaled pensively. In some strange way, he understood. Not that he agreed with her decision. But at least he understood it. "I'm sorry I let you down, Laura. I really am."

There was a prolonged break in speech. The rolling swoosh of the ocean grew louder as they advanced further into the woods.

"Me, too, Mitch," Laura said at length. She almost choked on the words. "Me, too."

MERYL SAT UP AGAINST her headboard in an unmade bed, legs mummified in layers of crinkled sheets. Within reach lay her phone and a box of tissues. An episode of *Law and Order* she had seen a thousand times dramatized on the mounted television. The gray track pants she had worn for the last two days were damp and humid with the sweat of an unwashed body. Her cheeks were dry from the salt of expended tears. The eyes from which the tears had trilled burned and itched. Despite her mental and physical strain, she ignored her suffering and steadied a weary engrossment in the fiction playing on the screen. She was afraid to close her eyes. Each time they shut, his face would appear. Those kind, lying eyes. That sweet smile of betrayal. The image of that stupid girl standing in his doorway, arms crossed, and a shit-eating grin of victory smeared across her face. The slideshow of memories twisted Meryl's stomach and robbed her of any unspent vigor. But no more tears were left to cry, only a perpetual dry heave from throbbing eyelids and a yearning for a never-ending tub of double fudge chocolate ice cream.

No, she thought. She wouldn't give in. She wouldn't let the liar or that skinny bitch ruin all the progress she had made in the last month. Roy had been an integral element in that progress, and his helpfulness was now a paradox that left Meryl scraping for a logical explanation of his actions, one which she tiredly concluded would never be found.

Her phone vibrated beside the box of tissues.

Not now, she thought. *No one right now.*

After a few rings, the device cut silent, and her coiling nerves unruffled. A singular beep notified her of a new voicemail.

Her gaze drifted from the television to her phone. *Maybe it's him*, was the first thought. *Who cares if it is?* was the second.

She forced her eyes on the television and focused on Detective Olivia Benson's interrogation of the obviously-guilty neighbor to the episode's slain victim. The culprit twitched in his seat as the detective laid out the irrefutable evidence of his transgression. Benson leaned, hands splayed on the table, putting the once-arrogant suspect in his place while simultaneously providing the viewers at home a nice gawk at her endowed cleavage. Meryl's glance returned to her phone as the suspect on the television broke into a sobbing admission of guilt. Reticently, she lifted the device and dialed her voicemail. After punching in her three-digit password, she raised the phone to her ear. She seized the remote and muted the television.

"Meryl, it's me," said the voice on the other end. It was the voice she had expected and dreaded all at the same time. *His* voice. Roy, Mitch, or whoever he was under all that bullshit. Her first instinct was to hang up and delete the message before she could convince herself otherwise. His selfish actions denied him the right to an audience. But there was no one around. No one to witness her powerlessness. Filled with inward loathing, she listened a bit longer, curious what guilty-neighbor-like excuse this deplorable scoundrel might contrive.

"Please, listen to this message..."

I am. Get on with it.

"I know I don't deserve your forgiveness," he began. "And even if I never see you again, I need you to know that you are not just a mark to me. You are not. Maybe that's how it started, but you have changed the whole way I see my life. And I need you to know that.

I have spent years lying, Meryl. And it was easy. But not with you. I want to be honest with you for as long as you'll let me if you'll let me. My name isn't Roy Hawkins. I'm not a recovering alcoholic. I'm not from New York City, and I'm not an Orthodox Protestant. I grew up in a trailer park in Albany. My dad was a drunk, and I ran away from home when I was nineteen. I made friends with a man who helped me start up the con, and I've been doing it ever since. I've hurt a lot of people from all over the country, and if anyone deserves your love, it isn't me. But I feel it. I feel it for *you*. And I haven't felt this for anyone, ever. It scares the shit out of me, Meryl. But I don't want to leave without seeing you one more time. Without some kind of closure. I'm at the place where we had our first kiss. I know by telling you this, I'm putting myself at risk of being arrested, but I don't care. I'd give it all up. Everything. I don't want money. I don't want adventure. I don't want to be a bandit. I don't want anyone else, Meryl. Just you."

Beep!

Meryl set down her phone and plucked a tissue from the box. Somehow a few more tears squeezed out the corners of her swollen eyelids.

A soft rapping came at the bedroom door. Meryl lifted her head and wiped her face clean of evidence. Her mother's head poked through the slim opening in the door, revealing solicitous eyes and a sympathetic frown as she asked her daughter if she was okay. Meryl sniffed and wiped her nose with the back of her hand. Her glance rose and fell. Her mother opened the door and stepped into the room, gently sealing the door behind her with both hands before joining Meryl on the edge of the bed. She peered around the room for a space, then said kindly: "Ronnie's been calling the house, asking for you. He really likes you, that boy."

Meryl wiped the hair from her face and shrugged in a stoop.

"You know," her mom continued. "You should consider yourself lucky. Some girls have a hard enough time finding one gentleman caller, let alone two."

Meryl rolled her eyes and fluffed her blanket. "Mom...stop."

Her mother patted her thigh softly. "I know. I know. It's none of my business. But I can see you're hurting, sweetie. I don't know what he might have done to you to have you in this sort. He doesn't seem like the type to be physical with a woman." She leaned a little closer. "He wasn't physical with you, was he?"

Meryl wiped her sandpaper eyes and shook her head.

"That's good," whispered her mother. Another silence prevailed. The two absently watched the television. Meryl fiddled tiredly with the comforter. Presently, her mother recommenced: "You know, dear...No man is perfect. Not even your father. Before you were born, your father was a bit of a wild man. A drinker. A gambler...he had one hell of a mouth on him, too. My father hated the man. He was never pushy with me, but that didn't mean I was never put at risk by his company. And there were times, many times, that I doubted whether he was the one for me. The real question was, did I love this man enough to help him change the things I could and accept the things I could not? I had to make that choice. And I would like to think I made the right one. After all, his bravery is what gave us this house, this life. And it was his tenderness that provided me with the most beautiful daughter I could have ever asked for."

A goofy smile hooked upward on Meryl's face.

"We all have to make that choice at some point in our lives, sweetie," her mother concluded. "And if you decide that the fight is not worth it, well, then maybe you should let yourself be open to someone who is."

She leaned in and pecked Meryl's forehead.

The gesture filled Meryl with comfort, hard-pressed as she was to show it. She was advised to think it over and her mother left the room, closing the door quietly behind her.

Meryl sat pensively for a minute, letting her mother's words resonate within. When ready, she reached for her phone and scrolled to Ronnie's number. She pressed the dial button and lifted the phone to her ear.

Ronnie answered the call shortly after the first ring. "Hey, Meryl. How are ya?"

"Hey, Ronnie," she said. "I was wondering if you had a minute to talk..."

THE COROLLA CREPT TO a park behind the Charger at the entrance to Oak Bluff. Joey cut the engine and yanked the key. He let out a long breath and shook off the less than passionate goodbye received from Joyce after he had dropped her back at home and used the bolt cutters in her garage to free them of their remaining shackles. The woman had been in no mood for exoneration, understandably, but Joey would have kindly forfeited absolution in exchange for one of those fervid 'goodbye forever' kisses that often climaxed to the accompaniment of a string orchestra on the silver screen. Alas, the time to wallow over the past had run its course. If the team was going to have any hope of a future, all that mattered was the present.

Joey exited the car and approached the Charger. He saw it was empty. He surveyed the enveloping dark for Mitch and Laura. Only the faint whoosh of the ocean in the distance and the throaty chirps of crickets attended his roll call. He stuffed his hands in his pockets, stooped his head to mitigate the chilled breeze sweeping through the reserve, and started briskly down the trail toward the forthcoming wooded area, where he imagined the rest of the team were waiting out of sight.

As Joey arrived at the mouth of the forest, there was an alarming succession of snapping twigs to his right. He freed his hands from his pockets and cocked his two fists like an Irish bare-knuckle boxer. Squinting through the blackness to identify the enemy, Joey spotted a furry white stripe wiggling its way through a web of underbrush. More twigs snapped and gave way under the nocturnal critter's scampering paws. The perpetrator, a portly and aloof stinkpot, confidently emerged from the underbrush onto the dirt pathway where Joey stood, heedless to the looming fist-toting human as it sauntered coolly in the direction from which Joey had arrived. Joey retreated from the malodorous beast one careful step at a time, offering no swift movements that could be misconstrued as antagonism.

Behind him, he felt two inches of hard metal dig into his spinal column. A familiar gritty voice warned him: "Don't try nothing stupid."

Sebastian.

The little Robertson had awoken from his Tammy-inflicted bat nap and didn't sound very happy about the prescribed sedative. How he had tracked Joey down was anyone's guess. Regardless, this new turn of events undoubtedly and grossly impeded Joey's whole 'having a future' thing.

Suddenly, getting sprayed by a skunk didn't seem so terrible of a destiny.

Sebastian snarled: "Now turn around. *Slow.*"

Joey obliged, and nearly gagged at the sight of the wounds bubbling over the younger Robertson's once charming visage.

In place of the handsome features that reigned, remained a grotesque perversion of flesh that would have made Frankenstein's monster feel as if he wasn't doing so bad in life. His pulsing, manic glower, quivered with fervent rage, belying his revolting and moribund countenance, as he proudly declared with an incidental spray of blood spittle: "Gotcha, bitch!"

He knocked Joey across the side of the face with the butt of the pistol. The sting was instant. A dull throbbing, reminiscent of the right hook he took to the jaw back at the construction site, lingered. Joey folded and clutched at the pain. Sebastian's callus palm squeezed Joey's neck and toted him deeper into the forest.

After approximately ten minutes, the whiff of sour, salty air started to overpower the scent of stone and pine. The crashing of waves noticeably intensified.

Sebastian broke the silence that had bound them at length: "You fucking bandits. You just don't quit, do you?"

Joey grinned. The dried wound on his bottom lip cracked open and he tasted blood. "What can I say?" he muttered tiredly. "Goonies never say die."

Sebastian was mildly entertained by the nostalgic reference. "Maybe not. But *saying* it and *doing* it are two *very* different things."

As the throng of forest dissipated, the bluff expanded to a dirt clearing riddled with patch grass and weeds. No longer concealed by the summit of the tree tops, constellations dazzled aloft in a cosmic panorama. Joey recognized Mitch and Laura, shoulder to shoulder at the bluff's rocky edge. Laura held a gun in her hand. Initially, Joey was inundated with hope, assuming the team had once again come to his rescue at his most dire of moments. Then it became clear that Laura wasn't holding a gun *next* to Mitch; she was holding a gun *at* Mitch. All too quickly, events previously veiled in obscurity sharpened into focus: how Sebastian found them, why Laura and Mitch weren't waiting by the Charger, and why Joey had yet to be shot.

Joey looked to Mitch for direction. His mentor projected a helpless gaze that begged his protege's forgiveness. Next, he looked to

Laura, who hardly returned his glance before she regarded Sebastian with an all-too-familiar expression of pseudo-endearment. Joey had seen the look before. It was a factory setting that Laura would dispense with impunity when she knew she was about to get her way.

"She's a looker, ain't she?" swooned Sebastian. He nudged Joey forward.

"Yeah, and loyal, too," Joey grunted. He spat out the vile taste that lined the walls of his mouth.

As the four congregated at the edge of the bluff, Joey glowered wordlessly at his turncoat associate. She offered no explanation, and had the temerity to crack a sideways grin at him as if to say to the fellow bandit: *Sorry, bud. Them's the breaks.*

"Real great, Laura," muttered Joey. He was too emotionally exhausted to thrust weight into his words. "You're a real gem."

Her triumphant grin held as she told him it was only business.

"Yeah, the business of being a grade-A cunt," Joey rejoined.

Sebastian spun him around to face the pistol barrel.

"Enough," ordered Sebastian. "Close your eyes, Laura. You won't want to see this..."

A gunshot rang out into the open night. For the second time that evening, Joey had been prepared to meet his maker. And yet, for the second time that evening, he did not. To Joey's astonishment, the aforementioned bullet had been delivered not from Sebastian's firearm, but from a position, if Joey's hearing had served him correctly, near the mouth of the forest. The slug had been aptly addressed for the gunman, and Joey witnessed its intended consequence as Sebastian's vacant remains collapsed at his feet.

Stunned, and allotted no time for supposition, Joey whirled and seized Laura's forearm just as her hitherto sealed eyelids started to peel open. Her peaceable tranquility immediately faltered to a rushing tide of boundless fear. Joey crushed bone and twisted her wrist. Her grip splayed accordingly. The gun dropped to the scraggy ground. Joey's foot cocked and drove into Laura's midsection. She tumbled backward with a panicked gasp and reached out for a hand that wouldn't come. Her balance gave way and she disappeared off the edge of the bluff. The faintest hint of a terrible scream was carried away with the wind and all that remained were the resounding crash of waves splitting against the jagged rocks on the shore a hundred feet below.

Mitch tapped Joey's shoulder, and pointed to the mouth of the forest. A young man in a brown Sheriff's Department uniform approached in hasty strides, holstering his firearm. Joey recognized the stranger as the officer who had helped the Sheriff bust up their house party.

"Holy shit," gasped Mitch incredulously. "It's Ronnie."

Behind the deputy followed Meryl. She was wearing gray sweatpants and a pajama top. The breeze blew her untamed hair across her face. She brushed it away and smiled at Mitch with tears in her eyes. Mitch was speechless, stunned, and grinning like only a dope in love ever could. Joey hoped to see Joyce appear through the trees, coming for him like Meryl had come for Mitch, but she did not.

Ronnie remained steely and authoritative upon his arrival. He asked if anyone else was in the vicinity. Mitch told him there wasn't. "All right, then," Ronnie replied. "You all stay put while I call this in." He set a gentle hand on Meryl's arm before walking ten feet and engaging his intercom.

Mitch stepped cautiously toward Meryl. "You came," he said under a spell. "You got my message?"

Meryl nodded.

"Does Ronnie know about who we are?"

Meryl shook her head.

Mitch processed her response's implications and said: "So...does this mean..."

"What it *means*," interjected Meryl, "is that I believe you when you say your feelings toward me are honest. I understand that. But I also know that your reason for pursuing me in the first place was sneaky, self-serving, and evil. *You* need to understand that. Trusting you is difficult. Not having you is worse. I called Ronnie to come with me because, well, I wasn't sure how this was going to go."

Joey raised his hands to the sky. "Thank God you did, Meryl! Thank that motherfucker!"

"Don't *ever* say that, that's horrible," said Meryl. She hurled a reproachful glare. "You're no angel, either, Sean."

Joey stooped hangdoggedly. "I know...I'm sorry. God's awesome."

Mitch stepped closer so he and Meryl were toe to toe. He remained thusly, searching her eyes. "So...how does this go?"

She lowered her gaze and said: "I don't think I can see Roy anymore..."

Mitch tightened like wet concrete on a hot day.

"*But*..." she added. "I think I could give Mitch a shot."

Color exploded across Joey's mentor's cheeks and his lips cautiously curled north.

"But *Mitch*," she warned with a stern finger and a beaming adoration. "And *only* Mitch."

Mitch pressed his lips to hers, and she returned his kiss. At the embrace's conclusion, he turned to Joey with a life in his eyes unseen before tonight. "What do you think, Jo? Feel like parking for a bit?"

Joey assented forthwith, charmed by the effervescent elixir of requited love. "You're the mentor, right?"

Presently, Ronnie reconvened with the group. "The Sheriff is on his way," he averred outchestedly. He spotted the lacing of Meryl and Mitch's hands and attempted in vain to stifle his antipathy. "I'm going to need you both to come back to the station for questioning. Let's head back to the car, and I'll get your statements."

The four of them started toward the mouth of the forest. Mitch and Meryl walked ahead. Ronnie and Joey followed behind. "Bet you weren't expecting to run into all that, now were you?" Joey asked the deputy as they strode.

Ronnie kicked a stone and shook his head slightly as he adjusted the holster belt slipping down his narrow waist. "She called me and asked me to take her to the bluff," he recounted with a musing grin. "I thought she was bringing me out here to make out..."

Joey threw back his head and laughed heartily toward the stars.

Chapter Twenty Seven

Now that the adrenaline coursing through Joey's bloodstream since he backed into Sebastian's pistol was starting to subside, there came an onset of a new type of fear, the dread that he had ultimately reached the final destination at the end of his long road to perdition. Separated from Mitch and placed in a small interrogation room, Joey braced the cumulative sense of encroaching walls. Memories of Martydale resurfaced. And this time, Joey hadn't just gotten into a silly bar fight with some meat-head biker; he had sent Laura off the side of a cliff to her death. He could face life in prison if prosecuted, maybe less on a manslaughter rap. Even still, he had no regrets for his actions other than his swinging boot didn't make it up to Laura's haughty chin.

The interrogation room door opened, and a slender man, formally dressed and slightly older than Joey, entered with a file folder under his arm and an FBI identification badge clipped to his breast pocket. The name on it read: Hank McAllester.

Joey swallowed. He was expecting Deputy Ronnie, or maybe the Sheriff, but not the FBI.

The agent waited until he was seated across from Joey before giving his presence any validation. And when the agent's gaze finally leveled, his dark eyes were self-assured and penetrating. "How are you, Mr...Harris?" he asked. He let the last name hang in the air almost mockingly as he sat back in his chair and crossed one leg at the knee.

"It's been a pretty wild night," answered Joey pitiably. He looked for signs that Meryl might have revealed more to the law than she had originally led on but failed to penetrate the stone-cold visage mirroring his regard.

"I'm Agent McAllester with the FBI," the equivocal agent declared. "Our department will be taking over this case. I've been looking over your statement. I'd say a wild night would be an understatement. You said that Sylvester Robertson and his son Sebastian came and took you from your home early this morning?"

"Yes, sir."

"Only you?"

Joey answered in the affirmative, half for Joyce's benefit and half for his own.

"Are you aware that Sylvester Robertson is currently under investigation by the FBI?"

"No, sir," answered Joey. This response wasn't *completely* a lie. He had only found out about Robertson's crime boss alter ego a few hours ago. *Where the hell were you when I was getting the shit kicked out of me back in Sandy Acres?* he wanted to ask.

"And you have no idea why these men may have wanted to harm you?"

"No idea," said Joey.

"Do you have, or have you ever had, relations with his daughter, Angela Robertson?"

Joey's throat clamped shut. His mouth grew dry and chalky, heartbeat slapping breastbone. "Can I get a water?" he asked.

"Glass or bottle?" asked McAllester with an inordinately servile inflection.

"Bottle is fine," said Joey.

McAllester chuckled malignantly under his breath. "It was a joke. You aren't getting shit. Why don't I just talk instead? You *do* know Angie Robertson. You were the best man at her wedding. Well, not *you* you, but the 'you' you were pretending to be so you and your team could defraud the Robertsons out of hundreds of thousands of dollars. Roger, I believe, was the name."

The agent cracked a cocky smirk, and Joey's palms secreted oil.

"I think I'd like to talk to a lawyer," murmured Joey with a downcast gaze.

"I'm sure you would," scoffed McAllester. "But why don't I save you the trouble? In legal terms: you are *fucked*. When Angie finds out that you were involved with the death of her father and brother, she will no doubt press charges. And with the high profile nature of such a news-worthy case, who knows who will see you on TV and come running to claim their pound of flesh? My guess is you'll be nothing but dry *bone* by the time all the folks you've ever swindled are done with you." Agent McAllester glared narrowly into Joey's eyes, wanting his words to resonate. And they did. Like a nail in the coffin. "You'll be looking at some serious jail time," McAllester continued. "How many years? I can't say for sure. That depends on your lawyer and how tightly the prosecution delivers their case. But it will be years. Years, and years, and *years*...that is unless you want to make a deal."

Suddenly Joey was at a poker table being pushed all in, and he didn't have a hand on which to stand. Conceding to his defeat, he slumped in his seat and breathed deeply, the inhale strained from a seemingly airless room.

"Okay..." Joey winced. "I'm listening."

IN THE HOUR OR SO THAT Mitch had been sitting in the small interview room, his thoughts were all he had for company. That, and the camera bolted to the top left corner of the close-quartered unit. The red light glowed just above the lens to let him know someone was watching. He didn't think about it. Mainly, his thoughts were of Meryl. He wondered if he would get to live up to his promise to her or if his past mistakes would squander his opportunity at a real future.

His head lifted as the Sheriff entered the room and closed the door behind him. Mitch wasn't sure if the Sheriff's solemn and yonder expression was something to be concerned about or if it was just a rational reaction to a grim situation. The Sheriff rested a brown-slacked haunch on the table's edge, removed his cattleman, and pensively set it down by his thigh. After what seemed to Mitch like interminable wordlessness, the Sheriff looked up at him with heavy eyes that engendered stomach-wrenching guilt.

"So...from what I can gather from Ronnie's report," he began wearily. "You and Meryl had something of an argument, and you had called her to meet you at the bluff. She had asked Ronnie to accompany her, and when they arrived, they saw you held at gunpoint by this Robertson fellow. My deputy said he fired off the shot that killed the gunman just in time. Another second, it would have been you who took the bullet..." Sheriff paused and sighed at length. "I don't know who these Robertsons were, but the same shell casings from the .22 he had on you were found at a murder scene in a motel room near the highway. They also found the casings in Sandy Acres at a junkyard owned by my friend Arnold; he was one of the people killed in this murder spree. I believe you two had some words when we came into the hardware store."

Mitch nodded that he recalled the encounter.

The Sheriff stared at the pale wall and continued: "Being a man of the law, I don't much believe in coincidences. In fact, I would go as far as saying there are no such thing. And Arnold was pretty certain that he had seen you dropping off a Porsche to park at his yard. That Porsche was found in Oak County. And now he's been murdered by the same man who had you at gunpoint..." His eyes drifted back to

Mitch. "So, I have to ask you, Roy...Is there something you want to tell me?"

Mitch weakened under the Sheriff's awaiting gaze. He felt old, beaten, and tired. There was no more strength to continue the lies, no motivation or logic. He opened his mouth to speak. As he did, the door to the interview room opened, and a man on the younger side of middle age entered the room. He was medium height, slender build, and the haircut combined with the FBI identification clipped to his navy blue button-down breast pocket told Mitch he was in the presence of high authority.

"Sheriff?" the agent interjected respectfully. "I'm ready."

"Great," said the Sheriff. He grunted as he shifted his weight off the table. He eyed Mitch and motioned to the young man. "This is Agent Hank McAllester with the FBI. He will be taking over this case." The Sheriff's eyes softened despite his magisterially grisly countenance. "Good luck, son..."

Mitch's gaze, and much of his hope, followed the Sheriff out the door.

The agent folded rigidly into the opposing chair and placed the file folder on the desk. He appraised Mitch and crossed one leg. "How are you, Roy?"

"A little in the dark right now," said Mitch politely.

Agent McAllester didn't seem to appreciate Mitch's babe-in-the-woods reply. "Well, let me go ahead and brighten things up for you," he offered curtly. "For the last ten years, you've been defrauding families out of wedding gifts, going from town to town, and running a con game on an assortment of rich, unsought women. Unfortunately, your last target, one Angie Robertson, had a father heavily involved in organized crime. He left a trail of dead bodies trying to track you down. You're lucky to be alive."

Agent McAllester might have been right, but Mitch didn't feel so lucky.

The fed continued: "I just came from speaking with your partner Sean. So, if you were thinking of denying everything, don't. Mr. *Harris* already made a deal."

Mitch refused to believe it. Laura's betrayal was at least digestible. But not Joey. Never Joey.

McAllester intensified. "I suggest you get on board with him."

"What deal?" Mitch croaked.

McAllester opened his file folder and removed a sheet of paper that looked similar to a job application. "The deal is this," he drew out. "Instead of you and your partner being charged and sent to jail for fraud, you can sign these papers that explain you were a civilian undercover employed by myself to weed out the Robertsons."

McAllester's words were like cool water on a fresh burn. Mitch had the urge to break out in laughter but wisely abstained. "You mean like a sting operation?"

Agent McAllester's mouth twitched a hint of a grin. "Just like in the movies."

As beautiful as the proposition appeared, Mitch was weary to accept. He glanced up at the camera. The red light was no longer glowing.

"You can trust me," the agent avowed.

Mitch searched McAllester's calculated gaze. "Why are you doing this?" he asked.

McAllester bit his lip as if weighing the truth against his reservations. "I could say that it would be good for my job if the people who caught the Robertsons were under my command, that it was me who orchestrated the entire operation. I could say that your testimony is paramount to this investigation, and without it, we might not get to look deeper into StrongBolt's financial records. But you look like the kind of 'no-bullshit' guy who appreciates a straight shooter. Maybe that's why the Sheriff likes you. So, I'll tell you...My father was in the oil business. I never knew him. My mom had me out of wedlock; from what I hear, my father wasn't the type to settle down. But before he and my mother met, he was kidnapped by some bandits who wanted the newly constructed pipeline he was working on, one that would bring oil from the U.S. into Mexico, shut down. It was big news. Anyway, the kidnappers ended up hiding out in Oak County, and it was the Sheriff who rescued my dad from his captors. Saved his life. So, when it comes down to it: I owe the Sheriff a favor. And I am a man of honor. Even if you aren't. So, what do you think, Roy? Play ball?"

Mitch was still waiting for the axe to drop. "Do you have a pen?"

The hint of a grin returned on McAllester's steely visage, and a short breath escaped through flaring nostrils. "All in good time."

He stood, placed the job application back in the file folder, and closed the file. He knocked the table's edge with his knuckle and gave Mitch one final shot across the bow. "Sheriff thinks you make a good match for his daughter. Don't prove him wrong."

Chapter Twenty Eight

"Breaking news today. This one is a strange one. A murder spree in California that left seven people dead, three of them being the gunmen. Owner of the nationwide construction conglomerate StrongBolt, one of the gunmen, Sylvester Robertson, was found dead today in the small southwestern town of Sandy Acres. His son, Sebastian Robertson, was shot by police in a quick decision stand-off at Oak Bluff in Oak County after holding two undercover FBI informants hostage. For their safety, the names of the informants have not been disclosed. Robertson had been under investigation as the suspected kingpin of a longstanding underground crime organization where he was known under the code name The Tyrant.

"The previous day, Robertson and his son killed four people spanning from Sandy Acres and Oak County. The motive behind these killings is still unknown. A junkyard operator, a young bartender, and two of the bar's patrons were among the dead. Police suspect there could be more. An investigation has now begun into the books of StrongBolt and the Robertson estate to determine how much, if any, illegal funds were filtered through the company."

"This is a bad time for the shareholders of StrongBolt."

"At a time like this, your heart goes out to the families of the deceased in what was just a senseless, brutal crime."

"And a big hand for the FBI for finally bringing this guy down. I heard this Tyrant guy was responsible for that kidnapping that made headlines some years back. Remember? Like thirty-something years ago? Some Oil Tycoon?"

McAllester clicked off the radio. The car went silent; his mind, however, was anything but.

Hugging the corner onto Lockstep Street, he spotted his house third from the end of the road. Despite expecting to be filled with comfort and warmth, he felt only the opposite: a black stain blotching his insides, a carbonaceous tar caked an inch thick against his now frayed sense of morality.

For the first time in his career, McAllester bent the law to suit his ulterior motives. Granted, it had worked perfectly; Assistant Deputy Director Martin was pleased with the investigation results and reverently declared McAllester's spur-of-the-moment promotion to ADD in the field office before his peers. Over the exalting applause, he wondered how long it would be until the truth exploded in his face. Agent Quinn was the only person who knew enough to object to the official story, and Quinn wasn't the type to blow the whistle. Hell, he was barely the type to wear clean underwear each day. Besides, after all their traveling, Quinn decided to use up some vacation days and stayed back in Cedar Falls for some R & R. McAllester couldn't imagine what was so special about Cedar Falls that Quinn wanted to spend any more time there than was necessary. Whatever the reason, McAllester took the happenstance as a blessing and didn't ask any questions.

He pulled the Buick into the driveway and stepped into the early evening air. Cool dampness splashed his face, a sensation sorely missed during his stint in the dry south. He sauntered along the pot-lit walkway and quickly shuffled up the front steps. The door opened before he had the key in the lock. Julia stood at the threshold in a crinkled shirt and slacks, one hand at her side, the other leaning against the stud. She offered him a welcoming smirk. Running up the rear was Jeanine. Her tiny footsteps pounded over the hardwood floor. "Daddy!" she screamed. "You're home!"

McAllester crouched down and let his little girl throw her arms around his neck. Suddenly, everything was right in the world. Though she was getting too big to be carried, McAllester made the exception tonight and lifted Jeanine in his arm.

He looked into his wife's gleaming eyes and planted a kiss. "Daddy's home," he said to her softly as he pulled away.

She stared at him expectantly, electric ebullience expanding her face. "So?"

Unable to repress his smile, he chuckled under his breath. "Yeah, I got it. You're looking at Assistant Deputy Director Hank McAllester. Can you believe it?"

Elation burned Julia's cheeks. She gasped with gleeful stupefaction. As a husband, especially a cop husband, these were the looks you took a mental snapshot of so you could refer to them on those nights you got chewed out for never being home, missing a play or parent/teacher interview, or being distant at the dinner table and failing to communicate. His wife pushed up on the balls of her bare feet and closed her eyes as her lips pressed his a second time. He inhaled the soft combination of her richly scented perfume and the coconut moisturizer she applied habitually in the evenings. A third aroma wafted through the door: the roast chicken cooking in the oven. "I'm so proud of you, babe," Julia said upon receding her heels. "Maybe we can afford that pool in the backyard now. You know...for Jeanine."

McAllester followed Julia into the front foyer and locked the deadbolt behind him. He squatted and let Jeanine to her feet. The spunky nine-year-old whirled and made a run for the television room. He rose and grinned at Julia with his eyes. "Jeanine...right."

While Julia continued preparing dinner and setting the table, McAllester went to the upstairs bathroom and took a long, hot shower, as scalding as he could stand it. While the steam vapor encircled his naked body, McAllester stood under the showerhead and let the water drizzle off his crown. He watched the droplets free fall from the soaked tips of his bangs into the swirling drain at the head of his feet. He was happy to be back in his home shower where the water pressure remained consistent and full-bodied; few things in life are as uncertain as the quality of a motel shower. And yet, he could not enjoy the home shower experience as wholeheartedly as he would have liked. Paranoia chewed at his conscious like a Rottweiler gnawing grizzly fat off a bone.

Someone will find out. Someone will catch you.

McAllester wiped the stream of water from his face and rubbed his eyes. Another more tender voice overpowered the shrewish murmurs of condemnation pinballing through his skull. It was Julia's voice, saying as sweetly as an angel in a dream: *I'm so proud of you, babe.*

Both voices disappeared. The hiss of the showerhead returned. McAllester stood under the spray with a newfound swelling of illumination. In that instant, he concluded that if he had done wrong, he had done it in the name of love and family. And while that particular line was nothing new, nothing that the ears in the courtroom pews had not heard pled from sundry frightened convicts on their way out of the courtroom, it endued McAllester with enough consonance to provisionally settle his anxieties. The only sound in his ear for the rest of the shower was the pattering of water pellets as they ricocheted off the shower curtain and joined the bubbling stream trickling down the drain.

After dinner, the home-cooked meal being a nice change from the week of eat-when-and-what-you-can in the Crown Vic, he helped Julia with the dishes. At the same time, Neil Young's *'Heart of Gold'* played at low volume on the stereo in the adjacent room and a scented vanilla candle burned on the ajar kitchen window sill. Jeanine lay on the couch in the television room under a blanket, watching her before-bed cartoons.

After Julia had put Jeanine to sleep, McAllester made love to his wife under the silk sheets of their marital bed, slowly and with great compassion. When it was over, Julia rested her head on McAllester's smooth, bare chest and threw her arm across him. She fell asleep to the slow rhythm of his breath.

It was good to be home.

THE FULL MOON BEAMED chalky light through the overhead skylight, transforming Angie and Quinn on the bed into thick geometric shadows and pale blue fragments. As her broad upper half convulsed with the exertion of tears, Quinn couldn't help but silently marvel at how the night's luminescence highlighted each of Angie's imperfections in such a way that was romantic, if not beautiful in its own right.

She sniffled and sobbed into his neck folds, arms wrapped around him so tightly that if it had been under any other circumstance, Quinn would have demanded that he be let loose and allowed to breathe. But Angie needed the cry more than Quinn needed the oxygen, so he gallantly inhibited his fleeting suffocation.

Outside Angie's desperate sobs and wailing moans deflecting a spectral reverberation off high ceilings, the Robertson mansion was dark and dolorous. A part of Quinn felt wrong for being there, yet a part of him knew there was nowhere else in the world he would rather be. Someone needed to tend to this sweet, broken woman whose family was now deceased due to a sting operation that played an innocent civilian as the patsy. Quinn felt as rotten as a three-day-old apple core for his part in it all. His only solace was that he wasn't aware of what was happening. In a way, McAllester had played Quinn for quite the patsy as well. Silently, the rage was bubbling and rising in Quinn's belly despite the soft reassurances he whispered into Angie's ear while rubbing gingerly on the flat of her back.

"It can't be true," she said as she pulled away from Quinn's dampened collar and wiped her nose with a fistful of tissues from the box of Kleenex resting at her varicose knees. "Sebastian would never kill Daddy. Why? Why would he do that?"

Quinn had no heart to tell her what the news reports omitted, that based on the testimony the civilian informants provided McAllester, Sebastian was under the impression that it was Daddy who set up the mob hit on his wife all those years ago.

"He wouldn't," Angie went on uninterrupted. "Whoever this informant is—rat, more like it—he has got it all wrong. Daddy is not a drug dealer. Whoever this Tyrant is, he's not Daddy!"

Quinn rubbed her shoulder. "We'll figure this out. Things are going to get better."

There was a flicker of softness for Quinn in Angie's glossy eyes before her face soured and twisted, and she burst into tears.

"There, there," whispered Quinn. He patiently guided her head back to his neck.

She continued to cry and moan at length, and when she had tired, she lifted her head—curls draped messily over her full, rosy cheeks slicked with tears. Quinn withheld the urge to wrap his lips against Angie's quivering mouth, though the temptation was strong, torturous.

"If they find out that Daddy was using his business to launder drug money, they could take the house! I'll be homeless!"

She buried her head in Quinn's neck and bawled.

At that moment, Quinn hated McAllester with all his heart. He had destroyed an innocent life for no other reason than his latent greed and selfishness. Quinn wondered if this reality had crossed the task force leader's mind as he accepted his new promotion to ADD. Probably not. He likely went home, played with his kid, ate a nice dinner, and fucked his wife with no regard whatsoever for the irreparable damage he had imposed on poor Angie. Maybe the world wouldn't care about Angie's woes because she wasn't so easy on the eyes and came from a bad family, but Quinn did. And he wasn't going to let her be forgotten. Not by McAllester. Not by anybody.

"Angie..." Quinn started. He let his address linger as if searching blindly for someone in a pitch-black room. "What would you say if I told you that your missing husband was really an informant for the FBI? The informant the news is saying blew the whistle on your father?"

Her sobs ceased momentarily, and her head slowly rose from Quinn's puddled collar. Red and swollen eyes locked onto Quinn's gaze with tractor-beam precision. "Clyde was the informant?"

Quinn gave a short, solemn nod.

Angie regarded Quinn suspiciously as if he exuded some horrible stench. "How do you know that? How *could* you know that?"

Quinn looked away, ashamed. "Angie, I work for the FBI...But I swear to you, I had no idea about what they had done to you. No one did. No one except for Clyde and one sneaky agent named McAllester. They planned it all. Him leaving you was a way to get your father out into the open, have him slip up, and incriminate himself. It was entrapment, really. How did they expect the man not to want to find the bastard who swindled his only daughter? But Angie, the man responsible got a promotion for it. A *promotion*."

Angie gaped as if she had been slapped in the face. She peered toward her stuffed animals on the shelves, washed in twilight. Blank button stares and aghast expressions reflected her consternation.

The room fell as soundless as the house around it.

"What would I say?" repeated Angie at length, gaze averted and dismal. "I'd say I'd like to kill them." Her entire body shuddered. Her lips shriveled into a scowl. She leered into Quinn's eyes with cold certainty. "I would kill them all."

Quinn pressed his lips gently upon her forehead. "I could help you," he whispered. "I could help make that happen."

She searched Quinn's vigilant gaze with a burning intensity, and released an exhale that resembled a whimper. Her lips balled over his and she kissed him passionately.

Epilogue

Meryl looked out across the reception hall from her center chair at the head table, graciously absorbing the array of white-clothed, candle-lit islands encircled by what felt like the entirety of Oak County's modest aggregation. Tonight, the rural community had arrived in their most elegant formal wear to celebrate her long-anticipated day of marriage. The evening's guest list included the entire Sheriff's Department, the hardware store, Meryl's new gym co-workers and her old colleagues from the call center, as well as the Assistant Deputy Director of the FBI and his family, and myriad other cousins, uncles, aunts, and shop owners who had closed their businesses early to make it to the church in time for the ceremony.

Betty, Meryl's longtime best friend, sat beside Meryl as the maid of honor. She had driven in from San Francisco and was at the church in her pink bridesmaid dress at the stroke of four p.m. for pre-ceremony pictures. With her arrived her husband Mark. He was a tall man with broad shoulders and a square jaw, classically handsome by all accounts. He worked at an advertising agency and recently received a raise that allowed Betty to quit her job so she could take care of the house and their infant son who was staying with his grandparents this evening. Meryl was happy for her old friend, knowing that being a housewife and present mother was all Betty ever wanted.

Betty was astonished at Meryl's transformation, both physically and metaphysically. The last time they had seen each other, Meryl was a size twenty-two and a bit of a mope. Now, she was a size twelve and teemed with zeal and charm. When Betty inquired to Meryl's secret, she explained that her gym job and personal fitness commitment were a big factor in her transformation. When some of the more handsome and muscular gym members approached her on the street, the jealous look in Mitch's eye didn't hurt her cause either. Even with a ring on her finger, Mitch was not unsusceptible to territorial anxieties. Of course, he'd try to subvert such insecurities, but her now-husband's skills of deception had since dwindled in the two years they had been together, and the one year they had been engaged to be married.

Meryl also had another reason to keep active and fit. A secret reason. And it had to remain a secret at least until a few weeks after the wedding. She had let Mitch in on the secret, as, having an equal part in the secret's creation, she felt it pertinent to apprise him of the situation. He was overjoyed at the news. But the Sheriff and extended family would have to wait, less reveal to the world that she and Mitch had not been as Protestant as they protested.

Meryl's moral standing on the use and necessity of lies in the weeks following her and Mitch's little secret had substantially mollified, if not entirely inverted. Her newfound wisdom on the topic grew ever more incandescent after her and Mitch's first wedding ceremony, which took place that afternoon in a small civil office with only a judge, the newlyweds, and her parents as witnesses. The wedding of Meryl and Mitch. The officially documented union. Then, for the rest of Oak County and her parents again, she married Roy, who *wasn't* an ex-con man and an FBI informant under identity protection.

"Hey," said Mitch beside her. He looked positively charming in his tailored penguin suit. "You know what I was just thinking?"

"What?"

"Now that we've tied the knot, we can finally stop lying about having sex."

Meryl chuckled lightly. "I was thinking that, too."

Mitch's best man sat beside him at the table and leaned in closer with a surreptitious grin. "So, are you guys going to tell everyone about the child Mitch shot into you?" Joey's grin broadened, carving out a dimple on the left of his face.

Meryl gasped and slapped Mitch in the arm. "You told?"

"Had to," said Mitch without compunction.

"I'm going to be an uncle!" Joey squeaked. Luckily, the ambiance of jovial chatter and clinks of cutlery against porcelain dinnerware stifled his enthusiastic proclamation from the ears of the other guests.

A succession of resounding falsetto tones pervaded through the reception hall. Meryl regarded the podium near the dance floor, where her father, the recently retired Sheriff, appeared prepared to speak. Tonight, he wore a black cattleman and black collared shirt, which he declared was to mourn the loss of his baby girl. Snug inside his belt holster was the prize six-shooter from the display case in their study.

"Attention, please. Attention, please," he announced into the microphone.

Oh, here we go, thought Meryl.

The chatter subsided. At the call center table, Chad yelled over the permeating silence: "Anything for you, Sheriff!"

Guests tittered lightly. The Sheriff smiled and tipped his cattleman with a wink to the distal heckler. "Now, now," her father said with a raised palm. "I appreciate the sentiment, but it's been a whole year since I retired. However, we do have the new Sheriff here tonight, keeping us all safe. Thank you, Sheriff Mayflower."

Sheriff extended his arm to Ronnie, who rightfully resided at the family table with Meryl's parents. The crowd returned polite applause in acknowledgment of their new peacekeeper. Ronnie remained authoritative and tried to act like he didn't love the attention.

Sheriff sipped his red wine, applying a fresh coat to the purple tinge accumulating over his lips. "As the father of the bride, I would like to say a few words. Over the last couple of years, I have watched my daughter flourish. She's a motivated, professional young woman with the world at her fingertips. I can't overstate how proud I am of everything she has become. And I know that the man sitting beside her tonight, the groom, one Roy Hawkins, has had a great deal to do with that. When I first met the young man, I will admit, I wasn't very sure about him. But since then, I have come to know the *real* Roy. He is a man of duty, a man of honor. And today, I am proud to be able to call him 'son.'"

Glasses raised high. Some, like Meryl, fingered tears from their eyes.

"Shoot your gun off!" Chad yelled from the fringe.

Sheriff shook his head lightheartedly. "Someone take the wine away from that boy. Sheriff Mayflower, maybe you want to check his ID."

Additional gaiety eddied the room.

"And now, I would like to call up the best man to say a few words." Her father extended a welcoming arm to Joey. He gave Meryl a tender wink and nod on his saunter back to the family table. He and Mitch also shared a brief but meaningful glance.

Joey slid back his chair and stood from the head table.

"Keep it light, Jo," warned Mitch. "The FBI is in the building."

Joey squeezed Mitch's shoulder, lurched, and whispered in his mentor's ear: "Fuck the police."

Mitch craned his neck and frowned.

"I'm kidding," chuckled Joey. He tapped Mitch's collarbone reassuringly. "Love the police. Love them."

The room hushed as Joey arrived at the podium. "Thank you, Sheriff," he said into the microphone. "You are a legend in your own time."

Meryl's father raised his glass as a show of gratitude.

Joey bowed his head respectfully, looked out at the crowd, and said: "Being the one who introduced the newlyweds is quite a special honor. I haven't had too many honors in my life..." Joey paused and chewed his lip. He scanned the room with a subtle air of mystery before peering to the head table at his best friend. Joey smiled and said: "You know what? I had a speech prepared, but I think I want to do this one from the heart... I've known Roy for a very long time. He's always been a big brother to me. I would follow him anywhere. He's taught me a lot about what it means to be responsible. The importance of holding yourself accountable. And I am filled with joy to see him so happy with Meryl. It's been a long road, but he made it here. And he was nice enough to carry me with him." He faced Mitch and raised his glass. "Love you, bud."

Mitch nodded knowingly. Meryl watched the exchange with a full heart.

"I will admit, though," continued Joey, impishly returning to the gallery. "When I first introduced the two, I wasn't expecting them to get married. I was just trying to get my buddy laid."

Chad's harsh laughter broke the uncomfortable silence pervading the room. Joyce, abreast of Chad, shot Joey an admonishing glare. Joey sniggered nervously into the microphone. "Anyway, that's my cue. Thanks, everyone, for coming."

He was ushered to his seat with a less than rowdy applause.

"You sure know how to dead a room, Jo," said Mitch as Joey folded into his chair.

"Usually, that line kills," Joey remarked, ostensibly confused over the crowd's dry reaction. "Anyway, good luck, you two. Fake marriages are easy. The real ones are hard."

Meryl softened. "When are you and Joyce going to tie the knot?"

Joey peered across the sea of tables and found his girlfriend of two years in the throng. The candlelight's soft reflection flickered against her cheeks. She and Tammy were in the middle of what looked to be a hilarious chinwag. For a moment, Joey watched her. His gaze returned to Meryl's, and he smiled warmly. "Soon," he said. "As soon as we're ready."

After the wait staff had cleared the dinner plates, the lights dimmed, and the DJ played a contemporary pop ballad. Gingerly, guests rose from their seats and started to mingle. Some headed to the bathroom, some for a cigarette out front, and the majority absconded to the open bar for a refill or two before the commencement of the first dance. Meryl and Mitch circuited the reception hall and thanked each guest for coming and for their gifts, many of which were envelopes of cash placed in an overstuffed white velvet sack near the buffet. Mitch brought Meryl to the McAllesters' table to personally meet the FBI agent who saved his life. They had sent him the invitation, unsure if he would feel comfortable attending. Evidently, he was comfortable enough to bring the whole family. Meryl thought his little girl was just the cutest thing.

"I wanted to thank you for coming," said Mitch, firmly shaking the ADD's outset hand. "I suppose I want to thank you for a lot of things."

"It's our pleasure," said McAllester politely. He had a formal and sober air about him that reminded Meryl of her father.

"And what's your name little princess?" Meryl asked the young daughter.

"Jeanine!" the girl proclaimed exuberantly.

"That's a beautiful dress," Meryl told her, referring to the girl's studded blue garb, frilled at the skirt and shoulders. A matching blue bow crowned the child's wispy blonde hair.

"Say thank you," urged her mother.

"Thank you," smiled Jeanine.

Presently, Meryl's father joined them at the table. "And how is everything here?"

McAllester beamed like a teenage girl with a crush. "Sheriff!" he boasted. "Great to see you. Enjoying retirement?"

"I can't complain," her father returned. "The Mrs. and I plan on doing some traveling. Mexico is first on the list. I might even come back with a tan."

McAllester and his wife emoted affectionately.

"Is that a six-shooter I see on your hip? Is that an antique?" asked McAllester.

Meryl watched her father's eyes swell at its mention.

"It's a gift that was given to me a long time ago. I hold it with the utmost distinction. But the reason I came over here, though," the Sheriff diverged, "was that I wanted to take this time to show the newlyweds *their* gift. So if you'll please follow me outside to the parking lot..."

Her father's plum-shaded lips grinned enigmatically and he started for the exit. Meryl and Mitch glanced curiously at each other and followed the Sheriff's lead.

"Well, I have to see this," said McAllester to his wife.

She rolled her eyes in a sagely and dignified manner. "We'll be waiting," she chimed.

"Mommy, I want to see," pleaded little Jeanine.

"No, let the adults go, sweetie," Meryl heard the mother say softly at her back.

QUINN WATCHED THE ENTRANCE of the reception hall from inside the rented Hummer. Windows down, the muffled music and banter from inside the building bled out into the hot, quiescent night and merged with his thumping heartbeat. He regarded Angie in the passenger seat. Her curls spread against the leather headrest as she reposed stiffly and with an air of agitation. Her eyes trembled desperately and invoked his compassion.

He reached across the center console and placed his hand tenderly on Angie's thick, yielding thigh. "Are you sure you want to be part of this? It could get ugly when it goes down."

Angie bit her lip and nodded resolutely. "They killed my family. The civil suit against Daddy's company ruined us. Justice has to be served."

Her commitment to the cause inspired him and, if feasible, engendered an even stronger veneration for her character. He leaned over the center console and, lips crashing upon hers like a stormy wave against a breaker, expressed his equally fervent dedication to egalitarianism. After parting from her gentle mouth, Quinn reached into the backseat and returned with a 9mm pistol that he placed reverently in Angie's quivering hands. Her fingernails, painted white for the occasion to symbolize a clean slate, coiled around the metallic grip. Quinn retrieved a second 9mm pistol and holstered it under his arm. Angie opened the glove box and withdrew two black balaclava ski masks. By this point, her hands had steadied as if the firearm's innate power and prestige had evened her nerves and galvanized her resolve.

Quinn had never seen her more beautiful.

"No turning back," she said quietly.

Quinn beamed into her fostering brown eyes, and a ready calm washed over him. "No turning back," he repeated.

THE DOORS TO THE RECEPTION hall sundered, and the convocation behind Meryl's father stepped into the parking lot. Meryl released Mitch's hand and raised her streaming gown over her ankles as an act of preservation. Mitch, Joey, and Agent McAllester gathered around the brand-new BMW XM SUV parked in the row of spaces parallel to the front entrance.

"Now, I know you're a big fan of the Charger," said her father while he stroked the tailgate. The comment engendered a sidelong glance between Mitch and Agent McAllester. The moment was fleeting, but Meryl detected a curiosity behind the exchange. She released the thought on account of it was her wedding day and little else save the newlyweds' love and future was cause for pause. "But I wanted to get you guys a new vehicle that could facilitate my grandchildren if you know what I mean."

He let out a raspy hoot into the toasty night air.

Meryl wondered if her father knew of the secret growing inside her. He was, and always had been, invariably apt at deciphering conspiracy. Again, she categorized the curiosity for a more appropriate time and place.

"It's amazing," said Mitch. He patted her father on the shoulder and wagged his head incredulously.

"Dad, it's wonderful," added Meryl.

"Very generous," McAllester pitched in.

Across the parking lot, Meryl spotted two people who had exited a yellow Hummer and were marching briskly toward their posse. She squinted through the gloomy night and discerned that the two approaching figures wore ski masks. One was a stout, portly man; the other was a tall, morbidly overweight woman. Her prodigious breasts and paunch pendulated as she advanced.

To her abject horror, Meryl also distinguished that the two masked newcomers were clutching firearms.

"Mitch?" uttered Meryl, immediately rife with panic.

Mitch glanced perfunctorily at Meryl and witnessed her horrified expression. He followed her paralytic gaze to the forthcoming armed strangers.

"Oh my god..." he gasped in comparable despair.

The short one raised his gun. He pointed it at McAllester and shouted: "Thought you were Thomas Blood, huh? Well, you ain't getting away with this one!"

McAllester's face twisted grotesquely. "Quinn?"

Two thundery shots fired from the masked man's gun and pierced McAllester's chest. He tumbled back on his heels and crumbled to the pavement. Alive or dead, Meryl wasn't certain.

The large woman raised her gun at Mitch. "This is for my brother, you asshole!"

"Look out!" Joey warned. He shoved Mitch from the line of fire as the woman squeezed the trigger. Mitch's unbalanced momentum flung him behind the BMW. Joey hit the ground. Meryl screamed. Her father drew the six-shooter from his holster and fired a shot that dropped the gunman forthwith. Concurrently, the woman shooter fired a slug aimed at Meryl. The bullet missed its target and shattered the BMW's back window. Glass shards rained down on the pavement inches from where Joey lay prostrate. Meryl's father squeezed off another precise shot that hit the masked woman under her right eye. She tipped backward like cattle, landed awkwardly, and did not relocate.

Mitch appeared behind the BMW and leaped over Joey to get to Meryl. "Are you hit? Are you hit?" he shouted as his hands frantically searched her body for wounds.

She attempted to respond to her husband, but her mouth clamped shut despite her efforts. Her legs had become steel anchors. Pins and needles ascended her arms to her shoulders, neck, and jaw. Soon, total paralysis consumed her.

Finding she was unscathed, Mitch peered deeply into her vacant eyes, rubbed her arm, and assured her he would return momentarily. He turned and attended Joey, prone on the ground. "I owe you for that one," Meryl heard Mitch say appreciatively to his best man. He knelt and rolled Joey on his back. Joey's bloody temple appeared in the margins of her blurred vision.

A bestial moan like none Meryl had ever heard exploded from Mitch's bowels and rang out into the still landscape. He hugged Joey's lifeless body as he cried and screamed, punching the pavement repeatedly, breaking the skin and slicking his knuckles with blood.

Meryl's desire to run to her husband's side and comfort him was futile. She could not feel her body. She could not feel her baby. The only thing she could utter as gelid tears spilled down her cheeks was a faint, weakened whisper: "Daddy..."

You're Also Invited

A shrewd con woman, a shady private investigator, and a modestly-endowed porn actor attempt to lure a billion dollar pharmaceutical manufacturer into a sexual harassment lawsuit in...

THIEVERY AND GRACE

Register for the newsletter to stay updated on new titles from Oswald Black.

www.oswaldblack.com

Oswald Black

Milton Keynes UK
Ingram Content Group UK Ltd.
UKHW030650090924
448088UK00004B/389